CREAM

A Poetic Drama

Mahogany Rose

Velvet Honey Press

Library of Congress Number: Pending

Published by **Velvet Honey Press**

Cover design by **Velvet Honey Press Design Studio**

Concept and Creative Direction by **Mahogany Rose**

Edited by Taelor Malcolm of **Elm Tree Studios**

Paperback ISBN: 979-8-9938754-7-7

E-Book ISBN: 979-8-9938754-6-0

Printed in the United States of America

First Edition

This is a work of fiction. Any resemblance to actual persons, living or dead, or actual events is purely coincidental.

For a lost love that has been found! My composition notebooks would envy this moment.

CREAM

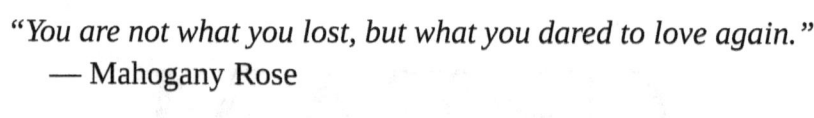

"You are not what you lost, but what you dared to love again."
— Mahogany Rose

Author's Note

This story came to me in fragments, memories, melodies, and mirror work. I didn't write it to glorify pain but to honor the survival of almost. I believe healing happens in stages, and sometimes you may be broken in ways that deserve silence in order to mend. Yari Gervais was created from the dashes of salt that stings our wounds. The tears we shed as we pull back the layers of our womanhood, and the emptiness that consumes us when we almost feel like enough. Curating this part of her story has given me the courage to understand that it's always been my pen my story.

But more than that, it's been my *becoming.*

Through Yari, I learned that survival isn't the end of the story, it's the doorway to softness. That grace is not the absence of grief, but the strength to return to yourself when love has stripped you bare. Every sentence I wrote was a conversation between the woman I was and the one I'm still becoming. Every book I write is an offering to the women who taught me to bloom in rooms that forgot their sunlight. *Cream* is a hymn for them and for us.

If this book finds you somewhere between who you were and who you're trying to be, may it whisper *you are still worthy of tenderness.* If you've ever questioned whether softness and strength can live in the same woman, this book is for you.

-Mahogany Rose

Prologue

Developing Light

I was ten when I first learned mirrors had teeth. Not the kind that cut to the quick, but the kind that bite slow, leaving dents you can't smooth out with lotion or new clothes. I tired myself out thinking of how to look different. Like if only I was able to shop at *GirlsWorld* like all the other girls in my grade. But that dream had been woken from for years now. I only wanted to show proof that I too had been able to fit in the glitter denim and graphic shirts.

It was now the spring of my senior year, I could hear the conversation spilling from the kitchen. The smell of whiting frying, cornbread cooling on the counter, coupled with the sound of my aunties' sharp laughter dripping from their mouths like grease.

"She gon' be thick like her mama," one said.

"Mm-hmm, she already is," another called back.

The room burst into the kind of laughter that makes your ears burn hot with shame.

I stood in the hallway, close enough to hear but far enough to pretend I wasn't listening. I wanted to disappear into the wallpaper, to melt into the floor. I wanted somebody, anybody, to say, *Stop. She can hear you.*

No one did. My grandma used to be that person, but she had been gone for two years, and now no one comes to my rescue. No one even realizes when I need saving. That was the night I realized grief had claws. The way it pierced my gut like salt, reminding me that home was now where truth carry sharp cheddar in its grits.

That night Jarell pulled up to the house, leaning against his daddy's old car like it belonged to him, like he was already grown. He had music spilling from the speakers, Aaliyah, or maybe it was Maxwell. He honked once, low, impatient but playful.

I ran out before my mama could ask me to set the table, tucking my shame deep down inside me, hoping he wouldn't see it.

He grinned when I slid into the passenger seat. He didn't ask what took me so long, just handed me a piece of peppermint gum and asked, "You ready?"

It felt like one of those summer nights had come early, We were going to some free concert downtown, when the city put speakers in the park and let the music do the rest.

And I felt rescued.

Enough to forget about the aunties, the kitchen, the mirror's teeth.

For a little while.

I was fourteen when silence became the soundtrack of my home and grief stretched itself across the couch like it paid rent.

My father's story ended abruptly with a bang and an exclamation mark followed by the conclusion of a period. My mother's ache turned into years of overtime, dinner dates, fancy silk dresses, and tear stained pillowcases.

It was now fall of my senior year I stopped sleeping in my room because it felt too empty, started sleeping on the floor of the living room instead because the memory of my father still sat in the big chair. The one that was perfectly positioned in front of the tv for Sunday night football and boxing matches that always managed to initiate a round of play fighting between the two of us.

That was until my mother found a runner up for the title that had wilted away with my father. My stepfather, Henry, demanded we throw it out. Saying he didn't want to watch his sports in a dead man's chair.

I could have smacked the taste right out of his mouth that day.

My mom gazed into my eyes mouthing, "I'm sorry," as she agreed it was time for something new. My tears wouldn't fall, so anger set in. My need to leave the house immediately helped me follow those movers as they carried my dad's chair out like a worn casket.

I stood on the sidewalk watching the moving truck until I could no longer see it. "I'll never forgive him." I admit while gritting my teeth before sending Yari a text.

> Jarell [5:20 PM]: When is graduation so I can get out of here?

> My Yari [5:22 PM]: 7 months 3 weeks 2 days and 18 hours but I promise I'm not counting

I find myself laughing at her accuracy. She wanted out too.

> My Yari [5:29 PM]: You wanna go to the fall festival?

I'm sure she could sense my need to busy my mind with something else other than what was causing me to try and find a cliff.

Jarell [5:30 PM]: Sure thing, I'll pick you up.

My Yari [5:31 PM]: Cool

Yari had always known how to be my peace. I didn't have to be anything but Jarell when we hung out. Not a son, a big brother, a star athlete, just Jarell.

I ran back into the house to shower and get ready. I could hear my mom in the kitchen treating Henry like a newly crowned king.

"Honey, I got it, don't move, watch your game." Her tone was tender, like she wanted so badly to fill all the empty spaces my father had left. I sat at the edge of my bed, staring at my baseball glove and ball as my tears found their way to the surface. Exhaling, I stood to pull myself together. I pulled my hoodie on thinking to myself, grief had no playbook. I had no tricks in my back pocket that would help me shake up the game and put me on the winning side. I rushed out the front door, slamming it behind me before Henry could try to claim another piece of what was mine.

The air outside smelled like fried dough and burning leaves, the kind of fall night that carried both sweetness and smoke. By the time I pulled up to Yari's block, I already felt the ache in my chest lessening.

She came outside in ripped jeans and a jacket with fur at the collar, her curls pulled back in a loose puff that framed her face like a halo. She slid into the passenger seat with a grin, the kind that told me she'd been waiting to pull me back down to earth.

"Thought you weren't gonna show," she said, buckling her

seatbelt.

"I needed out," I muttered, hands tight on the wheel.

She didn't push. Didn't ask. Just leaned back, let the music from the speakers fill the space.

The festival was already alive when we arrived. Bright lights strung across tents, the scent of kettle corn heavy in the air, a carousel creaking in slow circles. Kids ran past us with candied apples in their hands, parents shouting behind them. For a moment, it felt like the whole city had pressed pause on the grief I carried.

Yari insisted on buying a funnel cake for us to share. We walked side by side, close enough for our jackets to brush. She took the opportunity to dust my black hoodie with powdered sugar as she laughed. I let her. Maybe I even liked the way she didn't treat me like I was fragile.

At the edge of the field, a local band played on a small stage, brass horns winding through the cool night air. We found a spot near the back, laid out a blanket and nestled into the grass as the music wrapped itself around us. I could feel my anger quieting, replaced by something softer, something safer.

Yari looked up at me with powdered sugar on her lips and said, "You're allowed to be more than what hurts you, Jay."

Her voice was steady, no pity, just truth.

For a moment, I believed her.

Then the summer after graduation, Yari called me crying, saying she couldn't breathe. Something about the way a boy looked at her, something about not being enough and being too much all at once. I didn't know what to say. I only knew I couldn't let her cry alone.

So, I pulled up. Same car, different music. Nas this time, something steady with bass, something that made silence shrink.

She slid into the passenger seat; her face turned toward the window like she was embarrassed for me to see her. I didn't ask questions, I just drove. Downtown, past the stadium, past the lights, past everything. She kept saying, "I'm sorry. I'm sorry." While I kept saying, "It's okay. It's okay." Until she finally believed me enough to stop apologizing.

We ended up at the same park as before, sitting on the hood of the car, watching the city in the distance move around as if we never lived in it. Music drifted from somebody else's speakers. Her head dropped against my shoulder.

We didn't say a word, and maybe that was the loudest kind of truth.

The city kept watch while we both pretended we weren't breaking. Street lights laid golden across cracked sidewalks. Trains sighed through the night like they were tired of running. Saxophones moaned from basements where the doorways leaked neon. The city didn't care who touched you. It didn't care who left. It only asked what you were willing to lose.

Music and mourning lived in the same bars. Loneliness wore perfume and cologne. Secrets traded hands with dollar bills. The city whispered *stay*, even when all you wanted was to run.

I wanted love to look me in the face and stay. I wanted love to leave me alone before it broke me again.

We didn't know we were already holding the answer.

We just called it friendship.

Not On Duty

Yari

"Jarell, I'm not going to keep telling you she didn't deserve you," I growl at him from across the room. Sliding my keys across the island, watching as they crash into the vase of ivory roses my boyfriend André, had given me for missing our last date night.

"I know, but that doesn't mean this shit don't hurt Yari. Q and I've been together for two fucking years. I wanted to marry her," he says, as he closes the front door and throws his duffle bag on my couch.

I can't help but roll my eyes at the thought of the two of them making it down the aisle. This latest Q Drama seems to really have him frustrated. Jarell and I have been friends forever. He was my first kiss, right under the monkey bars in 7th grade. We swore to never talk about it again and I've been his wing woman ever since. I played it cool while he chased every girl with pretty hair and clapped the loudest when they eventually disappeared from his life. I've always been there when he needed me, but it was starting to

7

feel like I had invested too much time and energy telling him not to trust this girl for us to still be talking about her. It was in the way she always pulled him away from his goals, caused him to distance his self from his friends and the little bit of family he had left. He wasn't as focus as he used to be, all she wanted to do was shop with his credit cards and take vacations.

"You dodged a fucking bullet," I sigh combing through my bar cart before selecting two lowball glasses. "Jarell, I'm not going to say I told you so, 'cause honestly I was rooting for y'all, so I could finally be off duty," I smile faintly at him hoping to lighten the mood.

He shakes his head as he laughs, "Yari, I'm being serious. She was supposed to be Mrs. Drayton." He draws his hands across the space between him and the ceiling like the name was in lights, as he joins me in the kitchen.

"Boy please," I laugh. "Well, we're here now so what do you want to do?" I ask while fixing him a shot of bourbon from my cabinet of luxury, world class bourbons.

He throws back his shot and slams the glass down. "I don't know Yari."

I can hear the sadness in his voice as I look into his deep brown eyes, wishing I could remove the hurt.

"I can't have you feeling like this Jay."

Taking a sip of my old fashion, I walk around the island that separates us to sit on the barstool next to him. "You can stay here until you figure this shit out, you know I don't mind." He's a mess, the puffiness around his eyes tells me he's been crying all day.

"Thanks Yari, I swear you're my fucking peace!" He pauses, rubbing the back of his neck. "You're the only person I trust not to throw this in my face tomorrow." He looks at me giving me a half ass smile.

I'll take the defeated smile. It's way better than him losing his temper, or even worse, crying more. I can't handle anymore tears tonight.

"No problem, Jay, take the time you need. I know your place is tainted right now." I stand, giving him an empathetic look while running my hands through his beard. "I'm gonna go get the guest room ready. You can have the rest of my drink if you'd like."

As I walk away, I can feel his eyes following me. Stopping in my tracks without turning around I say, "Yes Jay, I'll spray your pillows with Lavender."

His laughter follows me as I enter the guest bedroom.

I don't know what I'm thinking, Jay can't stay here. What about André? He's not going to understand. We've been dating for seven months, and I barely let him stay the night. How am I going to explain my best *male* friend staying in my loft until well, … whenever? I still have to finalize things for this vacation with André to Mulancia next week, and now I have to figure out how to tell him Jay will be here.

"What the fuck were you thinking, Yari" I whisper to myself as I pick out sheets from the bottom drawer of the dresser. A shoe in the doorway startles me, causing me to tip forward and hit my head. "Damn!" I cry out "What the fuck Jay?"

He bellows "What the fuck were you thinking?" while laughing. "Huh?"

"Isn't that what you said?" He mimics my voice "What the fuck were you thinking, Yari?! So, what were you thinking?"

"Nothing Jay, stop listening in on my conversations with myself. Just 'cause you here don't mean you can be snooping around minding my business. This was an A & B…" Pointing at myself twice. "C Ya!" I say, throwing a pillow at him.

Catching it he walks towards me, close enough for his scent to dust the air between us. "I was just asking, don't do me like that." He expressed.

I find myself nibbling at my bottom lip as the bass in his tone shifts. His eyes were lost tracing my mouth, before realizing what

I'm doing. I quickly get it together and walk around the other side of the bed.

"What did you want anyway?" I ask while preparing the duvet cover.

"Oh yeah, I was going to ask if I could take a shower in your bathroom. I know there is one over here, but I poured myself another drink, and yeah, I need to take a shower now before I get too damn comfortable."

Looking at him I nod, knowing he must be tipsy if he thought he had to ask. Without saying a word, he turns to head to my bathroom.

I get lost thinking about just how much André will hate this as I finish setting up the guest room. Then I head into the second bathroom to make sure Jay will be squared away.

Jarell

I step into Yari's bathroom; it's decorated in her style. Everything has little hints of a bohemian touch and obsessively organized. Yari aimed for perfection in everything she did, her bathroom was no exception to that trait. I mean I'm clean, but this is next level.

I grab a washcloth and towel from her linen closet, sit them on her vanity bench and step into the floor to ceiling subway tiled shower, ready to cleanse myself of this day.

After what I just saw tonight, I need to stay under the spray of this shower for at least an hour. I can't believe Q could do me like this after all this time. I've been faithful, God knows I could've stepped out on her ass if I really wanted to. I thought I didn't have to play those games anymore. I really thought this was it. She was supposed to be the one.

My mother used to say love was supposed to feel safe. So, why has it always left me feeling alone, bloody, and broken?

I guess she got one thing wrong.

Yari's right, I dodged a fucking bullet for sure. Imagine if I'd started building that life with her. The one with the kids, and the Tuscan architectural style house. I wanted everything with her we talked about on the trip to the ski resort last year. The thought alone is enough to turn my stomach.

Scrambling out the shower I rush over to the toilet allowing myself to hurl freely. In this moment I appreciate Yari's need to be extreme in her obsession for perfection and aesthetically pleasing spaces. She's always prepared and has extra everything. Those tiny little rolled towels and extra travel mouthwashes came in handy after all.

"Fuck, I need another drink!"

I rinse off, dry down, wrapping the towel low on my hips before heading to her kitchen. Pouring myself a double shot of Booker's and swallowing it down, letting it burn my throat.

As the shot warms my throat, I hear music coming from the hallway with the extra bedrooms, sounds like Snoh, maybe. What the hell is Yari up to?

Before I can walk towards the sound of the music, there's a knock at the door.

"Who the hell's knocking on Yari's door at 2 AM?" I sneer, glancing back towards the music from the main guest room.

"Aye Yari, you want me to get that?" I'm met with her silence. Probably can't hear me over all that loud ass music. "Aye Yari, I'm answering the door!" I call out, cracking my neck and reaching for the doorknob.

"Who in the hell – What the fuck are you doing here?" I grit out through a clenched jaw.

I know damn well *this* dude ain't standing in the doorway looking me dead in my face.

Before he can say a word, I rear back and knock him square in his jaw, causing him to stumble back and fall. Without another word I slam the door hard on his sorry ass. I'm not trying to bring drama over to Yari's spot. I can't believe this shit at all.

"This dude has the nerve to follow me? Like he wants these kinds of problems." I seethe, pacing near the front door. It's then I notice Yari standing in the hallway, her eyes glued on me, a deer caught in my headlights.

"I'm sorry Yari, I didn't mean to scare you. Can you believe this dude had the balls to follow us here?" I ask, waiting for her response, but her reply doesn't come. It's as if she's frozen in time. "Yari, you good?"

Yari

I look at the time realizing how late it is. Almost 2 AM? Damn, Jay owes me for this shit. He's disrupted my Sunday evening self-care routine, and taken over my bathroom? My eyes roll as I realize that means I can't even take my spiritual bath tonight. I'll have to settle for a shower in the guest bathroom instead because it seems like he's taking his time in my bathroom.

I sigh, pulling my hair up into a messy bun and make a list of needs to help me get settled for the night. "Soap, moisturizer, and some jammies. Oh shit, I hope he's not naked, that would be awkward," I giggle to myself.

Tip toeing to my bedroom, preparing myself for anything, I hear the shower still running in my bathroom. I slip into the closet in search of my cream silk teddy.

"Yes, got it," I mumble, right as I hear the water shut off. I rush out my room heading back towards the guest bathroom. "Last thing I need is tonight to be more eventful," I mutter to myself.

Walking over to my record player housed in the corner of my living space, I pop Snoh Aalegra's 2019 album onto the turntable, before continuing to the main guest room.

"Give me all the vibes sis!" I exclaim as her voice surrounds me leaving me feeling like I'm having my own private concert as I step foot into the bathroom.

My sweats drop to the floor, the weight of tonight falling with them. Slipping into the shower, I drift into my own little world, hoping to grip a small bit of those good ole self-care vibes I crave every Sunday.

Stepping out of the shower, I see the pocket of my sweats light up. But I don't want to check it right now. I start drying myself instead, applying my signature Magnolia & Peonies body oil. Wiggling into my silk teddy, I turn on the faucet as the combined sounds of a phone notification and a slamming door cause me to jump.

"What the fuck Jay?!" I cry out, finally looking down at my phone. It's André. A nervous smile stretches across my face.

"Should I tell him Jay is staying here now?" I ask myself, biting my bottom lip. "No, that won't sound right. I can't just say 'hey babe, by the way my fine ass best friend is staying with me until whenever and he's currently somewhere in my loft naked' Yeah, no," I snicker, shaking my head. Reaching for my phone, I notice I've missed two messages from André.

> André [1:13 AM]: Baby I'll be over
> shortly… I got something for you!

He only ever arrives when it's convenient for him, never when I need him. He had something for me? Sure, but I know it's not peace.

> André [1:56 AM]: I'm going to have
> to reschedule our dinner plans for
> tomorrow night..

Lavender Pillows

Yari

"I lit the candles, I laid out the dress, and I was finally going to tell him I need more. And he cancels? Again?!" I seethe at my reflection in the bathroom mirror.

I'm so over him being distant. He doesn't even see me.

I watch my reflection, tracking a tear as it rolls down my cheek. "I can't believe him. He *promised*."

Yelling starts up somewhere in the loft as the record I put on finishes its final track.

"Aye Yo Jay, what the fuck?" I call, rushing out the bathroom to see what the deal is. "Yo, either you back drinking or-" I cut myself off because, *damn*.

My anger slips through my fingers like soap as I catch sight of his body. Still dripping, fists clenched, wrapped in my oyster-colored bath sheet, a thunderstorm in human form.

I can feel my lips moisten and my nipples stand to attention. I'm not moving a muscle because there's no way I'm depriving my eyes of this sight.

The smooth rumble of his voice interrupts my gawking. "Yari, you good?"

I throw my shoulders back shaking off those feelings. I can't be thinking like this, not about Jay. Not when André's supposed to be flying me to Mulancia next week.

"I'm good. What the fuck's going on Jay, don't you realize its after 2 AM? Why're you slamming doors and shit?" I ask, walking towards him. Purposely ignoring the slickness between my thighs. "What's up yo?"

He walks to the couch, leaving me gaping at him in awe. Wet and wondering what the hell he's so uptight about.

"This fucking fool really had the nerve to follow us here!" He says, rage rising to the surface. "Yari, I wasn't trying to bring this shit to you. It's bad enough you had to come scoop me after I saw her triflin' ass topping this goofball off, but him following us here and knocking on your door," he shakes his head in disgust, "that's some next level disrespectful ass bullshit. He lucky I ain't have my shit on me."

I walk towards the front door, swinging it open to look for who he's talking about, but there's no one in the hall.

Jarell snatches me back inside and locks the door.

"Don't do that shit," he scolds. "I need to get you a fucking ring doorbell. I don't trust this dude."

He grabs his phone from the side table, scrolling for and tapping around for a second. Finishing what he's doing he places the phone back down.

"The doorbell will be here later today," he says straight faced.

I'm at a loss for words. He's sexy when he's upset and protective. It's kinda cute.

"Thanks Jay, but I'm okay. I'm not worried about no lame seeking me out."

I gesture for him to open the side table drawer. "I got a little something that will put a hot one in his ass, and hold his ass right up."

Jarell gives a low impressed whistles as he slides the drawer open.

"Oh shit, and it's cute? Okay, Taurus Semi 9, with the gold accents, and mother of pearl barrel? I'm scared of you!"

I make a gun with my fingers and blow some invisible steam off the end before giggling and covering my eyes.

"Remind me not to get on your bad side," Jarell teases as he walks towards the bedroom with his duffle bag. Turning to look at me he says, "Thanks again, Yari. You're amazing, and I know you always got my back." He flashes his beautiful white teeth at me before walking into the guest bedroom and closing the door.

"Of course I got you," I whisper, turning all the lights out and gliding towards my bed. I need rest.

Jarell

7 AM and my alarm is blaring through my phone speakers blowing out my eardrums. At least that's what it feels like now that I start to feel a slight throb behind my eyes.

Grabbing my phone, I try to silence its disturbance of every bit of peace I have. After I switch off all my alarms, I decide not to go into the gym today. Opening my calendar, I realize I only have two appointments today anyway.

The first one's a three o'clock with my homeboy X. I shoot him a text to reschedule, keeping the details of last night vague. Knowing him he'll clown my ass for that shit.

My other appointment is with…Yari? Wait, what? Why? She's pretty healthy, and sure she's curvy, but all those curves are in the right places.

Yari and I have been cool since grade school. Everyone

could tell I was crushing on her back then, but she never noticed or maybe she never saw me that way. That never mattered to me though, cause I'd always do whatever for her. We're there for each other like that.

Sitting up in bed, I notice the blinds are still partially closed.

"Damn, I thought the sun was already all the way in the room." I stand to flip the blinds open. Moving towards the bedroom door, I head into the living room, smiling at all the sunlight spilling into her loft.

Yari must be sleeping still. I wonder what she has planned for today. The least I can do is figure out breakfast. I think to myself before heading towards the kitchen.

I decide on omelets and a few strips of turkey bacon. I fix them using egg whites, tossing in some spinach, peppers, mushrooms and cheese. We're both skipping the gym today, no need to add to the weight of the day with a heavy meal.

I scoop some fresh strawberries into a bowl and grab two glasses. Knowing Yari, she'll more than likely want some freshly squeezed apple juice with a touch of maple syrup for sweetness.

I finally found her juicer and get started on her drink when my phone vibrates on the island, her name flashing across my screen. My Yari.

> My Yari [8:21 AM]: Is that turkey bacon?
> Or am I dreaming?

Laughing, I instantly text back.

> Jarell [8:21 AM]: Sure is! You want
> some?

Bubbles quickly appear, signaling she's working on a reply, but disappear just as fast. I go back to making breakfast as I wait for her smart-ass response.

> My Yari [8:23 AM]: You mean to tell me
> you're in my kitchen and didn't think
> about me? You're the worst.

> Jarell [8:24 AM}: My bad

Seconds later, Yari graces the kitchen, hair all over the place, jammies rumpled from sleep. I've never seen her first thing in the morning before. She looks so beautiful, so naturally radiant.

She smiles once she sees plates on the counter.

"Did you honestly think I would forget to feed you, girl?"

Instead of replying she stretches her arms up with a yawn, bending forward before standing again. Taking a seat on the barstool across from me, she reaches for a strawberry bringing it to her lips and taking a bite.

My body reacts before I can stop it. She bites into that strawberry like it's a secret, juice glistening on her lips, eyes daring me not to look away. I need to pull it together. Grabbing my plate, I circle the island, subtly adjusting myself, praying my body doesn't betray the thoughts running wild in my head. This is Yari, I think as I shift my focus. "What do you have planned for today, Yari?" I ask, trying to relieve the pressure in my briefs with small talk.

She sips her juice, swallowing before looking in my direction. "Auditions for new Satin Dolls at Imani's Studio. Cream needs extra help with basketball season coming up."

I nod in agreement with her game-plan. "Smart, business woman."

Cream is Yari's luxury bar and lounge. I was proud of her, I'd watched her grind and save to make it happen. She came to me during the grand opening of FLEXD and said, "In two years I'm going to finally open Cream." That's just what she did. When she first opened the spot she had some push back. In a male dominated industry everyone thought she bit off more than she could chew, but she was still proving that when a black woman puts her mind to do something, not only does she do it but she does it with class and grace.

"Yeah the Lions are definitely on their big shit this season. James Johnson ain't playing no games, and Winterbrook been stepping up his playbook since he took over as head coach after retiring last year." I say while making an invisible shot, leaving with my arms hanging in the air.

Yari rolls her eyes, making me laugh at how close this conversation had been from going all the way left with those strawberries.

We finish breakfast and I stand checking my watch. 9:31 AM. I guess I'll get dressed and go for a run.

"Hey Yari, can we swing by my gym to pick up my car?"

She glances back at me, her eyes glowing, charged with the brilliance of the sun. A slight smile finding a welcoming home on her face.

"Sure, Jay. I need to run a few errands around there anyway. Give me a minute to get ready." she says, voice light.

I watch as she walks away, silk teddy caressing her curves in quiet appreciation, hips speaking a language I've done my best to not become fluent in.

She disappears behind her bedroom door, and just like that, the whole loft feels warmer. Familiar. Like *belonging.*

And that's a feeling I can't trust.

Body Smears

Yari

"Jay? When are you going to confront her?" I ask, keeping my attention on the road ahead, so I don't forget the upcoming turn like I usually do.

"I don't know," he says with a heavy sigh. "To be honest, I was just going to shoot her a text telling her to get the fuck out, hire a maid service to clean up her grime, and call it a day."

My brows and lips must be enough for him to realize how foolish I think he sounds because he quickly rephrases.

"All I know is I'm getting too old to go back and forth with any female about her dirt. I know what I saw. I have that shit on camera" he says, pulling out his phone to show me.

Usually, I would be down for a good World Star moment like this, but I'm not in the mood today. I side-eye him as he goes searching for the clip.

"Jay, I love you and all, but I don't want to witness that shit. I've been trying not to go see 'bout her out of respect for the situation. But you know I won't be able to hold myself back if I see that video. So please, just spare me." I say, swatting his phone from my view.

He lets out a halfhearted laugh. "Why I gotta go through this shit alone, Yari? You pose to be down in it with me. That's fucked up."

Pulling my cream-colored and gold accented G Wagon into the parking deck off Halsted Street, I see the sign for Jarell's gym. FLEXD.

Being a black man from where we're from, it always makes me proud that he's flourishing. Jay played sports while we were in school but he'd always dreamed of being more than an athlete. In his words "I want to build a legacy that will impact the wellness of our people for generations." So he kept his head buried in the books faithfully.

"You'll be fine. I think you should do more than tell her triflin' ass she has to go though." Rolling my eyes at him, I find a parking spot right next to his black on black Bentley. Putting the car in park, I look over at Jarell, but before I can say anything else he says.

"Hey Yari, I wanted to ask you something."

I brace myself, sitting upright in my seat. "Yes?"

He pauses, before getting to it. "I saw you booked an appointment with me today, why didn't you say anything?" He searches my eyes for the answer.

Dropping my head, I respond, "Jay, I need to drop a few pounds. You know how self-conscious I am about my weight." I sigh, discreetly wiping a tear before continuing with the humiliating truth.

"I went to put on my favorite dress the other night. For that celebrity event we were hosting, remember? Anyway, size twelves aren't fitting anymore, I'm a size fourteen now. I used to wear sixteens, but I don't want to go back to that now that I've been on the other side."

Jarell reaches over, placing his hand on my face, lifting my head while twisting my face towards him.

"Yari, you are an amazing woman with a healthy lifestyle. Your dress size doesn't matter. You take damn good care of yourself. You want to tone up? That's fine. You want to edit your diet? Cool. But baby girl, I promise, there is absolutely nothing wrong with your body. You should see the way guys look at you when we kick it, or when you come through the gym. All I'm saying is, I can help you maintain the body you have now, but I won't be a part of destroying a body you already take good care of."

His words make my tears fall fast. I want to believe him, but I can still hear my ex's voice in my head. The one who said, "You're pretty, but I'd be lying if I said I liked all that." The one who told me I was lucky he stayed at all.

Jarell is his opposite. His hands didn't flinch when they touched my face. His eyes didn't shift away when he spoke his compliments like my ex's used to. He wipes my tears without hesitation.

I nod, letting a soft smile bloom across my cheeks. "Thanks, Jay."

Smiling he says, "No doubt, baby girl. Listen I was going to take the day off, but how bout you come by the gym later tonight and we can get started on creating a plan for MAINTAINING. Deal?" He waits for me to give the okay.

I take a deep breath, feeling relief wash over me.

"Yes, it's a deal. Thanks, Jay."

He reaches his hand in front of him, waiting for me to join in on our handshake we had been doing it since 9th grade. We do our final salute and hug, and he jumps out the car.

He waves as he heads towards FLEXD, walking with that slow, easy stride I know too well.

For a second, I try to think of a time André has ever looked at me the way Jay just did. With eyes that say I'm here, I see you. Jarell's gaze always softens with me. André always seems so caught up in the chaos of the day. Since his dad gave him part in the family business that's all he seems to care about. Oftentimes I feel like he sees right through me into whatever reality has his undivided attention.

I shake off the thought and get back to reality. I have a business to run, a body to fix, a man to love. When I eventually figure out how.

My timing is perfect because when I get over to Imani's dance studio, she's right outside waiting for me.

Imani and I have been friends since college. She and I both majored in business since we thought it was the safest route and we didn't want to commit to just specific fields. We bartended together way back when too. She'd had a love for dancing long before I'd met her, but her parents never thought she could make a lucrative career out of her passion. Yet, here she is, three and a half years out of grad school, showing up and out with her own studio. I'm proud of her.

I pull into her lot and park, watching her wave from the front door. Jumping out of the car, I run around to open my trunk.

"Imani you didn't tell me you rebranded *and* remodeled the place."

Scurrying over to me she pulls me into a hug. "Yari babes I did it on a whim. One day I stood out front and said 'You know what? It's time to upgrade.'" She looks up at her studio with the joy of a proud parent. "Now here we are!" she exclaims, spinning around, hands in the air.

"Well honey it's beautiful," I say, while grabbing a crate from my trunk.

"Thanks girl. Can I help you with anything?" she asks, looking at me like I'm crazy for trying to carry everything alone.

"Sure! Here, take these," I say, handing her the bottle props and bags holding tryout uniforms. "I appreciate you letting me hold the auditions here. This way I don't have to disturb business at Cream."

When I first opened Cream I never imagine what living my dream would feel like. A dream that started while I had been working behind countless bars, wearing stilettos, cleavage all exposed. Four years ago, I started working two jobs, flipped a few investment properties, and stacked every dollar I made in tips to save up for this place. $8,000 plus every month, faithfully. At the end of each month, I'd walk into the bank and open a new CD. No nail appointments, no brunches, just discipline. Four years later, at 28, I don't just lease the building that houses Cream, I own it, paid in full.

I opened Cream for the girl I used to be. The one counting tips in the bathroom stall, wiping down her apron with tears in her eyes because the manager called her "thick" like it was a threat. I opened Cream to prove to that girl that her body, her voice, and her presence, are all luxuries.

Now, Cream's the hottest spot in the city. While I was bartending, I built a cult following by hosting the biggest parties and elite events. Celebrities were always pulling up to the bars I worked in, and they stayed with me when I opened my own.

Imani waves her hand in my direction. "Girl please, you've been a day-one friend. You know I got you."

We head inside to get set up for auditions when my phone rings. André? He wants to call now? I don't have time for this. He canceled. I'm still so disappointed he cancelled I can't find anything non-toxic to say to him. So, I send the call to voicemail and shoot him a quick text.

Yari [11:17 AM]: Hey babe I'm about to
start auditions, I'll give you a call when I

24

finish up!

Placing my phone on do not disturb, I toss it into my bag not giving him the chance to occupy anymore of my time today.

"He got some nerve calling now, regardless of his excuse, all the broken promises are not cool," I mumble to myself before heading back into the main room to start lining up my candidates. I'm super excited to see my business booming, and it's time to focus on that, not whatever excuse André comes up with this time.

Imani agreed to teach the Satin Doll hopefuls a dance sequence, and our signature entry stroll. She's standing in the doorway waiting on my cue to let the ladies into the main room. I look up, taking a deep breath holding in the happy tears trying to break the surface.

"Yari, I'm proud of you," she says, a smile on her face.

I smile, tilting my head to silently signal she can open the doors. She heads back towards me, starting up the music, as the clicking of heels and lengthy line of girls file into the room.

"Let's do this," I whisper to myself.

Jarell

I pull up to my crib, anticipating the worst.

I made a call to the cleaning service that handles FLEXD as soon as I picked up my car. The owner assured me his sister-in-law would be right over. Yari, mentioned I should do more than just saying fuck it, but right now, that's all I can handle.

A familiar face, dressed in khaki chinos, and a black polo waits to greet me as I approach the front door, bucket of cleaning supplies in hand. Trying to recall her name, I look up, searching my memory.

"Fran?" I guess, hoping I'm right so I don't look like an

asshole.

"Yes, I'm Fran, Mr.Drayton." Her accent however thick it was understandable none the less.

A relieved smile comes over my face. "Please call me Jarell... And thank you for coming over with such short notice. I had a few unexpected, and unwanted guests that made a mess. I apologize in advance for anything you may find."

She nods her head, gesturing with a shooing motion for me to just get on with it.

I take a deep breath and open my door.

The scent of *her* perfume hits me as soon as I step into the house. A wave of emotions hit me, bringing tears I have to quickly wipe away.

"I can't believe this bitch," I say softly while walking towards the living room.

Their grimy bodies had left smears on my windows, blurring the view of the garden mama and I had planted with our bare hands. The same windows mama helped me pick out when I had the house built. The same ones she came over to wash herself when I first moved in. Now, I can't even look at them because their bodies are like ghosts pressed into the glass. Their lust splashed across my house like blood at a damn crime scene.

Mama once told me, "Baby, on the long days when the world is loud and life seems hectic, you can always retreat here to pause, and you'll be right in the middle of God's peace. If you listen close enough, you'll receive that same peace as a parting gift. One that'll help you keep on keepin' on."

My phone's notification brings me out of my thoughts and back into right now. A group message from my boys about open mic tonight at Cream.

"Jarell!" I hear Fran calling me from the kitchen. "Jarell, yoo-hoo." I drop a thumbs up in the chat and slide my phone back into my pocket, then go find Fran in the kitchen.

"Ms. Fran, can I get you anything? The house is pretty big. You may be here all day."

"You staying while I clean?" She questions while slipping on her gloves.

"No, actually I'm leaving." I inform her. "Do you need me to get you anything before I head out." I ask once more noticing she didn't reply the first time.

"No, I'm okay. Are you okay?" Even with her thick accent I could hear her motherly concern. A concern that caused a lump to gather in my throat as my eyes tilted down to the tile floor. I nod hoping I can convince myself first.

"Yes, ma'am I'm okay." The lie is bitter to the taste but it gives me the courage to lift my head at once. Her eyes are now examining me as she uncrosses her arms to continue unpacking her cleaning supplies.

"Okay, then I start cleaning. Okay?" She knows better but I can tell she also doesn't want to pry.

"Okay." I say but remain still with my hands cradled and resting on top of my head.

"Okay, Go." She waves me off without even looking at me.

I reach into the pocket of my sweatpants to pull out a few hundred-dollar bills.

"Here," I say, sliding the money across the counter.

She looks at me like I've lost my mind. "No! I will not take that."

"Ms. Fran, I'm not asking. This is for you. If you don't want it, leave it. I'll just send it as a tip through the invoice."

She walks around the counter, pats my hand, then shoos me out of her way.

I take the gesture as my cue to leave. Heading back toward the front door, I pause, hand on the knob. I really hope Fran's cleaning can bring that sense of peace back and make my house feel like home again.

Closing the door behind me, I pull out my phone and open the notes app and get to typing.

Again, you were right. Peace isn't a place, it's who's in it.

A few salty tears slip from my eyes and land on the screen as I stare at the words for a moment.

Then, I delete the whole note, whispering, "Miss you, Ma."

I tilt my head back and exhale.

"Ughhh, I need a fucking drink," I groan, sliding my phone into my back pocket and heading to my car.

Pack Light

Yari

Auditions went well. We selected a trial troupe of twenty-two ladies. They'll all have a week of intensive training, and a chance to show what they've learned at an event we're hosting this weekend for some sport executives.

Imani and I are cleaning all the gold streamers off her studio floor when a thought makes me pause.

"Imani, I don't know what to do about me and André," I voice, posting myself against the mirrored wall, arms crossed.

Pausing her own cleaning to walk over to me, she comes to stand next to me, placing her hand on my shoulder.

"Yari what is going on? I don't know much about him, but I feel like he's dimming your light." She widens her eyes, shaking her head before continuing with, "Every time you speak on him you're in a funk. He's giving bad vibes, babe. No harm, no foul, but I don't like the sound of this goofball."

I snicker at her quick shift in attitude. "I know Mani. He's great though, I just feel like we keep missing each other, like there's never enough time. We're supposed to be going to Mulancia next week," I trail off for a second as my mind wanders. "I really hope that he doesn't cancel." Dropping my arms to my hips and turning to face the mirror as I say the hard part out loud, "I can't deal with this distance between us, we live in the same damn city. Come on, you know? Am I holding on for nothing? Like, am I trying to convince myself there is even something still there?" I needed to say that while looking into my own eyes.

Imani faces the mirror looking at me while she speaks, "Yari, honey, look at yourself. You are worth making time for. We all get busy, but we also make time for the things we want and love."

She sounds so matter of fact with it I can do nothing but nod in agreement. André was running out of time with me. The clock was due to strike soon. I really wanted who he had shown he could be, but waiting on him to return was causing my curls to drop and my heels to come off. I was tired of dancing.

"Girl you right, he better make things right." Switching to a sing song tone, *"If he don't get his act together, he gone have to,"* I pause to look at her smiling as she joins in, *"Pack lite!"*

We burst into laughter and get back to cleaning the studio.

"I'm gonna catch you later, boo. I have to meet Jarell at FLEXD. Are you and Naveah still coming by Cream tonight?" I ask in a light hopeful tone. "You know we have open Mic on first and third Mondays of the month."

"Girl yes, I did put in a request for us to get a section but it's pending," she answers, while I'm popping the trunk of my car to place the uniforms in.

Nodding absentmindedly, I pull out my phone, taking it off do not disturb to text Jarell. It's then I notice three missed messages from André are waiting for my attention. Rolling my eyes, I swipe right past them.

Yari [3:27 PM]: Jay I'm running a little
behind schedule, but I'm headed to you
now! See you soon!

Like clockwork he texts me right before I can put my phone back in my pocket.

Jarell [3:27 PM]: It's all good I'm here
whenever you're ready!

For some reason his response makes me blush, and I forget Imani is in front of me.

"HELLO, earth to Yari!" she says sarcastically, waving her hands in my face.

"Oh, my bad," I giggle, coming back to earth. "I'll make sure we have our section of course, don't worry."

She's side eyeing me as I give her a hug.

"Umm girl, you're glowing and blushing. He must be fixing something!"

She's assuming I'm talking to André. Laughing at the thought, I shake my head, "No, it's not André."

Her jaw drops and her head does a slight tilt to the side. "So you already stacking up a little roster?" She suspects and I find myself giggling.

"No, but don't get my wheels turning, we both know I'll take it to far."

She laughs. "You know what you're right. I don't want you back in your college days when you were jumping frat houses."

My jaw drops. "Oh, see you didn't have to go there Miss. Waiting By The Phone."

Her laughter quickly turned into a giggle. "You didn't know what was in that package girl. You would have been waiting by the phone too."

I walk around to the driver side of my truck with Imani following me. "Yeah, I bet" I state before turning to give her a hug. "I'll see you later."

Pulling out of the hug "See ya" she says lightly jogging back into the studio. I wait for her to get back inside then head towards FLEXD.

Pulling into the parking deck I look for Jarell's truck. I smile, parking in the spot right next to him. As I get out of my car I hear someone call out my name, "Yari!"

I turn to see a familiar face walking towards me with a hoodie on. "X?" I smile realizing who it is. Xavier Duvall, Jarell's right-hand man since middle school. I inherited his friendship because of their brother like bond. X was a class clown. Always getting into trouble for trying to impress the ladies. A bad boy turned entrepreneur. After his run in with some trouble a few years back he took his love for the street life and decided to use it for good. He's now the proud owner of X-Force Security Solutions. Employing the city's most known ex-cons and OG bad boys who wanted to do things right the second time around.

"What's good girl?" he greets, hugging me. "Sorry if I'm sweaty. I just finished a few rounds of kickboxing with Cam's crazy ass," he says pointing behind his left shoulder with both his thumbs.

I laugh as Cameron walks over towards us pretending to still be kickboxing.

"Don't come over here with all that extra shit," Xavier yells out throwing up a block.

"Y'all crazy," I laugh, shaking my head.

"What's up Yari? Looking good girl," Cam says casually, as he reaches out for a hug. Cameron Banks has a way of filling a room without raising his voice. Where Jarell is steady and Xavier is sharp, Cameron is the quiet thread that keeps their trio from unraveling. His locs are always pulled back, his patience steady, and when he finally speaks, people listen.

"Thanks, Cam. I'm just meeting up with Jay for some much needed 'maintenance'," I say, using air quotes on maintenance, remembering my earlier conversation with Jarell.

"Oh, he gon' help you drop a few pounds in that head of yours?" Xavier teases, mushing my head.

Cam laughs, adding his two cents, "Right that's all he gone be able to do."

I roll my eyes crossing my arms. "Shut up yo, my fucking head ain't that big!" I spit, trying to hold back my laugh at their slick ass compliments.

"Sure," Cam concedes, rolling his eyes.

I chuckle and playfully punch him in the arm. "Are y'all coming to Open Mic tonight at Cream?" I probe, grabbing my gym bag out the backseat of my car.

"Of course! After the weekend I just had, I could definitely use some spoken word, a little live jazz, and a smooth ass cigar," Xavier admits.

"Oh yeah, Yari, I've been meaning to set up a meeting with you so we can work on amping up security at Cream for the coming season." He pulls out his phone creating a reminder for himself.

"Sure thing. Let's set something up before end of the month."

Looking down at my phone, I notice the time, 4:31 PM. Before I can dismiss myself from the conversation, I see Jarell standing at the entrance of the building. I bite my lip nervously, worried I've been holding him up.

"Jay," I say, pouring as much innocence into my voice as possible.

"Ma'am, are these jerks harassing you?" he asks, a smile on his face.

I sigh in relief. "Oh, he's not mad," I mumble under my breath.

Jarell walks towards us, dapping up Xavier and Cameron before wrapping me in a hug. He smells so good.

"No, they were just begging for change," I laugh, covering my mouth to hide it.

Cameron looks at me in disbelief, jaw dropping. "Oh, you got fucking jokes?" he shakes his head, throwing his hands up in surrender to my sarcasm.

"Wow, it's like that?" Xavier asks, nodding his head.

Jarell turns to me, probably feeling my hesitation about our session. "Yari, you ready?" he asks, tone confirming he can feel my energy.

I take a deep breath and give him a gentle smile, "As ready as I can be."

We say our goodbyes to Xavier and Cameron and head into the gym.

Jarell

I had already set up everything we'd need for our session in my private training room next to my office at the back of the building. So, I lead her there, watching as she drops her gym bag on the floor near the weight station. I keep my eyes locked on her as she puts on her gloves, trying to gauge what weight she should be lifting. I must be staring too hard cause she quirks a worried looking eyebrow at me.

"Yes?" she asks, her tone hesitant, almost scared.

She's either judging herself or afraid of my judgment. That's not going to work. So, I look into her eyes. She's holding back tears. I can see her fear in her stance.

"Yari," I say as softly as I can. Reaching for her, I embrace her and feel her worry melt away.

"Jay," she whispers, and I can hear her sniffling into my

hoodie.

Lifting her head, I wipe her cheeks. "Talk to me, baby girl. What's up? Is this about the setup," I ask, waving at the room.

"No!" she quickly replies. Pausing for a second before continuing, "well yes, but it's not just this, it's everything."

At this point I'm beginning to feel like I've taken up too much of her mental space. Maybe my bullshit is causing her extra stress and that's the last thing I want to do. Yari was always so kindhearted with the people she cared about that she would put their needs ahead of her own, without ever considering herself first.

"Yari, I called a cleaning service for my place. I can definitely go home tonight and work through this shit on my own. I'll be fine. I don't want – "

"Jay, no!" she cuts me off, her eyes wide. "This isn't because of you. You don't have to go home until you're ready to, I meant… It's just… I have so much going on and it's making me feel," she drops her head in frustration.

I reach for it, lifting it once again. "Making you feel?" I ask, hoping she'll allow me to be a shoulder for her to lean on for once.

"As if I'm not good enough. I feel so fucking stupid," she whispers the last part but I hear her loud and clear.

Her words hit me like glass shattering in my chest. Stupid? Not good enough? If only she knew how many nights I'd prayed she'd see herself the way I see her. Her radiance, too much for any room and yet never enough for herself. The way she talks down on herself makes my jaw tighten, like I'm standing on the sidelines watching somebody I love take punches they don't deserve. I want to catch every single one, carry the whole damn weight just so she doesn't have to.

"Yari…" I let her name settle between us, softer this time.

"I'm trying my best not to overstep, but if you gone talk to yourself like that in front of me, then you need to know I'm gone be all up in you're A and your B. I'm not just gon' sit here quiet. You say you not enough? Then I'm gon' spend every word I got reminding you that you are. All of you."

She gives me a little smile. I'm glad I can lift her mood, even if only for a second.

"I know you haven't met him yet, but André keeps ditching and dodging me. He canceled our plans for dinner tonight, even though we promised we'd make it a point to take time for each other."

I shake my head in disbelief. I know she ain't feeling like this over no dude. She's too smart for that, and whoever this dude is, clearly isn't if he's fool enough to be playing with her time. She's top tier when it comes to holding someone down.

This situation is not about my feelings on this dude though. I need to focus on her feelings, not mine. She needs me to be her shoulder to lean on, and I'm going to make sure I'm a damn good one.

"I hear you Yari, your feelings are valid for sure." Embracing her then leaning back to look at her, I continue, "Have you tried speaking to him and finding out what happened? Maybe this time was different and he wasn't on bullshit. Try talking to him. It doesn't have to be tonight, but at some point, when you're ready," I say, wiping the single tear that falls from her eye.

"You're right, Jay. It's just, being here, while dealing with him avoiding me, is making me feel like maybe I have gained too much, and he's not attracted to me anymore or something."

I almost laugh at the ridiculous statement. Inside, it hurt to hear her talk like that, like she couldn't see what was plain as day. She's enough exactly as she is, always has been. But it wasn't just her body she was doubting, it was her whole worth tied up in it.

That's the part that stung, because I knew better. I always knew better.

So, I told her, "Yari, don't do that to yourself. You're more than enough always have been. Don't let one man make you question that.

Remembering I'm supposed to be her shoulder. I continued, "Yari, any man would be lucky to even orbit your world." I wanted to say, especially me. I wanted to say, you don't even see the way you light up a damn room.

But I stick to the script because this ain't my scene to steal.

"I can't believe he'd ever be thinking that." I'm really talking this dude up like I know him now, when he really needs his ass kicked for making her question herself. Meanwhile, I'm here wiping his girl's tears, making her juice, watching her glow in the morning.

But nah, I need to chill, it's not my place to judge what they have going on when my girl can't keep her panties to herself.

Taking a deep breath and dropping her head before looking back at me she asks, "You think so?"

I chuckle at the giddy look in her eyes, smiling and biting my bottom lip while nodding. "Yeah, I think so."

She smiles squeezing me tighter. "Thanks, Jay."

She lingers in the hug. Maybe half a second too long. Just long enough to make me wonder if her embrace could mean something more.

I pull back slow, because wanting her right now would be selfish.

She punches me in the arm.

"Damn, what was that for?"

She laughs, shaking her head at me. "Don't ever play with me thinking you're the reason for my tears."

I rub my arm, laughing through the sting. "Okay, damn. You pack a fucking punch, huh?"

She tosses her head like her hair isn't in a bun. "Yep, and don't fucking forget it."

"Alright then," I grin, "Let's do this."

She fixes her bun and pulls on her gloves, a little lighter now, but I can tell something still lingers. There's a weight holding down the corners of her smile.

I want to say something, to remind her again that she's not hard to love, but I stay quiet. It was his words she needed to hear. Those were the words that would comfort her.

"You still coming to Cream tonight?" she asks.

I nod, unwinding a fresh pair of wraps. "Wouldn't miss it."

I look away, giving myself a second to ponder, reminded that she doesn't need saving. She just needs someone to stand still long enough to stay.

Yari's session goes well. She perked up after our talk which allowed me to focus on the plan I wanted to create for her. Even though she's self-conscious, she's beautiful inside and out. I don't mind reminding her of that any chance I get. Besides, everybody's body is different.

"Aye Yari?" I call out, swinging my gym bag over my shoulder.

She looks up at me while tying her shoelace, then stands to walk with me. "Yeah? What's up?"

I hand her a bottle of water as we approach the main lobby. "You did amazing today. We can do twice a week if you have time in your schedule," I offer.

She smiles. "Twice a week? Yeah, I can swing that. I feel great, thank you so much, Jay."

I can tell she's blushing as she goes in for a hug. Wrapping my arms around her I glance at my smart watch and see I have a missed message from Q.

I still haven't confronted her. Kissing my teeth when I realize I can't keep avoiding her makes Yari pulls out of the hug.

"What? Do I stink?" she asks, sniffing under her arms.

I chuckle, my brows raising in amusement. "Naw you good." My chuckle dies down as I snap back to reality. "I got a few things to handle before I head out. I'll meet you back at your place, baby girl."

She stares up at me; her eyes piercing my soul. If I stand here any longer, I'll start taking up too much of her emotional space. So, before she can inquire, I assure her, "I'm good, promise. I'll be there, at Cream, tonight."

She nods, giving me a partial smile and a fist bump before heading to the parking deck.

"Hey Siri, call Q," I command, as I place my bag on the front desk.

"I don't see a contact for Q. Who would you like to call?"

I really need to change her contact. Fumbling through my phone, I stare at her contact card before selecting the phone icon. Seconds later she picks up.

The Way Pipes Burst

Yari

The call ended fifteen minutes ago, but I'm still in FLEXD's parking deck. Sitting in my car, staring into my own eyes in the rearview mirror, trying to ground myself. My phone's face down on the dashboard as if showing its screen is too shameful after it betrayed me.

André said all the right things, or maybe just enough of them. A soft "sorry", a tired "I've just been slammed", followed by a "you know how I feel about you." That last one didn't hit like it used to.

After all that, here I am. Heart not quite healed, and hope not quite gone.

The windows are fogged from the warmth of my breath. I press my fingers against the windshield to clear it. Outside, the city hums in a way that lets me know it thinks I'm pretending again.

Jarell's gym lingers on my skin. Eucalyptus in the towels, faint lavender from the locker room soap, his silence and presence pulling out the tension in my shoulders.

And now, André's voice in my ear, pulling me in another direction.

I don't think, as women, we talk enough about the way memories soften a man's absence. About how love restructures itself into highlight reels when things start to stretch too thin. That we often forgive based on the beauty of what was. The joy we women find in keeping 'good enough' company way past its bedtime. So easy to forget the only things open that late, are the legs we part to give room to stars we wish would turn into something we could actually hold on to.

Sometimes, I remember the version of André that hasn't existed in a while. The one who used to know when to show up without being asked, who knew my moods without me naming them. I used to think that version of him was the only version I would ever have to love. I hadn't counted for the multiple stages of a person. Or how comfort allowed room for shoes to be kicked off and feet to rest no matter how much time passed.

Some men have the power to make you remember, even in their falling short, they once knew how to hold you right. When I try to remember moments he's held me down, I usually start with the day the pipes burst.

It was the week everything fell apart. One broken pipe, two canceled vendors, and a bank statement that made my stomach cramp.

The floor at Cream had flooded overnight. Just water at first. Then mud. Then mildew. Then doubt.

You get what you pay for, right? I was paying for using discounted labor.

I'd been sleeping in my office, high off resilience and low on backup plans.

My throat burned from yelling at contractors, and my eyes hadn't seen a clean eight hours in five days.

I wore the same hoodie each day, out of necessity, and surrender.

The morning he came, I didn't hear the door. Didn't hear the rain slapping against the brick outside or the wind knocking on the boarded up windows. I felt his presence, before I saw him.

"Yaya?"

No one called me that anymore. Especially not when I was working.

Not my granny before she passed, God rest her soul. Not even Jarell.

Only André.

When his voice goes soft like that, I know it means he can sense I'm drowning.

I turned slowly, expecting, a lecture, a demand. Instead, I found him standing in the hallway holding a bag of takeout in one hand, a toolkit in the other, wearing my old CAKES crewneck. The one I'd left at his place last spring.

"You didn't answer my texts," he said. "So, I brought your favorite. Griot and plantains, and a wrench."

My breath caught. I wanted to cry, or laugh, or just fold into the feeling of being handled.

Instead, I blinked at him, too tired to be cute, too worn to perform.

He didn't wait for permission.

He set the food on the front desk, kissed the corner of my forehead treating it as fragile ground.

Then, he crouched near the busted pipe like he'd done it a thousand times before. Looking like he was always meant to be there.

"I called a plumber," I whispered. "He canceled."

"I'm not a plumber," he said, "But I watched enough YouTube last night to fake it."

A beat passed. And then I let out a small laugh, one that

reminded me I was still alive.

We worked in silence for a while. Me sweeping debris, him under the sink with a flashlight between his teeth.

It wasn't romantic. It was real.

By the time the leak slowed, the sun had started bleeding through the back windows. The rain had stopped, but everything still smelled like wet memories.

"Let's eat," he said, already opening the box, laying out napkins.

I sat next to him, not across from him. Usually, the distance seemed natural. Like we were getting to know each other. But in this moment, I felt like I knew him, like he knew me. So, I let my guard down, allowing myself to melt with him. Shoulder to shoulder, like we were on the same team. Like maybe we always had been, because in that moment that's what it felt like.

He poured Cola into two cups and handed me one. I didn't realize how thirsty I was until I gulped it down like it owed me something.

"I've been thinking about your logo," he said after a while. "I think you should have it etched into the concrete right at the entrance."

I blinked at him. "That'd be fire."

He nodded his agreement. "It should feel permanent. Like you ain't going nowhere. Cause if I have anything to do with it, you not."

That's when I felt it. That nasal sting that comes right before tears.

He'd been listening. He'd heard me through all the mess, through all my doubt.

"André…"

He looked at me, lips glistening from the oil of the fried plantains, eyes soft. "Yeah?"

"I know I've been hard to read lately, but thank you for

showing up today."

He leaned back, arms spread along the back of the couch, a man settling into his home.

"I didn't come here to fix pipes," he said.

I turned to him slowly. "Then why did you come?"

He looked at me forehead wrinkled like I was asking a dumb question. "Because you didn't ask me to."

That night, he didn't leave. He stayed on the pull-out couch in my office. I curled up in my chair across from him with a blanket, remnants of hope and the smell of leftovers piercing the air between us.

At one point, around 3:00 a.m., I woke to him whispering what sounded like a prayer to himself. I didn't ask what it was. I didn't need to. Some things don't need translating.
And even though we didn't say anything at all, it felt like a conversation anyway. It was in the way he covered me with a second blanket I didn't know I had, in the way he muted his phone before I even looked up, in the way his breathing slowed when mine did.

In the morning, before the contractors came, he made coffee in the busted coffee machine I kept forgetting to replace. He handed me a mug and kissed my shoulder with the ease of a man that'd been doing the action for years.

In that moment, for the first time, it felt like we were building something. Not just repairing damage.

I remember that morning more vividly than the night we first kissed. More than the time he told me he loved me in the middle of a thunderstorm. Because that morning, he didn't say anything big. He just, stayed.

Later, he measured the floors without being asked. Sent me three flooring samples the next day. Tried to front the cost of the new tile. Even told me he had a connection at a bank who would look at my loan terms again.

I refused all of it, not because I didn't trust him. Because I needed to believe I could still do it myself.

But the fact that he even offered, that he came without needing to be asked, that stayed with me. Even now, months later, when he feels more like a voicemail I never listen to, I still remember the exact sound of his boots on my tile. The way he hummed to himself while tightening bolts. The way he didn't ask for anything in return.

A part of me is still in that moment, still sitting on the couch with cold griot, rain in my hair, and a man beside me who brought tools, not flowers or apologies.

That day, that was enough.

But, that was then.

I blink back into now. Into the hum of the parking deck, the echo of my own in my ears. The rain's stopped.

My phone buzzes once.

Jarell [6:06 PM]: You good?

That's it. No pressure, just presence.

I don't respond right away. I just hold the phone in my hand, a reminder that being seen isn't always loud. Sometimes it sounds like eucalyptus towels and a man who waits for your silence to turn into a sentence.

Jarell never demands anything from me. Doesn't try to outshine the chaos. He just waits, still and steady as a porch light.

I close my eyes and let the silence between us do what André's promises haven't, give me peace.

That, too, is something to remember. Not passion, plans, but peace.

The kind that doesn't knock, doesn't rush, doesn't try to fix with empty words.

Love isn't always fireworks. Sometimes it's a man sitting

quietly in your corner, waiting for the storm to pass, and never asking you to come out before you're ready.

The tap on my window mid thought causes me to jump a little, before I realize it's Jarell standing at my passenger door. Rolling the window down I proceeded to curse him out. "Jay what the fuck? You trying to give me a heart attack?"

His laughter helps me find my footing.

"Yo, are you good? It's been at least 20 minutes. Aww, were you waiting for me?"

I squint at him, "Boy please, my life don't revolve around you."

He pulls on the door handle, his mouth twisting. "Yes it does," He states, mushing my head while jumping into the passenger seat. "Let me bum a ride with you, then you can bring me back to my car in the morning." He dumps his bag in my back seat.

"Oh, you just bought the audacity platter for dinner? Oh ok, would you like any sides with that?"

"You're so corny."

"And, you're definitely paying for my gas."

"We're going to the same place."

"So?" I deadpan, popping him in the back of his head.

"Just drive, lady," he demands, clicking his seatbelt and waiting for the car to move.

I can't help but laugh.

Interlude

The Body Remembers

There's a difference between being looked at and being seen. I learned that early eyes can trace you and still miss the point.

The curves of a cheek or the bend of the brow, all the fine details that makes the picture whole.

Most days, I wear my confidence like a gloss, shiny enough to distract from the cracks underneath. The world likes its women polished, not honest.

Sometimes I wonder what it would feel like to stop performing for an audience, to let my skin be skin instead of a statement, to not have to turn everything into armor or invitation.

My grandmother used to say I walk like I know something no one else does. Maybe I do. Maybe I just knew from a young age that I would have to learn to hold myself up on my own. Her wrinkles revealed that time wouldn't last forever.

The mirror catches me before I leave, it always does. The makeup, the dress, the body, all remembers the late nights, the almosts, and the places I left too much of myself behind.

Still, I roll my shoulders back.

My body. It keeps the rhythm, the lessons, the proof that I've lived.

And that's enough, for now.

Slut Candy

Yari

The notification on my phone reminds me I haven't texted André back. I pull into my complex's garage, park, then grab for my phone.

"Jay, I'll be up shortly. You got your key right?"

"Yeah. Is everything ok?"

I smile at his concern, knowing that I was about to lie to his face. "Yeah, all is well."

He squints at me, tilting his head slightly. "Yari, come on, stop it. What's up?" he questions so tersely that his eyebrows draw marks across his face.

"I just forgot to text André after I was done with auditions."

His brows raise in shock at that one.

"Damn, Yari, it's almost 7," he says, shaking his head and opening the car door. "Yeah, you go ahead and text him. I'm gonna order sushi. You want some?"

Thinking, I respond, "Yes and some-"

49

"Miso soup, edamame and jasmine green tea. I got you!" he interrupts, finishing my thought.

I smile at his attention to detail. I would have had to tell André what I wanted. Granted, he's never around long enough for me to get hungry. I shove that thought to the back of my mind, scroll through my phone and hitting the call button next to André's name.

"Damn baby I thought you got kidnapped!" he says, once he finally picks up.

Why is he in such a good mood? Usually, if I take an extended amount of time to call him back, he's a jerk about it.

"Hey, yeah. I got all behind schedule…I'm about to eat dinner now."

"Oh, I was gonna ask you earlier if you'd be open to going out for dinner. I know I canceled before, but I took care of everything early today so…."

I'm not canceling my plans. He wants to act like he's doing me a favor after he's the one that canceled on me? Nah, I'm good.

"Oh, you did? Well, I wish I would've known sooner. I have plans at Cream. I have to be there. How bout we raincheck. Unless… you wanna come by Cream?"

I regretted the invitation as soon as it leaves my lips. I don't want him there, I just don't want to have to explain why.

"I understand. No big deal. Honestly, I would go to Cream, but open mic nights aren't really my thing, and I don't want to be a buzzkill. I'll finish up some work instead."

I quickly mute my phone. "Thank you, God! You always looking out."

Unmuting, I respond, "Ok, maybe we can still connect before vacation. I know we're both busy, but..."

"We definitely will. Could you slide over here before heading to Cream?"

Rolling my eyes and muting my phone again. "For what?" I

ask the air, beyond annoyed at this point.

Unmute. "Yeah, I'll head there real quick."

"Alright bet, I'll see you in a few."

With that, we hang up.

I can't even pretend like I'm excited to see him.

"It's just going to be a waste of time, but play along, Yari. Maybe he'll realize you're pulling back."

Looking at my reflection in my rearview mirror, I pull my hair into my signature messy bun. Trying not to cry, but the tears start falling anyway.

"Get it together, Yari."

My phone rings, interrupting my thoughts. It's Jarell. I answer without hesitation.

"Yari?"

His voice melts me. I hold nothing back. I start openly crying, my head pressed to the steering wheel. I hear the call end. Three minutes later, Jarell is opening my door, pulling me into his embrace.

Neither of us speak while I get myself together in his arms.

"I'll be back," I say, once the tears have slowed. "I'm going over to his place."

He lifts my head and our eyes meet. "I'll be here waiting for you. Call me if you need me. OK?"

A smile lights my cheeks as I release my eyes from his stare. "I will."

He steps back and waits for me to look at him again. "I'm serious Yari." His tone is stern, protective, firm. It makes my panties wet unexpectedly.

"I promise," I whisper, biting the corner of my bottom lip.

He hands me the keys. "I'll be waiting," he assures me. "Be careful, baby girl," he says, closing the door, waiting for my departure.

I smile, cranking the car and pulling out, heading towards

Andrés.

♩ ♩ ♩

André's very well off financially. He lives in a two-story mini mansion in Oaklin Hills. A five bedroom, four and a half bath gift from his dad for making junior CFO of his dad's finance company. Seemed more like a bribe than a gift to me!

Even when he had nothing going for himself. His parents were the type to make it happen for him. It was the one ick that caused me to gag. Once they bought his bachelor's degree, he was given permission to just 'live a little' while they footed the bill.

He popped up at Cream at the height of his party days, the night of the Valentine's Ball, and asked me if he could have the honor of buying me a drink. I blushed so hard my cheeks matched my lips. It wasn't until Arias, one of my lead Satin Dolls, handed me the drink and spilled the beans on tonight's occasion. Which got him all fired up. "For You Birthday Girl," she said slyly, wiggling her eyebrows in his direction.

My eyes shot towards him as he lifted two fingers and signaled for Arias to come to his side. As he whispered in her ear she looked over to me, all smiles and nods, then walked straight over to the DJ. Within seconds Arias had a mic in hand and was informing the entire lounge that we had an open bar until the end of the night.

She gave me the biggest smile, lifting her glass for a toast as she finished her announcement with, "A gift from a special friend on your special day. Happy Birthday, Yari!!"

We were so much happier then. Now, I can't get solid date plans to stick. I know we've both been busy, but this relationship has been too spacious for me. We can lose the status, if it's going to be stuck like this, I'd rather not deal.

Once I arrive at his place, I notice all his lights are off. I pull around to the double car garage that meets the curve of the driveway, park, and jump out the car.

"I can smell the privilege, and it stinks," I say to myself. turning my nose up while walking to the door.

Before I can knock, I'm greeted by André standing in the doorway.

"Hey Baby, come in. Wait! Close your eyes and put this on," he says excitedly, handing me a blush pink blindfold.

This is different. I wonder what he's up to. I can't help but blush a little. I take it while looking at him suspiciously.

"Don't be on no freaky shit Dré. I still gotta go to Cream," I remind him as I slip the blindfold over my eyes.

He grabs my hand and guides me inside. For the first time in weeks, he's reminding me why I gave him a chance to begin with.

Taking a few steps forward, I hear the door close behind me, and R&B softly playing in the background. André's hand tugs at the blindfold and he instructs me to open my eyes. My jaw drops as I look around his living room at what seems to be hundreds of lit candles.

"What is all of this Dré?" I ask, walking over to the couch.

"It's me making it a point." His voice gets lower the closer he walks up behind me. Kissing my neck, he slides his hands down my breasts, resting them right at my stomach.

Goosebumps raced along my skin as the heat inside me swelled, impossible to hide. Turning me around, he kisses down my neck, slowly trailing his tongue down to my breast. I let out a moan, giving him permission to continue. His hands grip my ass lifting my legs around his waist.

I've been wanting this, wanting us in this energy, for weeks.

He sits me down on the couch removing my biker shorts, sliding my panties off along with them.

"Dré, I have to get to Cream!" I exclaim breathless.

He looks up at me while kissing my island. "Not before I

make you." He punctuates his sentence by throwing my legs over his shoulder and using his tongue to lap at my wetness like a man dying of thirst.

I wrap my feet around the back of his neck, hips floating higher while I ride his face. Arching my back to bury my head into the couch pillows. Forgiveness begins to pour from me as I inhale. Except, hold up.

"What the fuck?"

He sucks on me, unaware of the shift in my mood, assuming I'm giving him a climax medal. But I've fallen out of the mood. What the fuck is this smell? Fruity, cheap, and bold notes scream through the couch pillows as I fight my orgasm.

"Dré, stop," I whisper, a tear falling down my cheek.

"Come for me Yari!"

I'm so disgusted. Why does his couch smell like some cheap, dirty ass female? Trying to ignore the ledge I'm hanging off, I lift my hand to wipe the tear and let out the fakest version of ecstasy I can muster. Then, "Dré, I... I have to go."

He lifts his head smiling. "Okay baby, I just wanted to let you know that I know I have a lot to make up for. This is just the start. Go handle your business. Call me tomorrow. Ok?"

I sit up, slipping my panties and bikers back on.

"Sure thing. I gotta go."

I don't look back. Just grab my keys and walk out doing my best to imitate a woman who wasn't about to fall apart.

Sliding into the driver's seat and closing the door, I'm still breathing in someone else's scent. It's clinging to my skin.

I don't need saving! I just need someone who doesn't disappear when the mask comes off. Instead, there I was, half-naked on a couch, soaked in perfume that wasn't mine. Faking love and orgasms for a man who kept mistaking performance for presence. Trying to convince myself this was love, and that all it would take was forgiveness to make it feel like desire.

I don't cry this time. I just drive. Straight to the only place I always feel seen.

Home.

Bottom Of The Glass

Jarell

I finished my sushi, my shower, got dressed, but Yari's still not back. I'm starting to worry. Checking the time, I start to pace. I wonder if Yari is okay. It's damn near nine o'clock.

As if she can read my mind, my phone rings, lighting up with her name. I swipe right to answer.

"Yari! Where are you?!"

"I'm on my way."

I know something's wrong but I'm not going to push her. I need her to make it back to me first.

"Ok, how far are you?"

"I'll be there in 15 minutes."

"Bet, I'm about to make myself a drink if that's cool. You want your old fashioned?"

"No, I want Vodka."

"Vodka? Since when you with the clear?"

"Since right now. I'll be there soon!"

She's snappy but also hurt. She's doing her best to mask it, but I can tell.

"Alright I got you! But Yari?"

I have to say something.

"Yes?"

I can hear her sniffling. The sound of her tears had become known to me over the years. I do my best to pay no attention to the picture I had painted in my head. Her driving through the city, face puffy, and eyes bloodshot red.

"You're amazing. Just know that. I'll see you in a few."

I hang up and try to imagine what could be wrong. I can't imagine what's got her all worked up. Whatever it is, it better not be about some dude. She's way too well put together for some lame ass to be snatching her smile.

Trying to shake the thoughts of what could be going on with her, I head over to the kitchen to fix her a drink. I'm squeezing some lemon juice over the crushed ice I've added to her martini shaker when her front door opens.

Yari walks in, eyes as wide as a deer caught in headlights. They're swollen too, and ringed red.

Walking over to her, I try to grab her arm, but she pulls away.

"I should have fucking known!" she yells, throwing her keys on the counter.

"Yari, what happened?" I question, wishing I could get her to calm down long enough to let me in.

"Jay, I can't believe this shit! I need a shower."

I sit on the barstool, grabbing for her hand. This time she doesn't pull away. "Baby girl, you have to calm down. I'm here. I'll wait for you to take your shower, then we can talk."

She drops her head, letting out a sigh before tears start pouring over her cheeks.

I stand to embrace her. She's a wreck.

I've only seen Yari this way once before, and that was almost

5 years ago now. It was when her mother was first diagnosed with breast cancer. She spent weeks disconnecting from the world, isolating herself in pain. I promised her then that I'd never allow her that type of isolation again.

She gained the weight that makes her so self-conscious now during that time in her life. Her curves have never bothered me, I think she's beautiful inside and out. But, I think the standards of the world make her think otherwise, and she beats herself up about her weight every chance she gets.

I refuse to let her unravel like that again. It would do nothing but break her.

I step back, giving her time to purge before I slip my hand under her chin lifting her head. The salt in her tears have burned the whites of her eyes even more. I use every bit of energy in my body to transmit a sense of calm to her through my eyes. I send her love and understanding with no judgment.

She softens under my gaze and her breathing evening out.

Cupping her cheeks with my hands, I say, "I'm here."

She blinks away the last of her tears and they splash onto my skin. Transferring her pain into my palms because, right now, I'm the only one she trusts to carry it.

"Can you sit with me while I shower?" she asks, searching my eyes for an answer.

Without hesitation I nod. "Of course. Whatever you need, baby girl."

I tilt my head into the direction of her room, never taking my eyes off her. I lean into her, close enough so my whisper doesn't echo "Whenever you're ready."

For the first time since she walked into the loft her dimples deepen as she gives her face the chance to express a closed-lip smile.

Walking into the bedroom I stop as Yari continues towards her bathroom. "Would you like me to stay here until you're finished?" I ask, taking a seat on the chaise lounge in the corner of her room.

"What, can't you take the steam?" she teases, her back to me.

I watch her peel off her shirt, her disgust with the article of clothing clear in her every move.

My eyes trail down to the floor. "I can handle the steam, I just didn't know if you wanted some privacy," I state, trying to let her know her comfort is what's important.

"That's up to you," she replies, dropping her pants down to her feet.

I keep my eyes on the tiled floor so I can control the life rushing through my body.

"Damn," I mumble to myself.

"Jay? Can you hand me my towel please?"

I spot her towel from where I'm sitting, getting up to grab it. "Yeah, I got you!"

Turning back to her, I squeeze my eyes closed, stretching my arms out blindly to hand her the towel. I can hear her giggling as she grabs it from me.

I head back to my seat and continue to wait for her story. I hope she tells me what was wrong soon because it's going to bother me all night if she doesn't.

"We're still going to Cream right?" I hear her call out from the bathroom, steam spilling out of the shower and into the bedroom as she appears in front of me. I'm in awe at the sight of her.

She's standing across in the doorway of the bathroom in a champagne-colored silk robe, her hair in a looser version of her messy bun. She does the effortless beauty thing so well.

Picking my internal jaw up off the floor, I stand up to regain my focus.

"Sure. Are you gonna talk about what happened before we go?" I ask while she hunts through her closet for what she plans to wear tonight.

"No." Her response is so fast it catches me off guard. She backtracks just as quickly though. "You know what? Actually, yes," she says popping her head out the closet. "André must be crazy if he thinks I'm stupid," she says, apparently ready to really get into it now.

I sit again, I think I'll need to be relaxed to stay calm for this story.

"I'm over there thinking he's stepping up and starting to realize that he has been distant," she pauses, peeking out the closet again. "Jay, I walked in blindfolded. Completely vulnerable, gave him all my trust," she shakes her head as she say this, stepping back into the closet.

"A blindfold?" I scrunch my brows, tilting my head to the side. "That's different. Why a blindfold?" I ask, anticipating a story worth hearing. Though, whatever it's about definitely can't be good. The way she was crying doesn't give off 'Man of the Year' energy.

She's slightly breathy as she responds, "Oh, so he could put on a show for his so called apology."

I can tell she's putting on clothes with the sound of tussling coming from the closet. I check my watch to make sure we'll have enough time to get to Cream. We're fine.

Yari pops out from the closet in a chocolate brown lingerie style dress, a pair of heels dangling from her hand. Her skin is glowing, and I can smell a luxurious mix jasmine and vanilla bean radiating off her. She walks over to her vanity and sits as she loosens her bun.

"The apology definitely didn't go over smoothly, by the way you called me," I say, trying to distract myself from her body so I can focused on what she's talking about. I look at her through her vanity's mirror so she's aware she has my attention.

"No, it definitely didn't, Jay. It truly didn't." Her eyes are locked on mine and I can tell she's yearning for something.

I stand walking over to her keeping my eyes on hers. Her shoulders raise as I approach, her head starting to drop, but I catch it turning her face up towards me. Forcing our eyes to reconnect. "Tell me what happened, baby girl," I coax, using my thumb to wipe the single tear rolling down her right cheek. She raises her right hand to meet my left. A thick silence falls between us, as our eyes continue to draw portraits on each other's canvases. "Just tell me what happened, I'm not going to judge you or say some off the wall shit. We can even take a shot after."

Moving my hand from her face she gives me a pinched smile that barely uses her dimples and turns back towards the vanity to finish her hair. I lean against the exposed brick wall waiting.

"So, like I was saying, he blindfolded me and walked me into the house. We get over to the living room area and he removes the blindfold. And Jay, there were candles everywhere. It looked like one of those sexy movie scenes."

Yari stands, smoothing wrinkles out of her dress, as if it will help her smooth out the crumpled edges of her story. Then she sits back down to continue.

"I won't lie; it was beautiful. And for a second, I thought, maybe this is his way of showing up. From the floor to the coffee table, the fireplace to the banister, there were candles everywhere." Her face lights up at the thought. But drops as she continues. "We immediately started kissing and peeling off clothes, things just got hotter and hotter."

Side eyeing her I clear my throat. She pauses, eyes flicking up to meet mine in the mirror. "I know, I know. Spare the details. I'm getting there." She brushes a stray curl behind her ear, an attempt to tame her racing thoughts at the wildness of her story.

She giggles, "But this part is important though." She looks at me for my consent to continue.

"Ok Yari, go ahead," I concede as she sprays some foam stuff in her hands and applies it to her hair.

"I'll be as PG as possible, I promise. Ok, anyway so we're kissing when he picks me up and walks me over to the couch. At this point I'm anticipating what's about to happen. So, I throw my head back as things start to unravel."

I interrupt her "Yari? Come on."

She's throwing her head back? I don't want to hear about her being with another dude.

"Jay, just listen. I'm about to fall into ecstasy, right? I arch my back throwing my head back only to smell perfume that doesn't belong to me. I don't wear fruity skanky perfume," she says rolling her eyes before looking up at me.

My eyes widen in shock. "You what?" I grit out, starting to pace again.

Her breath catches, and she stands, getting ready to pace too, but she stops herself, sitting back down abruptly. "Jay, I don't even know what pissed me off more. The fact that I stayed, or that I tried to fake my way through it."

Either of those would have definitely pissed me off. I'm pissed off just thinking about it.

"Jay, I faked an orgasm so I could leave...It was disgusting." She swipes her makeup brushes off the vanity in one sweeping frustration coming off of her in waves. "At least respect me enough to just leave instead of playing games," she rants, grabbing her shoes and sliding them on.

My own anger is building too, but I pace faster trying to calm down. This isn't about my feelings towards his lame ass. I have to protect how she feels right now.

Except I can't hold it in. "I'll kill him, Yari!" I state, stretching my neck left and right.

She shakes her head at me with a small laugh. "Jay he's not worth it."

I kneel where at her feet. "You want me to fix us those

shots?" I wait for her answer as she finishes buckling the strap on her left shoe.

She nods, "Yes I need a double. And make it clear."

I side eye her pausing before walking out the room. "I'm pouring Casa Azul. No Clear."

I hear her suck her teeth in frustration as I head towards the kitchen.

Tonight we're leaving our troubles in the bottom of our glasses.

& To Me

Yari

The only word that can describe how I feel right now is, overwhelmed. Which is why I'm so happy Jarell is staying with me until whenever. Jarell's presence is like a steady hand on my back when I feel like I might topple, but at the same time he knows how to crack a joke or just listen until I breathe again. With André feeling so far away lately, I guess I've needed the extra reminders that I'm still worth showing up for. Having Jay here makes the weight feel a little lighter.

Fastening my right shoe, I get up to join him in the kitchen. I'm not going to let all this shit going on with André ruin my night.

"Alexa, play My Monday Meltdown Playlist," I command as I turn to exit my room, pausing to savor the notes from John Coltrane's tenor saxophone stack as they float up to touch the loft's high ceilings. I feel the tension in my body begin to melt with every note; that's all I want tonight, relief.

I spot Jarell as soon as I wrap the corner. His back is to me as he pours our shots. His stance steadfast and strong. He's wearing a pair of milk chocolate tailored trousers and a Brown Sugar & Ivory crisp tee topped off with a camel Kurabo denim jacket. His outfit pairs nicely with his Cole Haan penny loafers the color of sultry smooth Pierre Ferrand Cognac and a gold Cuban link. The monochromatic brown hues melt against his skin making him appear edible. His potent cologne tickles my senses as I enter the kitchen.

He turns around when he hears me, extending his arm to hand me my double shot.

"Thank you, Jay. You look clean by the way."

He smirks placing his glass down on the island, giving me a once over. "Ditto. You ready to head out?"

I down my shot and nod. "Now I am!"

I love Monday nights at Cream. When I opened the lounge a year ago, I knew I wanted Mondays to feel different. Grown, mellow, sexy, and sultry in a way that slowed the world down. That's why I set the dress code to nudes and neutrals; colors that melt into candlelight and mirror the smoothness of jazz chords smoked whiskey. Open mic takes the stage, and the whole place hums with something deeper than entertainment it feels like communion. The crowd is a living mosaic: shades of mocha, caramel, mahogany, and deep chocolate swaying beneath low amber lights. Conversations drip low and easy, glasses clink against tables, and every laugh carries the warmth of a room that knows itself. Mondays aren't just a night at Cream; they're the heartbeat I prayed this place would have.

We pull up to the front of the building parking in my reserved spot. Tony, Xavier's director of security for his company X-Force, meets us at the door.

"I knew that had to be you," Tony says, shaking his head and reaching to dap up Jarell.

"You would've handled it if it wasn't me. How's the family?

Did you guys enjoy the cruise?" I ask, releasing him from our hug.

Xavier and I just sent Tony and his family on a vacation as a thank you.

"Absolutely, Rachael and I can't thank you guys enough. It was the break we needed."

I smile, "Tony, it was no issue at all. I appreciate all that you do for me here. I can't thank you enough. I do have a few emails to send over to you this week though. One for a meeting about the contract events we got coming up this season. Also, some information about my plans for expansion opportunities. I want you to be a part of all of that."

His eyes widen and his face lights up, "Yes Ma'am. You know I got you. Let's get this work." He turns opening the door for Jarell and I to walk right into the vestibule that leads right to the lounge. We stop at coat check so Jarell can drop his jacket before finding our crew in our favorite section.

I slide into the booth right next to Imani, catching her off guard while she and X fumble around with something she's showing him on her phone.

"Girl where are Nevaeh and Cameron?" I ask. She shifts her eyes over her right shoulder using them to point in the direction of the bar that sits in the center of the lounge. Then turns right back to whatever her and X were chatting about.

My eyes land on Jarell's, the look of concern on his face warns me of the check in he's about to attempt. "You good?"

I reassure him with a closed-lip smile trailing my eyes behind him to catch Sasha's, my other lead Satin Doll, attention.

When she arrives at the table, I let her know, "I'm ready to get my night started."

"Amen to that!" I hear from behind me. Which can only mean one thing, Nevaeh and Cameron had walked up damn near at the same time as Sasha.

"Aye, aye! What's going on gang?" Cameron calls out before

plopping down next to Jarell.

"Hey Boss Lady! What y'all eating tonight?" Sasha questions as she scans the table for anyone's response.

Before I can answer, Arias walks over interrupting, "Yea, cause we already got y'all's usual drink orders on the way." When she sees Jarell at the table, she gives him a flirty, "Hey, Jarell," batting her eyes at him.

He doesn't even look up from scrolling through his phone as he replies with a, "Sup!"

"Damn, Arias," X scolds. "Is he the only person you see at this table?"

Jarell's eyebrows raise as he tucks his phone away perking up at Arias and X's getting into it.

"No!" she huffs, rolling her eyes

"Ok, then HELLO ARIAS!" X says way too loud, determined to redirect her attention to him.

"I just haven't seen him in a while, X. Yo ass be in here damn near every night," she quips.

The table harmonizes in laughter. She had a valid point. She saw all of my crew often, but Jarell wasn't around as much as the rest of us. But she wasn't fooling anyone, we all knew she had a little crush on him and wanted his attention. All the while X wanted hers.

"I'm too sober to listen to y'all go back and forth. I hope this is us right here." I admit as one of the other Satin Dolls passes a tray off to Sasha; waving at our table before moving on to her next task.

"Here y'all go," Sasha says, expertly passing out the drinks. "Yari, I'll let you think on food I'll come back later."

"Yeah, give us some time. I'll let you know when we have it all figured out."

She nods, excusing herself from the table.

Arias and X were still throwing little jabs at each other. I decide it's time for me to cut in and break it up.

"Hey, Arias, do we have the lineup for the showcase tonight?" I ask.

Her attention now on me, she thinks for a moment before replying, "Yes, we do have a small problem though. Which was why I came over in the first place," she explains, overemphasizing 'in the first place' and throwing a whole lot of attitude X's way.

"Okay what's going on?" I ask, ignoring her jab.

She gives me a tight-lipped look of worry. "So, Jim, you know our Saxophonist, right? Ok, well he has to leave early tonight with his band. I tried to schedule our secondary band, but the Jazz & Juke Fest is in Roseville this week. So, we have no live music for the last hour of tonight's showcase. They usually play exclusively during the last set for the poets."

I take in what she saying, trying to think quick since showtime is starting in 10 minutes. "Tell Isaiah to meet me in my office," I finally say.

Her face scrunches with confusion "Bartender Isaiah?"

"Yes, bartender Isaiah. He played Sax for his first two years of college before he went back to Track & Field. Which is really beside the point. Anyway, tell him to meet me in my office. And I'll need you to move some folks around. He's off for the rest of the night."

Shrugging, she gives a thumbs up and walks away.

"And that's why you're the owner, Yari. It's smart as hell for you to have people who have multiple talents working in-house in case some shit like this happens," Imani says, shoulder bumping me as I tap Nevaeh's thigh so I can excuse myself from the table to handle my business.

Within the next 20 minutes the night was flowing along smoothly. I stood near the side of the stage admiring the vibes spilling throughout the space. At this point the crowd at Cream was dense, a sea of brown tones, chestnut lined glossy lips, doorknockers, gold grills, fresh fades, locs, braids, blow outs, afros and multiple shades of melanin. The smell of shea butter, sweet French vanilla and amber permeated the room, dancing around the high notes and smooth baritones coming from the stage.

Local artists and those from surrounding cities showcased their talents during open mic night. It was definitely a vibe.

I set up an event planning committee for Cream last year once I realized our popularity was a blessing that needed to be honored. I didn't want Cream to be just another place for folks to get drunk and act a fool. I wanted to curate a space that would have a lasting effect on the culture of my city. Tears began welling in my eyes as I took in the energy of tonight, realizing that's exactly what I had achieved.

A hand on my shoulder catches me off guard, causing my head to spin around and those tears to fall.

"Hey, Jay! What's up?" I say, brushing away the tears.

"Baby girl, I'm proud of you! Look at this!" He lowers his head to my shoulder, turning me back around to face the crowd. "It's beautiful. It's like a family reunion in here."

I smile, taking it in once more. "I know I can't believe this vibe. Jay, I've been dreaming of this."

He comes to stand at my side, "Your dream is reality now. All those long nights, the money you had to save, all the things you've sacrificed, you deserve this. Girl this is better than we both expected," he pauses, "You coming back to the section? We've been waiting on you so we can toast to this shit!"

He stars walking towards the section, the question obviously more was more of an expectation. Shaking my head, I follow him back, finding a tray of shots and all my friends waiting for me.

"Yari, it's sexy as a motherfucker in here, with all these sexy motherfuckers in here, girl!" Xavier states excitedly, dapping up Cameron and grabbing his lowball to take a sip from his whisky.

"Hell yeah, man. Listen, Yari, it's lit in here!" Cameron adds, nodding in my direction causing me to blush.

"All facts girl. And it's MONDAY!" Nevaeh laughs

"Right? Everybody in here definitely got to work tomorrow!" Imani agrees.

"I most definitely gotta work tomorrow. Unless you giving me the night off Boss Lady?" I hear Arias ask from behind me as she walks past me, handing Imani another tray of shots and smiling before heading to the stage.

"That girl is a pain in my ass, but she handles the Dolls and makes sure everything is tight with them. Can't help but love her," I laugh watching as Arias grabs the mic from Quest which causes my forehead to wrinkle with a question.

Quest's a local poet who frequented our open mic nights. The crowd always had love for him. He's usually the last one up but we were about 10 minutes too early for that.

"What is she up to?" I ask, watching as my friends grow quiet. "What are yall up to?" I ask getting suspicious because the only time they get this quiet is when they're being sneaky.

"Yari, please grace us with some of your poetry tonight. It's been forever." Nevaeh pleads, batting her eyes in my direction.

"You should seal the vibe tonight, Yari. You created it!" Imani chimes in.

Before I can decline, Arias finishes her mini speech thanking everyone and is calling me up to the stage with her hands opened out to me.

The crowd turns in my direction, clapping. I don't know what she said but I was starting to get overwhelmed by all the love and appreciation.

Stepping away from the table once more, I stroll up to the stage. Arias wraps her arms around me in a quick embrace before she passes me the mic.

Turning around to face the crowd I search for my section of friends that have just put me front and center during our busiest open mic of the season

"Hello, beautiful people. I want to thank everyone for the support you guys have given to Cream. Curating this space has been a dream of mine for so long." I feel the tears coming back as everyone cheers and claps at my emotional expression of gratitude.

"WE LOVE YOU YARI!" Nevaeh and Imani yell and the whistle blowing and claps slowly fade.

"I haven't done spoken word in a while, but I was asked to seal this night off. I don't have anything prepared so Isaiah," Turning to look in his direction. "I'm going to need your help with this."

"Come on wit it!" Some pretty Afrocentric queen encourages from the corner of the room.

A chuckle leaves me as I lock eyes with her and see her melt back down into her seat.

"Just, inspire me," I request, looking back toward Isaiah.

He nods in my direction then begins to create magic with my grandfather's Saxophone. I give him a few counts to bring everyone inside the magic of his sound. I look over towards my section, only to spot Jarell with his eyes closed vibing. Closing my own eyes, I inhaled before I begin.

"He reminded me of Jazz. With his ability to calm me, allowing me the permission I sometimes needed to just, be.

We bare cadence to one another, a rhythm like swing. It guides us through wide ranges of expression and gives us a safe space to ride whichever wave chooses to brush against the shore of our emotions.

Horns ache beautifully blaring pen strokes of love notes written in symphony.

He reads me. Like melodies and lullabies and hymns. Like music. Like blue. Like gray. Like chords struck to meet bridges.

He cradles me like saxophone players in Barrelhouses. Or trumpet blowers in Juke joints.

He gives me the permission I somehow need to just, be. And to me,

He. Is. Jazz."

I flutter my eyes open as I hear the snaps clicks of appreciation start up around the room. Isaiah continues to play. My breath deepens as I place the mic on the stand ready to find the fastest route to my office. But, before I can grab the railing of the staircase that leads to my office, I feel a tug on my wrist.

"What the fu-" I lose my words at the sight of André standing in front of me with a bouquet of ivory roses. He's dressed in code, as if he had always planned to come. His linen ivory suit and white button up, show off his iced out 18 karat Cuban chain, almost making me forget what happened earlier back at his place.

Kissing my hand, he extends his arm to offer me the roses. "For you," he says, his voice so deep and low so that only I can hear him in this crowded room.

I leave his arm extended midair, gripping the apology he's desperately trying to present me with.

"What are you doing here?" I press; I'm not in the mood to be in his company. I don't want to play cat and mouse tonight.

"I finished my plans for the portfolio I was working on. I had you on my mind, so I figured I'd come peep open mic for once. To my surprise I got to witness you in an element I never get to enjoy."

Squinting at his words, I search them for signs of lies. Is he being honest? But what about that damn perfume? I can still feel the "slut candy" burning my nose hairs as I tried to decipher the truth of it all.

Crossing my arms, I turn to head down the tiled hallway that leads to the private glass elevator only used for private events and to get up to my office. Smiling tightly at everyone I pass so I don't cause a scene before I give him the curse out he's waiting on.

Before I can reach the elevator Arias comes out of the lady's room blocking our path. "Boss lady, you good?"

I nod, "I'm good."

She moves in front of me, "You sure?" she questions noticing André.

"Yes, I'm sure."

"Mmm-Hmm."

I can tell she doesn't believe me but she moves along watching us continue down the hallway to the elevator.

André hurries behind me to keep up with my pace, confusion written all over his face.

"So, you've seen me in my element and now, what?" I say, while we wait for the elevator doors to open. When the elevator arrives, I step through its doors and turn to face him. "You show up in a suit with roses like that's supposed to erase everything. What do you take me for, Dré? Some girl who needs gifts to keep her quiet? You don't see me. You perform for me. Boy please! Don't waste my time."

Walking into my office I hear my phone ding with a notification. Fumbling with my keys and my phone I peer at the screen to find a Neveah calling me.

"What up Nay? I'm kinda in the middle of something."

"Arias told us you seemed upset and Andre was with you? Where are you?"

I cringe. I knew she would say something.

Andre walks towards me getting ready to mansplain his bullshit. I'm not having it.

With both palms facing outward, I halt his steps so I can respond before this night turns into a melting pot. I take a deep breath to compose myself.

"Nay, I'm good. I told Arias that. I don't need rescuing. Are y'all fucking lifeguards or something? I don't need no little life coach trying to guide me through every step of my life. I'm a businesswoman above everything and I know how to handle my business. The best thing to do is let me handle on my own. I'll catch up with y'all later."

Nevaeh laughs a little then she responds so quick and witty. I can tell she's annoyed by me avoiding her help. I didn't mean to push anyone away but I needed to just face whatever this lesson was with André.

"Glad to know you can swim all of a sudden."

"Nay my bad, I'm just saying."

"Whatever Yari, save the spiel. It's not needed and I'm not interested. I'm going to swing Jarell over by your place since you're 'handling your business' and you must have forgotten y'all came here together."

"No, it's ok. Just – "

For the first time in a long time Nevaeh hangs up the phone on me.

I take another deep breath so I can give myself time to find the energy to address André. Then, I look him dead in his eyes.

"Answer me, Dré. Am I supposed to be happy?"

He steps forward to calmly place the roses on my desk, backing me up against it and caressing my face. "Baby, I told you, I'm going to do better. I'm here because I can't get you off my mind. How are you mad after all those words you spoke about me out there?"

I turn my head away from him. "Dré..." He pulls my head back towards him and starts kissing me. He feels so good, and this is what I missed but I couldn't get the smell out of my head.

I try pulling out of the kiss but Dré has me locked in. His arms wrap the small of my waist as he lifts me onto my desk, sliding my dress up my thighs.

"Andre, we aren't done talking. What are you doing?" He stops abruptly, pulling his vibrating phone out of his pocket.

"My bad baby, I need to answer this."

Rolling my eyes, feeling very much played with, I cross my

legs along with my arms so I can be in full attendance to what could be important enough for him to take a call right now.

"Hey Angie, you good?"

He paces back and forth a few times. Looking over at me every couple seconds as he entertains this conversation.

Who the hell is Angie? I just know he ain't on the phone with another woman right now.

Before I can stand, he utters words that draw me back and snatches my fury towards him right away from me. And I feel just a little stupid.

"Alright sis, let me know when you land. Don't stress too much. I can help you through prep for your CFA exams. Just let me know once you set a date to take them."

Sis? I mean I was partially correct, it was a female who left that smell in the couch pillows. I just didn't know it was his sister. He had briefly mentioned her before but we never went deep into conversation about her. All I knew was she was in finance school so she could join the family business as well.

"Ok that's cool don't sweat it. Oh yeah, umm…..Yeah..… Dad told me... OK then I'll send you something to hold you over til you start getting your stipends from your externship. We'll have enough time to plan out all of those details Ange, listen let me go okay and don't forget to let me know when you land. Love you."

André hangs up the phone and swipes through it once more before addressing me again.

"Baby, I apologize my sister was just letting me know she was leaving my house to catch her flight." He took a deep breath like something was bothering him.

"Dré is she ok?"

He nods, "Yeah, she's straight. I'm gone make sure she is."

I exhale fully for the first time since he answered the phone. "Dré…"

He places his pointer finger over my lips. "Come home with

me."

Without admitting that I was upset because I thought his distance had something to do with the "slut candy" I now know is "breast milk", I nod. Mostly out of exhaustion. Out of wanting to believe I overreacted.

I uncross my legs to allow my natural aroma to penetrate the space between us. But even as I stepped off the desk, I could still smell it.

That cheap, fruity scent. My gut was unsettled but I didn't want to fight about it tonight.

I grab my keys without looking at him. I didn't trust myself to make the smart choice, just the quiet one.

I switch off the lights in my office as he follows me out, closing the door behind us.

Interlude

Weights & Echoes

The gym is quiet for once. No bass, no breath, no clatter of plates, just echoes. The kind that reverberate through your bones.

I stand in the middle of the floor, hands on my knees, sweat cooling against my skin.

I wasn't chasing a lift goal tonight. I was chasing the sound of her laughter that filled this place when she'd stop by after closing, the way her perfume would float between the mirrors and the chalk dust.

I looked at her forgotten water bottle on the counter – half full, label peeling. It had been there for weeks. I kept saying I'd throw it away, but every time my hand reached for it, something in my chest said, *not yet.*

They always said time heals all wounds, but no one talked about the passing of time feeling like opening new wounds. About how healing still sounds like her name on my tongue.

Sitting down on the bench, elbows on my knees, watching

the red digital clock blink 2:54 a.m. Everything in me wanted to call, but my pride was stronger than my grief.

The mirror across from me shows a man I don't recognize, strong but hollow. The kind who can lift anything except the weight lying between us.

I exhale and the sound bounces once, then it disappeared somewhere in my mind.

Its weight held such an echo, longing.

What Still Lingered

Yari

I'm back in his bed. Lying against thousand-thread count sheets that still can't cover the ache. His breath on my shoulder. Warm, steady, comfortable. It's like nothing happened. Like cheap perfume doesn't live in his couch.

The overhead fan whirs like a lazy whisper. My body stays still, but my thoughts kept pacing. I stare at the ceiling for what feels like hours. Not because I can't sleep. But because I can't lie to myself in the dark.

My poem's still echoing in my ears. The snaps. The hush that came over the room. The way Jarell looked at me like I had just said something sacred. Eyes beckoning me as if they were calling me home.

But here I am. In a house full of luxury and leftovers. All I can hear is the hum of a refrigerator somewhere in the distance. And the breath of a man who thinks silence mean safety. I'd been faking forgiveness for a man who still hasn't said the words. I let him kiss me like that kiss erased everything he never admitted to.

Maybe that's my flaw. I crave acceptance so bad, I sometimes confuse it with silence.

I think about calling Jarell, I don't. I think about leaving, I don't. Instead, I slide my hand under the pillow, find my phone, and open my Notes app:

Maybe love isn't supposed to fix you. Maybe it's just supposed to stay when you can't.

I never hit save. Just stare at the screen until it goes dark. Just like everything else lately.

I slide out of bed, bare – emotionally, mentally, and damn near physically as I make my way to his bathroom. The light buzzes as it turns on, harsh and blue. The cold tile stings my feet. My legs feel too heavy, like the weight of regret had settled in my knees.

I didn't recognize the girl in the mirror. Mascara is smudged under one eye. Lip liner faded. My silk teddy bunched at the waist like it was tired of being seductive. I reach for a washcloth and run it under cold water, I hold it to my face.

"You're not stupid," I whisper. The tears begin to roll. I want to feel new, I want to feel untouched. I drop the washcloth into the sink and pull down the hem of my teddy, concealing what had already been exposed.

Reality is, that is not what I am. I feel washed-up, like a lady singing the blues in a ran down juke joint. But even as I try to wash his touch off my skin, I can still smell that cheap, fruity scent. Not mine. So, whose? I just can't muster up the strength to fight about it tonight.

Maybe that's the part that hurts the most. That I don't even have the energy to argue anymore. That forgiveness feels easier than confrontation.

I stare at myself, then stare harder.

You said you wanted love. So why do you keep settling for the cosplay version of what it should be?

I asked, but the mirror didn't answer.

I grab my phone from the bathroom counter, open the Notes app, and hover a finger over the pen box in the bottom corner.'

Maybe love isn't supposed to fix you. Maybe it's just supposed to stay when you can't.

I delete and type something else.

I can't fake it anymore. Right?

I delete that too.

I stare at the blinking cursor until the screen dims. Letting it fade to black just like everything else lately. I walk back to bed and lie down next to him. When he reaches for me, I let him. Not because I wanted to, but because pretending still feels easier than being alone.

And maybe that's the worst part. I don't need a savior I'd settle for someone who'd still be there when the applause dies down.

Someone who knows the difference between here and there.

This time, I don't need a hero. I just need someone who knows how to stay. And somehow, I still choose the one who disappears with the light.

I close my eyes and count my breaths. Not to fall asleep, but to keep from unraveling. Here I am again, pretending this bed doesn't feel colder with someone in it.

I know tomorrow will come with questions I'm not ready

to answer, with routines I'd outgrown, and with a man who keeps calling this relationship love even though he's never even taken the time to ask what I need.

I'd grown so used to performing love that now I have no clue how to even ask for the real thing without feeling like a burden. I'd become fluent in pretending. Fluent in, 'It's fine,' and, 'I'm okay,' and 'Maybe next time.' But tonight, I could feel it. The show was ending. And I'm not sure I have the strength to take a bow.

I must've drifted off at some point. But it wasn't rest. It was survival. The kind where your body surrenders because your spirit's exhausted.

When I woke, the sun was already slicing through the blinds, warm and merciless. André's already gone and with him went the scent of candles and apology. All that lingered now was thick, stale air.

I sit up slowly, the sheets tangling around my legs like consequences I hadn't agreed to. On the nightstand, a note scribbled on custom stationary read:

Had an early meeting. You looked peaceful. Let's reset tonight. Dinner? Your favorite place.
–Dré

My favorite place? He still doesn't get it. My favorite place was never a restaurant. It was the nostalgia for support and comfort. Consistency. Being chosen in daylight, not just when the lights are low. Not just for convenience.

I fold the note in half, then in half again, and tuck it in my purse. Not because I wanted to save it. But because throwing it away feels too final, and I'm not quite ready to admit that truth yet.

The quiet presses against me as I walk toward the master

bathroom.

Same cold tiles, same mirror, same girl. Only this time, the mascara is gone. But the ache? The ache is still there.

I reach for my phone, thumb hovering over Jarell's name. I type a message,

I have no words....

Backspace. Try to type it again.

Thanks for always....

Backspace again.

I turn off the screen, shutting it down like everything else lately.

And then I get dressed, not because I feel like myself, but because pretending still feels easier than starting over.

Still Rooting

Yari

The first thing I notice is the silence. Not the kind that screams and not the kind that settles in after someone leaves and you're forced to sit with the echo of everything they didn't say. No, something about this is softer.

It's the hush that follows a conversation you're not sure meant anything, but you keep replaying it anyway. The type of silence that lets the weight of something land fully, finally, without interruption.

André had tried. Really tried. Candles, music, and my favorite tea. But all it made me feel was how far apart we'd drifted. How easy it is to perform closeness when the real thing feels unreachable. I wanted it to work. Hell, I still do. That night in the lounge when he gave me the world in a glass and announced he was opening the bar's tab in my honor. I believed then. I believed in the possibility of him.

But I also remember the slow drift away from me. The way

his absence arrived in small ways first. Missed texts, changed plans, touches that felt more like habit than hunger.

That's what makes tonight so hard. Because part of me does want to be held, wants to believe in whatever apology his body could offer. But then there was that scent... fruity, cheap, loud. That smell on his couch wasn't mine. And neither was the version of myself pretending it didn't matter.

It's morning and I'm driving back from André's with the radio off, letting the night air press against my windows and the scent of someone else's perfume still coating my sweater. That smell ain't mine, but I'm stuck wearing it anyways. The gas light on my dash prompt me to pull into Lucky's.

A quick stop for gas and maybe some brown liquor wisdom from Ole Man EJ before I retreat home to my own daunting thoughts. Pump 3 is my favorite, right in line with the front door, the one that made it easy for the gas attendant to come out and lend a hand. Lucky's is your average gas station, but what made it feel like more is the man who had become its heartbeat: Ole Man EJ.

He never seems to be in the way. Everybody knows he just wants money for his brown bag, but nobody minds. We support him because he's a reminder that any one of us could be one tragedy away from slipping. Still, EJ never begs. He works for every bit of pocket change. The owners even let him become part of the station itself, and with the help of the community, they renovated the old shed beside Lucky's and turned it into his home. Now he tends the pumps, washes windshields, even fills your tires if you need it. He's the community's uncle, and we cared for him as such.

Hopping out my ride, I catch my own reflection in the glass. I don't look sad. I don't look angry either. Just... rooted in some version of myself I no longer recognize. That scares me more than anything.

"What's dat dere look on yo face miss lady?" I hear a

drunken slur from the other side of my truck and know Ole man EJ is already working on his tip.

"Hey Ole Man, how's yo night going?" I try to switch subjects even though I know he'll notice. He may be a drunk but he is no fool. His eyes peer around the back corner of my truck as I try to pump my own gas.

"Now, why would you try and do that?" He questions, jumping in between me and the gas pump.

I can't stop myself from snickering. "I'm sorry I wasn't trying to take your duties."

"Thank you." His hand reaching for the nozzle. "Now, who got yo spirit crushed up like this?"

I try to play it cool. Shrugging softly, I slide my hands in my pockets like the weight on my chest wasn't try to push the air out of my lungs.

"You know it's always somethin'," I say, my voice barely strong enough to hold the sentence upright.

Ole man EJ doesn't say anything right away. Just hums to himself like he was attuned to a frequency I couldn't hear yet. The pump clicked on, and I watch him lean into it like the ritual of fueling somebody else's car gives him purpose.

"You still tryna love somebody who don't know how to hold they own damn hands," he finally says.

It wasn't a question.

I look at him, startled. "What?"

He turns slowly, eyes cloudy but sharp enough to cut straight through me. "That smell on you ain't yours, miss lady. I done pumped enough gas for broken women to know when they drivin' away from somethin' that look good on paper but ain't never fed they soul."

I look away.

EJ keeps talking. "You ever seen a bird stay in a cage even when the door wide open?"

I nod slowly. "Yeah."

"Well, that's you. Sittin' there singin' for somebody who don't even listen. Wearin' somebody else's perfume, speakin' somebody else's peace. Tryna shrink yo shine just to feel held."

I swallow hard.

"I guess I just thought… maybe if I loved him the right way, he'd show up different."

EJ chuckles, low and tired. "Ain't that the first lie every woman tell herself? That love gon' build a man who already comfortable livin' small? Baby, love don't raise grown folks. Love don't teach people how to not be careless with a heart they ain't earned." He claps then rocks before speeding around to the other side of my car.

I stay quiet, letting his words lay against my chest like warm bricks. He walks over, grabbing the squeegee, and starts to clean my windshield without asking.

"A woman like you," he says while wiping in circles. "You don't need fixin', you need rememberin'."

"Rememberin'?"

"Yeah. Rememberin' who you was before you let somebody treat you like a favor instead of a miracle."

I feel something crack in my throat. My lips part, but nothing comes out, just the sound of my own breath thick with realization.

He finishes the windshield and tosses the tool back in the bucket.

"Now you go home," he says, wiping his hands on his shirt. "Don't call that man. Don't explain yourself. And don't go layin' down in sheets that still smell like another woman's shadow."

I blink. Tears threaten, but don't fall

"You gone be alright, miss lady," he adds, his voice softening. "Sometimes God gotta let a woman rot in the wrong soil long enough for her to stop callin' it growth."

I reach into my wallet, pulling out a folded blue note and

press it into his palm.

"Thank you," I whisper, "For seeing me."

EJ grins, that old gold gap-toothed smirk of his still shining despite the decades. "Don't thank me," he says, stepping back. "Just promise me next time you feel lonely, you don't go lookin' for company in a room that already emptied you out once."

The pump clicks off.

His eyes lock on mine. "You know, folks always talkin' 'bout movin' on like it's some train you just catch when you ready. But some things... some people... they ain't meant to be left at the station."

He wipes his hands again, this time on a rag, and leans against the pump, looking past me like he's talking to a version of himself he used to be. "See, when a flower don't bloom, you don't yank it out the ground. Naw. You check the soil. The sunlight. You see if it's chokin' on somethin' that ain't its fault."

He glances back at me, more sober than before. "Ain't always 'bout who stayed or who left. Sometimes it's about who *listened* when you got quiet. Who *waited* long enough to see you bloom again. Even when you didn't believe you would."

I blink, holding his words like water I'm afraid to spill.

He taps the side of my truck gently. "You gon' be alright, miss lady. Just make sure the garden you water don't keep killin' your joy. Root for *you* sometimes."

I nod, the lump in my throat making it hard to speak. "Thank you, Ole Man EJ."

He smiles again, crooked and gold gap-toothed. "Go on now. And get some rest. That spirit of yours look tired."

I get back in my car with silence still riding shotgun...but this time, it isn't heavy, it's honest.

And that's enough to get me home.

I get home and don't turn on the lights. I just stand in the middle of my loft, letting my purse slip from my shoulder onto the floor. My sweater follows. I don't shower. Don't change. I just sit on the edge of the couch and stare.

And just like that, I remember the garden. Not a real one. A memory. It was late spring. My grandma had just trimmed the back hedges and laid new soil for the rose bushes. I was eight, maybe nine. I wore little jelly sandals and a yellow sundress that never managed to stay on both shoulders.

She let me help. I was proud of that.

"You gotta talk to 'em," she said, showing me how to pat the soil gently, fingers curved like prayer. "Flowers don't just grow. They need to know you're still rooting for 'em."

I didn't get it then. But I do now.

Because loving André has felt like planting seeds in dry soil. Me praying with my hands. Watering a garden that keeps giving me thorns.

I know he loves me. Or something like it. But I can't keep calling neglect, love just because I'm thirsty for connection. And that's a truth that makes my chest tight.

Still, I miss him already. Not because of tonight. Not even because of the way he touched me. But because I'm grieving the woman I wanted to become with him. The softness I was willing to give. The surrender I was willing to practice.

Maybe I just wanted to be good at love.

My phone lights up on the table. A missed call, André.

I don't answer. Instead, I reach for the lighter tucked beneath the incense tray and spark the cedarwood. Let it smoke its prayers into the ceiling. I lie back on the couch, letting the scent soothe me.

I want this to work, I do. But wanting something ain't the same as being wanted. I close my eyes, whispering a name I don't want to admit is already forming behind every inhale, "Jarell."

Not because he fixed anything. Not because he showed up. But because when I break, he doesn't try to sweep it up. He just sits in the wreckage with me.

And somehow… that feels like faith. Like something that's still worth rooting for.

Broken Halo

Jarell

I haven't had a night like this in forever. I don't know what's going on with Yari, but after seeing how flared Nevaeh's nostrils were after their call, I wouldn't be surprised if she didn't let whatever it was get the best of her.

I open the door to Yari's place and the Meltdown playlist is still going. Even though the vibe was appreciated I wanted to have some time in silence, so I shut it off.

I strip down to my briefs, tossing my clothes into the laundry basket of the guest bedroom's closet. Yari had this room set up like a 5-star situation. Rolled fresh towels lined a closet inside the bathroom. A Bluetooth speaker inside the shower I could connect to my phone.

Turning on the shower, I walk out to the room to grab it seeing I have two missed calls and a few text messages waiting for my attention. I can't even believe this, two missed calls from Q. She's probably wondering where I've been. She has some fucking nerve. I'll call her after this shower. I need to relax before I speak to her. My jaw clenches as I shoot her a quick text.

> Jarell [1:17 AM]: I'll hit you
> back, pick up

> Q [1:18 AM]: Of course

I glance at a text I received from Yari.

> Yari [12:22 AM]: At Dré's. Make yourself at
> home!

I couldn't even be concerned about what he did or said to convince her that he was worth entertaining because I needed to find the words to speak to Q. Tossing my phone onto the bed, completely forgetting the speaker set up, I head for the shower.

Feeling torn on what I wanted to do about finding her, MY girl, in my house, in positions of submission, submitting to another man, discarding what I had been nurturing, her immensely disrespecting me in the worst way. I wanted revenge. There was rage in my heart. Not only did she dishonor herself but she broke a part of me that I've spent time healing.

I'd already struggled for damn near my entire life with trusting women. For years I carried a bad taste in my mouth from adolescence about the havoc they could wreak when chaos interrupted their plans. After years of therapy, I did my part, I did the work. I hadn't done anything to deserve this, none of it. Not my stepfather mistress throwing stones and hiding her hands, not Q pushing up on me at FLEXD in the middle of my healing and interrupting that progress years later with this fuck shit.

I wanted to marry her. At least I thought I did. I'd had the conversation with her father 4 months ago, asking for her hand in marriage. Since he's a Pastor he took that as honorable and commended me on thinking of a future with his daughter.

"Most young men don't think about creating a foundation," his words echo in my head like a broken record on a warped loop.

Foundation huh? Ha! That's comical. His fucking daughter just jackhammered the hell out of what I was prepping to build on.

Her mother overheard the whole conversation and swore to secrecy. I spoke to her best friend to assist with the decor for the proposal dinner. I bought a new suit and got thousands of fresh flowers ordered for the occasion. I had a spa day planned out for her the day before, a dress custom fitted for her, makeup artist, hair stylist, the whole nine, just so she would be picture ready. I was even flying in her entire immediate family and a few college friends for the occasion.

She would've had a flawless 3 karat D color cushion cut double halo diamond ring on her finger just in time for snow to begin dusting the ground.

Oh yeah, I'm getting my revenge.

I throw on a pair of red FLEXD joggers, grab my phone from the bed and head into the kitchen to make me a drink so I could give Q a callback.

I loved that Yari had the most unique range of liquor. Her bar was staged and designed like a library. It had an entire wall with built-in cabinetry designated to the craft of spirits.

Making myself a drink I slide the prompt on my phone to Q's contact and hit call. Without hesitation she answers. She must have been holding her breath waiting for the phone to ring.

"Hello," she greets, trying to search for my voice on the other end of the line.

I pour a quick double shot and throw it back, with hopes I can get my anger to subside.

"Hello?...Jarell?...Can you hear me? Hello?"

I move to the living area to find a seat on Yari's couch before answering, "Hey, yeah, I can hear you. What's up?" I mutter with my jaw clenched and my hand tightly gripping my drink.

"Baby, I miss you, I thought you would have called to let me know you were back in town, or I would have seen you at the gym tonight since you just got back today."

Her voice was no different than usual, she had no fucking remorse. You would think she would be feeling guilty or at least showing signs of it in her voice. But there was nothing. I didn't understand how we got here. She's not who I believed her to be. I have every intention of showing her I can be a better man than any other she could get.

"Naw, I'm not in town yet ma." Needing a second to collect my thoughts, I wait before continuing. It wasn't like me to lie to her, I just couldn't face her deception just yet. "I have some things I'm getting situated with the gym expansion," I was lying and it tasted disgusting.

I came back into town a day earlier than planned. Ready to share good news with her. That moment was ruined. So, now here we are. It wasn't like me to lie; I never had the need. I'd made it my mission to be a different type of man.

The tears started to roll as my mind replayed the sight of her the night before. I didn't like her having this kind of control over my emotions.

"Fuck," I hiss.

"What's wrong?" her question draped with the kind of cape only a concerned girlfriend would have.

"Nothing…I'm good," I quickly respond, placing my drink on the coffee table and wiping my face. "What's been up with you though ma? I haven't heard from you much since I've been gone."

Glass back in my hand while I wait for her rebuttal. I'm trying to give her another chance to show signs of regret and for me to calm down before I take my revenge to the next level.

"I've just been working like crazy baby. This new job has me in a chokehold. I haven't had much time out of the office since we have some new clients to secure."

She's fucking lying. She has definitely had time out of the office.

My anger starts to reach the point of explosion. Gripping my glass tighter, I stand to walk back into the kitchen, as she begins again. "I didn't know what to do this past week without you. So, I just poured myself into my work."

Poured herself over some other man's lap. She was compulsive with her lies, lies that she didn't even have to tell. Before I could realize I had glass shards, liquor, and crushed ice in my hand. Yari's hardwood floors cradle the remaining remnants of my drink.

"Shit…"

"What happened?" she asks.

"Nothing, I'm good."

Looking up at the ceiling, with hopes that I'll be forgiven. I rush to grab the broom and a towel."Yeah umm, sounds like you need a vacation. You think you can take some time off?"

She giggles at my words, yet nothing is funny.

"Time off sounds great. Just you and I?"

I chuckle maliciously, "Naw, just you. All paid. I'm thinking Raynol's Island. Beautiful beachfront penthouse. In-house spa services and 24-hour room service."

She squeals, "WHAT!!! We've been wanting to go to Raynol's Island for almost two years now! Wait… but why alone?" she asks.

I can't help but laugh out of annoyance. "I don't have the time to waste vacationing right now. FLEXD has just become a top priority for me. Business is expanding, so I have business to handle."

She goes mute after letting out a deep sigh. " I always thought we would explore the island together. I don't want to go alone."

I shrug, spitting out my next words, "You're going to have to go alone. I'm not going."

"What's up with you Jarell? All of a sudden FLEXD is top priority? What about us?"

She got some fucking nerve asking me about 'us'.

"Listen, it's damn near 3 in the morning, I'm not in the headspace for a deep conversation. We're good ma! I'm about to turn in for the night. I'll hit your line with flight details and shit."

"Jarell, are you dismissing me?"

"Naw I'm getting off the phone before this conversation goes left, and I've been drinking so that's not what I want."

"Okay, goodnight, baby," she says.

I just hang up. No need for all the extra shit.

I finished cleaning the floor and discarding the broken glass. I'll replace it. Flipping off the lights in the main areas of the loft. I head towards the bed.

I need sleep.

The next morning, I wake to music blaring and Yari singing at the top of her lungs. Guess she's feeling better. I still don't know what happened with ole dude last night that had her up and down in her feelings. So, I decide to not even bother asking.

I walk out of the room to see Yari dressed in a gray cotton shirt style dress dancing around the kitchen. Once she notices me, she grabs a remote to turn down her sound system.

"Don't let me ruin your vibe," I state crossing my arms and posing against the exposed brick wall near the kitchen.

"Stop it, Jay. You could never ruin my vibe," she smiles dancing over towards me still doing her little one, two step. "What's up with you?" she asks, examining the lack of emotion in my face.

"I think I'm going to go back home tonight."

Her face quickly drops along with her shoulder and she clicks the remote to turn the music off. "Jay, it's no rush for you to go back home, you're not ruining anything here," she promises.

"I know, Yari. It's just better for me to be out your space before I start all the toxic shit I'm about to be on," I admit as I pour myself some of her expensive ass local pomegranate juice.

"And what toxic shit is that, Jarell? Don't be stupid," she inquires while looking up at me, standing in between me and the fridge.

"Baby girl, don't look at me like that. I'm stating facts," shrugging at my comment because the fucks I gave had run out. I decided to place the juice on the counter since Yari was still blocking the fridge.

"Answer my questions Jay, what toxic shit you bout to be on? You aren't even that guy."

Taking a sip of my juice I lean in towards Yari. "I think that's the issue. I'm not toxic enough. No problem though, I can be."

"Are you still drunk? What are you even saying? I think you should stay right here until you are for sure ready to be at home and be civil."

"The thing is Yari," I say, finishing off my juice and placing the glass in the sink. "I didn't ask what you thought. This isn't a discussion, Yari. It's a decision. One I already made to protect you from the version of me I don't even like right now."

Her expression is puzzled and shocked as I walk back into the guest room.

I could hear her following behind me as I moved through the room, throwing things into my duffle without thought.

She stands still. Arms folded tight, jaw clenched. Trying not to snap.

Then she did.

"So, let me get this straight."

She uncrosses her arms, crosses them again. Paces the room twice, then plants her feet. Ready to say this thing she's been holding for too long.

"You think you can just call me when the bottom falls out and lean on me when you need a shoulder but the second I check you on your own shit, I'm the problem?"

Her voice cracked just enough to make me look up.

"I've always had your back, Jarell. But you're not about to spit fire in my direction just because you're finally feeling the burn."

I pause, thinking about how to address her question. "Yari, listen," I start, walking around the bed to where she stood but I was quickly silenced.

"No Jarell, you listen. I care about you and what you have going on. You're my best friend. When you hurt, I hurt. But if you want to shut me out and go home and be toxic, so be it. I don't want to babysit you anymore. I never liked this girl; I always thought that she probably was up to no good. I warned you that I felt that way after meeting her at the FLEXD Wellness Event over a year ago. And you chose to continue with her, and now here we are. She has fucked you over and broken your heart, and I'm the one being disregarded? Have you even spoken to her yet? Huh? Have you done that? While you're wanting to be toxic, and fly off the handle, and be 'big bad boy Jarell', have you even faced her yet? Huh? Have You?" Yari says, obviously upset.

I don't answer. My silence is loud enough.

She scoffs. Crosses her arms tighter. "Exactly," she mutters.

I can admit I was putting the heat on the wrong stove and that wasn't my intention.

"I did speak to her. Yari, I'm sorry. I never intended to disregard you. I just don't give a fuck right now. I don't want to feel it. I can't be in your space with the mind set I have right now. That's why I want to go home. It's to protect you from this part of me."

Uncrossing her arms, she meets my eyes as she says, "Jay,

take the time you need here. I'm about to be out of town anyway.
André and I leave out on Sunday. I'll be gone for two weeks."

I allow my eyes to surf the ceiling. She's out of her mind.

"Two weeks? For what? You know what... Don't answer
that. Cool, I'll kick it here. I still need to go back to my place
though. I'll be back this way tonight. I gotta handle some things."

She gives me a closed-lip smile as she backs out of the room.

"Wait, what happened when you spoke to her?" she asks.

"Let's just say we had some time to catch up."

She squints at me. "You're up to something Jarell, and I don't
think I want to be in the know. There is no way y'all just 'caught
up.' I wouldn't believe that even if I was there witnessing it."

I raise my hands in the air to surrender to her allegations. She
shakes her head and leaves me to finish packing.

Boundaries.

Plate Full of Crumbs

Yari

It's Saturday, the week is flying by and I'm trying to get things in order before going out of town tomorrow with André. He'd given me a list of thoughtful items to bring as a just in case thing.

I'm in this new boutique, Cheeky, on Scottsden Ave in uptown Roseville looking for a few vacation dresses when my phone rings. It's Imani. I fuss around trying to answer.

My girls and I hadn't spoken since open mic night. Today was usually when we together to grab brunch, get a massage, or mani-pedis. But Nevaeh wasn't responding to any of my texts.

"Hey, Imani!! What's going on girl?"

It sounds like she's at her studio from the background noise. "Hey Boo, are you up for a mani-pedi playdate?"

I giggle, "Yes! I need some relaxation. I tried reaching out to Nevaeh, but I guess she's still upset with me."

I can feel hesitation in Imani's response. "Yari, just meet me at Posh & Polish in an hour. Cool?"

So, she knows Vaeh was upset. I'm not sweating it, she'd come around. She always does.

"Yes ma'am, I'll be there."

I finish up the call and about to grab my held items off the rack when I feel a tap on the shoulder. Turning around to see, "CeCe? Hey girl!"

CeCe and I used to run together back in our late teens, and early twenties. She started off as a bartender too. Until Vince, the owner of Cakes, a club we worked at, realized how beautiful she was.He was insistent about her being one of his dancers. Once she gave in and her money started growing, we kinda lost touch.

"Hey YaYa! I haven't seen you in ages and we in the same city."

I shake my head, "I know, it's kind of crazy how that's even possible. The city ain't that big. We should've been crossing paths since I moved on from Cakes."

She extends her arms pulling me into a hug. "Girl, yes! Cakes ain't been the same since you left. Vince hates to admit it, but he knows you were big business. I heard your spot be bumping. I need to come through."

I nod excitedly in agreement, "Yeah, come through girl! Are you still at Cakes?"

"Yes and no! I no longer dance, and you're standing in one of my many investments," she shares, spinning around with her arms in the air, smiling from ear to ear. "Girl, that was never my end game. Now, I honestly just manage the girls. I run it like a regular job. They report to me, and if they do any foul shit they gotta go. I also now made a mandatory course they have to take to learn about investing their money. No one is meant to shake ass forever, you know?."

I tilt my head in her direction to agree. "Facts. I hear you girl. You know what? You should come by Cream tonight. It's Satin Saturday. All my Satin Dolls will be dressed in their house style costumes and the drinks will be flowing. And, because it's ladies night" I pause building suspense, *"it's free champagne,"* I sing, hoping that's enough to convince her.

"I think I can swing it tonight," she smiles.

"Great to hear. I'll see you tonight," I say, giving her a quick hug and heading to the front to make my purchase.

I shoot a text to Imani with my ETA before heading over to Posh & Polish for those bottomless mimosas and hours of relaxation I so desperately needed.

🎷 🎷 🎷

The salon looked different than what I remembered. The ambience was sultry and romantic with dim lighting. The walls were dark gray and slightly textured with hints of metallic gold flakes in the wallpaper. Notes of salty vanilla and neroli merlot folded effortlessly over the foyer. There was a whisper of Jazz dancing in the background and I instantly began to melt into the down-regulation this vibe was providing me.

He's everywhere, I thought to myself as I spotted Imani signing us in at the reception desk.

"Girl, they have turned this place into a slice of heaven," I state, greeting her with a hug and kiss on the cheek.

"Yes, I love it even more now than before," she says handing the guest book back to the young lady behind the counter. We grab the champagne flutes that were prepared for us and find seats near the floor-to-ceiling bay windows.

"So, they told me 15 to 20 more minutes because our appointment is for a private room, and everyone has to be here for us to get started." She breezes through the last part of her statement as if she hopes I don't give any rebuttal. Knowing that's not who I am she looks at me waiting on my response.

"So have you let her know she's holding us up?" I ask.

"Well…" she starts but is sharply cut off by the sound of keys and an annoyed Navaeh ready to state her case.

"I'm not holding up anything. I'm here when I said I would be," she spits, rolling her eyes. "Imani, here you go lovely," she continues, handing Imani a white gift bag with tissue paper.

"Thanks, girl! What's this?" Imani asks, peeking into the bag.

I roll my eyes, I'm not here to have her do this whole 'you're invisible' thing.

"It's the, '5 Year Plan', planning journal for black business women I told you about," Navaeh explained, refusing to make eye contact with me. Even though I know she felt the lasers I was burning into her face.

"Nice, thanks. Did you bring one for Yari?"

I waited for her answer.

The pause was heavy, like she wanted me to know she had a choice in this moment. A choice she wasn't ready to make.

"I have more in the car," Navaeh finally mutters, "if anyone would like one."

My eyes squint in her direction at the snarkiness in her tone.

"Naveah, I'm not here to be consumed by your drama. I tried apologizing for brushing you off Monday night. It's now Saturday. We're either going to address it, or not. Either way, today, for me will be relaxing," I say, leaving no room for her to counter.

Before she could respond the young lady from the front desk walks over to let us know our private suite is ready.

"Look at that, just in time!" Imani cheered.

Our suite had gotten just as sexy of facelift as the foyer. A selenite crystal chandelier hung in the center of the room, pedicure pedestals for three on one wall, an en-suite room that had to be for our mini facials and massages, and a mini bar equipped with everything we may need for our bottomless mimosas.

"If this don't get y'all both relaxed enough to move past Monday night…" Imani says, turning to look at both of us, "I don't know what will."

Navaeh and I lock eyes, we knew she was speaking all facts.

By the end of the afternoon, the three of us were back in sync.

Taking a sip from my mimosa, "Ladies I have to get out of here, it's Satin Saturday, and if I'm not there for uniform checks, I don't even want to imagine what I'll walk into."

Standing to leave, my phone rings. Xavier's name flashes across my screen.

"Hey X! What's up?" I greet as I'm walking out to my car.

"Aye Yari, Cam and I just picked Jarell up. We're taking his drunk ass home. He was at a bar down on Vines and 5th. The owner called me."

Vines and 5th was the touristy side of town with bars, clubs and hotels. There was always a party going on.

"Alright, I was headed to Cream, but I'll re-route to link with you at his place. Give me 20."

Ending our call, I send Arias a quick text giving her permission to takeover Satin Saturday. It doesn't look like I'll be in attendance any time soon. I toss my phone into my car's center console hop in and pull off, rerouting my GPS but not my emotions.

Drunk? Jarell? That wasn't like him. Even when things were rough, he never drowned in liquor, not like that.

Maybe this was my fault. Maybe I'd pushed too hard. Or maybe he just needed a night to fall apart without the world watching.

I didn't know what I was walking into. But I knew I needed to show up. As someone who cared enough to stay.

I looked up through the windshield, watching the sky dim into that kind of lavender gray that always made the city feel quiet.

Cream would run itself tonight. But Jarell? Jarell had been holding so much in, I guess he's at a breaking point. I don't think he ever properly grieved his mother and now losing this relationship with Q must have him quite upside down. Maybe tonight, he needed someone to hold him.

I park just outside his house and cut the engine, but I don't move.

The air feels too still. Like it knows something I don't.

I sit there with my hands on the steering wheel, staring through the windshield like the answers are out there somewhere, floating between the streetlights and the sky.

What if I make things worse? What if me showing up right now feels like pressure instead of peace?

I don't want to be another person he has to perform for. Another person he has to prove he's okay to. I want to show up soft... not strong. I just didn't know if he'll let me.

I glance at my reflection in the rear-view mirror. Not to fix anything, just to see the girl who always showed up anyway. The girl who was still trying, even when she didn't know what to say.

"You don't have to be enough," I whisper to myself. "You just have to be here."

I grab my bag and get out the car.

I don't know what I'm walking into. But I know whatever it is, I won't be leaving.

Cream of the Crop

Yari

Once I step out of the car and onto Jarell's driveway I notice droplets of blood on the ground, causing me to run inside panicked.

"What the hell Jarell? Why is there blood in the driveway?" I ask a slumped version of my best friend.

He's draped over the corner of the sofa with a bottle of water sitting on his lap.

"Get your shit together. So, this is what you're going to do now? Drink your life away?"

I take a look around his house. It was so out of order. Jarell had sat his ass in this house rotting all week. Take out containers covered in leftover greasy food, sauce packets, pizza boxes, and empty liquor bottles flooded his kitchen. Last I saw or spoke to him was Tuesday when he left. He never came back to my place and turned his phone on DND. I had plans to come by after dropping by Cream today just to make sure he was alive. Good instincts because clearly, he's barely hanging on.

"Yo, Why you here?" Jarell asks me with a slur in his speech. When he sits up, I notice his right fist is wrapped up.

"I called her, she's probably the only one who can get through to yo ass," Xavier responded while walking out of Jarell's room.

"Look man I don't know what's going on but you gotta talk to somebody. It's weird as shit seeing you like this," Cameron admits following closely behind X.

That's when it clicks that Jarell hadn't told his boys what he saw that night.

"Y'all, I got it from here. Thanks for calling me X," I say looking over at him.

X nods, "No doubt, we headed to Cream. I'll be in the spot all night, so I'll keep you updated if there are any issues."

I turned to hug him and Cameron. "I have an old friend coming by tonight. Her name is CeCe. Can you make sure she's taken care of? Let her know I had," I look over towards Jarell, "other business I had to handle, and I'll catch up with her another time."

"Sure thing, Yari," X assures me. "Hit us up if this knucklehead gets out of hand," he says, walking towards the door.

"Oh, there won't be any of that, right Jarell?" I ask pointedly.

"Yeah, whatever," he slurs trying to stand.

I watch him struggle for a little while, then give in, assisting him up. Shaking my head, "So, are you going to tell me what happened?"

His eyes cut me as he walks past me to his master bathroom. "Naw."

My eyes roll, "I don't want to baby sit you anymore Jarell. You didn't hear me when I said it the first time?" I call after him. I can hear the sounds of his regret as I walk past his room to the kitchen.

Looking around at the mess, I don't know where to start.

I grab a trash bag and start to clear the island. Plastic cup, after empty bottle, after pizza box, after wing sauce. I slowly work my way to the sight of marble. Jarell joins me at the island as I begin washing it down.

"I don't need you to do nothing for me," he says bitterly.

"Oh, really? I can't tell. Who gone do it? Cause you damn sure ain't." I turn off the faucet waiting for his answer.

"I'll call Fran, she'll get me right," he shrugs.

"Jay, she's not your personal maid, and she damn sure ain't your woman, or your momma." I catch myself, realizing I may have struck a nerve I wasn't intending to hit.

His eyes shoot in my direction as he waits for me to retract my statement.

"I'm saying Jay, you may be hurting and there is a possibility that you hate every female in the world, but allowing yourself to get out of character is stupid."

He throws his bottle of water back, finishing it, before placing it on the island. "Listen I don't want no fucking speech right now, Yari. I'm going to shower then go to bed. If you want to play Ms. Maid, do that, but I don't need you for anything else." He finishes his rant and reaches into his pocket, grabs a wad of cash and throws it up in the air towards me.

I watch the money fall onto the counter and floor.

"Lock up when you're done," he says, turning to leave.

"YOU DONE LOST YOUR FUCKING MIND JARELL!" I yell towards him as he slams his bedroom door.

I finish cleaning the kitchen and made sure I left a note for Jarell before 'locking up'.

He had never been so disrespectful towards me. Instead of putting him in his place while he wallowed in a lost drunken slump. The note I leave should let him know where I stand with him.

I take my spare key to his house off my keychain and place it on top of the note, locking the door as I leave.

Jumping into my truck I wipe tears from my face. I'm losing my best friend, I thought to myself, as I cranked my engine, turning up the volume so the music could drown out my feelings.

I decide to just head over to Cream instead of going straight home. I did want to catch up with CeCe, she and I used to be thick as thieves. That was before life showed me we needed to split so growth could happen. Which seemed to be the best for the both of us.

When I arrived, I noticed a familiar Porsche parked out front with its hazards on and a broken backseat window. I spot Tony out front as well. Pointing to the car, I pull into my parking spot to see what's going on. "Aye, Tony whose car is this? It's blocking the expressway. I don't want no citations."

He walks over explaining and apologizing. "Yari, I was just finding out who it belonged to. I went inside to holla at X. I came out and it was here. We just made an announcement. If they don't want that pretty motherfucker towed, they'll be out here. I got our tow guy on alert already."

I nod, "Looks like y'all got it handled and I'm glad cause I don't plan to be here long tonight. Thanks, Tony. Preciate you. I'ma head in. Keep me posted if you end up needing that tow."

As I step inside, the signature smell of Cream fills my nostrils. It smells like home.

Walking through the building, I spot the booth X had given to CeCe. It was so like her to be tucked off in the cut, away from heavy lighting. She always looked like she was up to something. Her dress was form fitting, all those sheer cut-outs meant her curves were on heavy display. And the fact that it was red made her stick out like a sore thumb, in a room of mostly black clothing.

Shaking my head at her, a smirk appeared on my cheeks until I recognized the reason for that familiar Porsche out front. I stopped dead in my tracks. My stomach turned before I even saw his face. Some ghosts don't knock. They just show up, wearing the same cologne you tried to forget.

My body stiffens and my glare sharpens.

A hazy Vince walks in my direction, his smile, conniving.

"Nice to see you again YaYa," he whispers in my ear, close enough for me to feel his lips drag along the side of my face, right before he kisses my cheek. His eyes now focused on mine. He shoots me a smile as he lifts my chin to close my parted lips. "I'll see you around," he announces before turning back towards CeCe, who is sitting on the plush velvet tufted cushions with her legs crossed.

I watch as he exits the building before walking over to CeCe.

She stands to greet me, "Hey girl.I thought you weren't gonna make it tonight."

I roll my eyes at her, "Why is Vince here? I don't want no parts of the foolishness he brings." My hands are on my hips as she simply sits back down in the seat that brought her comfort enough to give me attitude.

"YaYa, we were discussing a small business hiccup if you must know. You trippin' for real. Maybe you should go home and get some rest. We can catch up some other time."

I see everyone is on one tonight. First Jarell, now CeCe. One thing for certain, Cream is something *I built*, and I wasn't about to have it fall due to the reputation of people like Vince frequenting the place.

"Naw, I'm not trippin' CeCe. Vince's presence in my lounge is not needed. If y'all have business, cool! Meet up at one of your 'many investments,'" I quote her, hoping she didn't think I misunderstood what her little flex earlier at her boutique really meant. She wasn't slick and I want no parts of it.

She stood once more, closer this time. She clearly had something to get off her chest. And she did, "You may have moved on and left Cakes, YaYa, but don't think anyone has forgotten the part you played." She runs her fingers gently down my arm. "While you over here playing Miss Goody Two Shoes thinking you're the cream of the crop, just remember, it would only take one phone call to shut this whole shit down."

I push her hands from my shoulder. "I never wanted in on that shit. I've built a whole different life for myself, with a whole nother set of rules. I don't need baking soda to make this rise," I spit, leaning back in my stance to assert my position on the situation.

She laughs, reaching behind her to grab her purse, throwing it over her shoulder. "The thing is you may not need it to rise. Without it the cake will fall and there wouldn't be a need for cream, now would there?" The smirk that accompanies her words puts a bad taste in my mouth.

"Listen…" I start, but she shakes her head.

"I'm not gone bring no drama to your doorstep. I wasn't coming here to ruin your good girl act, or out your past boo. We can be cordial. I can be Cynthia," she points to herself, before turning her finger towards me, "and you can be Yari. But don't forget I know YaYa." Her eyebrows rise as she walks away.

"Oh, and Yari," she calls from behind me, causing me to turn in her direction.

"Yeah?" I respond, only giving her a half look over my shoulder.

"I like what you've done with the place. I'll see you around." With that she's gone.

It wasn't her tone that scared me. It was the fact that she knew just how far I'd come and exactly where to aim if she wanted to tear it all down. I quickly shot a text to Xavier to move up the meeting for increasing security. I didn't know what CeCe had up her sleeve, but I wanted to leave the drama of Cakes behind me.

Jarell

Waking up the next morning, I had the worst migraine I've ever had. I couldn't bare light and was blinded by the partial opening between my blackout curtains. I didn't want to move so I stayed in bed. Scrolling through my emails before noticing a voice message and pictures from Q.

She sent me little snippets of her trip thus far, with hopes she could convince me to come join her. That loneliness she despised, she was going to have to get used to. I wanted nothing to do with her, but I wanted her to hurt first. I wasn't going to walk away and let it just be. I wanted her to feel just as embarrassed as I did, just as disrespected. I wanted her to feel my wrath.

I slowly unraveled myself from the covers, remembering to be careful of the cuts on my hand. I needed food, my stomach was in my back.

Walking out the room I notice the aroma of the house. It was clean and decluttered and smelt divine. The scent of bergamot and hinoki lace the entire house bringing a smile to my face.

My Yari.

I knew it was her. She left imprints of feminine essence everywhere she went. I felt grateful that she looked out for me.

I walk into the kitchen about to press send on a thank you text I was sending to her, when I halted at the sight of a note and key on my island. Confused I pick up the note. It was from Yari.

Jarell,
Once you are sober enough to notice this note, I'll be off on vacation. The way you disrespected me tonight, speaks not to who I believe you to be, but who you are choosing to become. I meant it when I said I was done babysitting you. And I meant it when I said I wasn't going to stick

around to watch you drink your life away. You were right to leave my place that night. And you're right that this isn't the version of you I want to be around. I have always supported you. Through it all we have never treated one another like this. Like how you treated me tonight. If you want to be slumped over wreaking of alcohol and living in a pigsty, you do just that. Maybe you need help with this from someone who has tools that I don't. That's perfectly fine. I've finished cleaning up your mess for the last time. You have a fresh start now. Do with it what you will.
BTW: Thanks for the tip. I took every single bill you threw at me. As for your key, because after all it's yours, I have no use for it anymore. Until you're better, take care of yourself.
-Yari.

I drop my head, trying to put together the pieces of my night. Everything was a blur. I tried calling Yari so we could talk, but I get her voicemail.

Confusion sets in. What the hell happened last night? I threw money at her? Last, I remember X and Cam were walking me out the bar. I checked the time to see if I could possibly catch up with them before they left their kickboxing class. 12:17pm, perfect timing. Just enough time for me to get over to FLEXD before their class let out.

I ran back to the bathroom to brush my teeth and wash my face before grabbing my keys to meet them. I needed to know what had happened, so I could at least try to fix it.

Tap Out

Jarell

Speeding down Halsted Street, I park before seeing X and Cam shuffling through the doors of FLEXD. They spot me as I hop out my ride.

"Look who's vertical," Cam jokes. "Damn man, you good?"

I guess X could feel or see my panic. I take a second to dap them both up before getting to my only reason for being out in the daylight right now.

"What up y'all. Thanks for looking out last night. I was definitely on one. Thats why I'm here. Please tell me y'all know what the fuck happened last night."

Cam drops his head and X places his hand on my shoulder. "Man…," X whistles out, "you were running rampant last night my guy. I haven't seen you like that in YEARS!"

My eyes shift between the both of them. I hope they have more to tell me than just that. I could *feel* the actions of the night just fine, I needed to know what I'd *done*.

"Yo what happened bro? Let's umm," I point towards the building, suggest we get some privacy. They follow me back inside of FLEXD. Once we get to my office, they head for chairs as I close the door. Leaning against my desk I wait for X to continue.

"Naw, real shit all I know is Mr. James from Tap Out Bar & Grill called one of my guys to get my contact. He knows you my bro, so he hit my line. Said you got into it with some dude, and you had been drinking since you got there round 2 or some shit. He took your keys, and you were bleeding. He said he didn't want to call the law, so me and Cam came to get yo ass."

My eyebrows lift, "Ok, that explains my hand, I guess. So, what happened with Yari. What did I do?"

Cam shrugs, "Well shit we decided to call her so she could get you right. We figured she could talk some sense into you or something. You been moving like a zombie since last week. You wouldn't tell us what was up so we figured she could get it out of you."

I threw my hands up in frustration, I still have no idea what happened. "So what happened once she came over? When did I throw money at her?"

X's eyes stretch wide, and he lays back in his seat, damn near fallin' out of it. Cam jumps up, his jaw dropping wide open before he slaps his hand over his mouth in shock.

"YOU DID WHAT?" they yell in unison.

"MAN WHAT?" Cam asks in disbelief, pacing across the floor of my office.

"No, you didn't man, please say you didn't," X pleads, hands now on his head as he stands too.

I shake my head with confusion, "I must have, she said I did. What happened?"

Cam looks at me. "We don't know man. We called her, wrapped your hand, cleaned up your vomit – I still don't understand why that shit was purple by the way. Like what the hell did you eat?"

"Cam!" I snap, so he can get back to the point. This wasn't about purple vomit or my hand. I need to know what I did to Yari.

"My bad...she came to the crib, said she had it handled. We left and went to Cream. That's all we know."

"Damn! What did I do?" I ask them as much as myself. "She left me this note," I say handing the handwritten note over to X. I watch him and Cam read their faces awestruck.

"Whatever you did man...." X starts as he hands me back the note. "It was fucked up dog."

"You know Yari, man. She don't do things to get attention, it seems like she's done with yo ass," Cam shakes his head.

He said exactly what I was thinking. She wasn't the type to play games or seek attention.

I drop my head in my hands and take a seat at my desk. My mind is all over the place. I can't believe I had thrown money at Yari, and she still cleaned up. Why would she do that? Based on her note it appeared as if she wanted a clean end to our friendship, but that can't be. Right?

Standing back up, I thank Cam and X for looking out for me, letting them get on with their day. Sitting once more I toggle on my computer to pull up my security cameras from the house to find more answers.

I get so focused on my computer screen, the ring of my cell phone scares me, causing me to slide the reel too far. Q's on my line and on my screen.

I hadn't taken the time to review the footage from that night. I'd forgotten to check if it existed.

There she was, with her ass pointed straight into the ceiling camera that captured my living room. Her body bent over his as she cradled his head to her breast before sliding down onto his lap.

She had oiled up her body, which prompted me to go further back in the footage and search for how all this had started. If she'd oiled up, she'd been preparing for this.

I could feel the heat rising in my chest, my eyes beginning to burn. I watched as she walked throughout my house, wrapped in the satin robe I bought her during our Italian anniversary getaway last year. She was preparing plates for two. I watched as she served him. I watched as she played house in my home with another man. My eyes got heavy with regret for all the trust I had given her.

I made a mental note to return to this video later; Yari was my concern right now. I couldn't let this distract me from finding out the truth. I had hurt the one person I never should have hurt because I couldn't deal with my shit, and I needed to know how.

Fast forwarding to the footage from last night I see X and Cam carry me into the house. While studying the video I connect the speakers so I can hear.

I sit still.

Stiller than I had in days.

Watching her on my screen. Not crying loud, not breaking dishes, not slamming doors, just... cleaning.

Quiet.

Like her heartbreak didn't deserve to echo.

She wiped down my counters with one hand, wiped her cheek with the other. She moved like someone who had already made peace with leaving. Like her silence was louder than anything I could've yelled.

That's what broke me.

Not the tears or seeing the mess I'd made. Not even her note. It was the way she tucked the rag under the sink, like it was the last time she'd ever cleanup for me. The way she folded the dish towel before she left like she didn't want to be messy on her way out, even if I had been.

I don't want her forgiveness.

I want her to know I saw the damage I'd caused. The version of me she'd been met with last night.

And I'm not gonna leave it there.

The disappointment had sunken in by the time I realized the security cameras had switched back to a live view of my house. My phone began ringing once more, Q's name flashing across my screen. "The Queen", yeah right.

"Yeah," I answer, realizing I needed to change that name as soon as possible.

"Yeah? Boy don't play! What you doing?"

"Handling business. What's up?"

"Damn Jarell, I've been gone for almost a whole week. You haven't responded to any of my messages, answered any of my calls, I'm all alone on this beautiful ass island. I miss you! Don't you miss me?"

I laugh, "Naw."

She laughs, "I'm not playing with you."

She thinks I'm joking, which I find funny. All signs point to fuck her, but she sucked at reading the fucking room. Fucking clueless.

"Well baby my trip ends in two days, can you pick me up from the airport?"

"Naw, I actually won't be in town. Got to handle some important shit for FLEXD. Catch a car, I'll touch base with you when I return next week."

"Jarell, seriously? I haven't seen you since you left the last time! It's like you're too busy for us now that you're making plans to expand the gym."

"Hey, listen I gotta do what I gotta do. When I get back, I'll make it up to you, that I can promise. You don't need to worry. I want you to be carefree and relaxed. No stressing. Ok?" I question, wondering why the little guy on my shoulder helping me cope with all this was having me speak this nonsense.

"Ok, I'll see you when you get back!"

With that I hang up, time to put plans into actions. I shoot my assistant a quick email to inform her I would be out of the building for the week. Now, time to send all the invites out and get reservations finalized.

I smile to myself, determined to put my plan in motion.

Interlude

Between Air

There's a quiet that happens before you go. Not silence exactly, but a vibration that sits behind your ribs. Like your body is anticipating a change is coming.

I packed my bags deliberately slow, folding clothes I bought for the occasion. With hopes that once I arrived to my destination they would pair nicely with the bandages that dressed the battle scares I had gained from the neglect of absence love. I tell myself it's just a trip, but my reflection stares back at me like she knows better.

Maybe I need distance to remember my own sound. Maybe I just wanted air that doesn't carry his cologne. Have the chance to remember something other than his voice. Maybe the excursions would carve new memories that help me release the ache of nostalgia.

The city is still when I leave, the air heavy with rain. My phone quiet for once, no calls, no promises. Just me and a ticket to a place where no one knows my name.

They say vacations clear your head, but I think they just turn the volume down so you can hear what's been whispering all along.

And right then, between the goodbyes and the boarding gate, I hear it. A small, steady voice that says, *"Don't go to escape, baby. Go to remember."*

Rain, Baby!

Yari

Time sure does fly when you're having fun. Dré had pulled out all the stops. Sunday, he whisked us off to Mulancia, a small exotic country off the coast of Raynol's Island. Mulancia was known for their tropical flora, photogenic excursions, and unreal views of the night sky. The moon appears unnaturally large against muted skylines where volcanoes dust the hilltops with smoke from the Earth's core. The coastal waters separated organically, giving space for the black sand to drift along its edge.

We were greeted with these signature drinks called Moontinis. They were delicious, blackberry gin and cherry bitters infused with hints of hibiscus flowers and orange zest. The flavors instantly made me unravel.

André said he would make it a point to prove he's all in, and I was starting to see it. We settled into our shorefront bungalow, winding down from our trip to the countryside of Mulancia where we spent the day touring multiple wineries and stomping grapes.

I walk in and head straight for the walk-in shower inside the master suite. André follows close behind, laughing as I hobble to keep as many remnants of grape seeds off the marble floors as possible.

"Baby we already rinsed our feet, what are you doing?" He asked once inside the shower alongside me.

I turn to respond but my words wouldn't come out. My internal jaw had found its place on the floor of my wet panties. André had begun stripping his clothes off, his body toned and muscular. I lean back against the shower wall to enjoy the show he had yet to notice he was putting on.

His back to me, he reaches to turn on the water. I don't even realize I'm underneath one of the rain-shower heads until the water starts to drown me.

"Ahh!!!" I jump out of my trance to alert Dré to turn off the water.

Instead, he pulls me closer to him, placing his mouth upon mine. Our tongues begin dancing as he gropes my ass. I can hear the waves crashing on the shore, through the open French doors in the en suite. The sun was starting to set, splashing hues of orange and pink across the bathroom through the skylights.

I wrestle to undo the buttons from my shirt, stripping down to the coco-colored lace bra that holds my breasts perfectly. André freezes mid kiss to take the opportunity to watch me remove my shorts. My eyes never leave him as I slide the denim down my legs, the air catching between us like static before a storm. André's gaze follows, deliberate and unflinching. The kind that makes you forget your own skin. When his hands find my waist, it doesn't feel like hunger guiding him; it feels like knowing.

He lifts me easily, every muscle flexing like a promise making me feel lightweight. The distance between us vanishes. My breath hitches, caught somewhere between fear and fire, both familiar. His mouth meets mine and everything slows. The kind of slow that rewrites time, where seconds feel like hours and want sounds like harmony.

Water whispers against tile as his fingers trace the back of my neck and then the line of my spine, learning me all over again. I feel heat bloom low in my stomach, a slow unraveling that makes it hard to remember how to stand still. His palms cup underneath me, finding the places that remembered him, the places that had awaited. Each touch feels like punctuation, commas of breath, ellipses of longing, full stops of surrender. I feel the pulse of him through every layer of me. The connection I had begged for had found me. Its warmth, its tremor, and its ache traveled up my spine until it reached something deeper than flesh. He whispers my name like a vow, and in that whisper, I heard every version of love I had prayed for and never believed I'd find. My body softens into his rhythm, a quiet undoing that feels both sacred and dangerous. The lights dimmed, and the edges of everything blurred. Waterdrops slide down my curls as the steam rises between us, the steady thrum of heartbeats keeping time. When the moment crests, it isn't loud. It's a breaking, soft and passionate surrender disguised as breath. I feel my body melt into his hands, feel the weight of the world lift just enough for me to remember what it means to be alive.

He holds me there, lips tracing the curve of my shoulder, whispering something low and rough that I almost don't catch. It doesn't feel like a command. It felt like a request.

"Get cleaned up," he murmurs, voice rough and gentle all at once.

"I've got a surprise for you."

I nod, still catching my breath, the air thick with warmth and quietness. And as he steps away, I realize I'm smiling. Not because of what just happened, but because of how seen I suddenly feel.

Roughly half an hour later we're both dressed for whatever surprise Andre has in store.

"So, what's this surprise?" I called out to Andre while sitting on the end of the California King, oiling my legs. He's still in the bathroom finishing up.

"I got us an in-house private chef to prepare a full five course meal!" He responds, walking out the bathroom. "Are you ready to eat dinner? I know it's a little early but…"

I cut him off. "I'm definitely hungry. I mean after all that I don't want to walk too far, so that's perfect."

He chuckles walking over, lifting my chin to kiss me. "You can take these off." He grabs my leg, making me fall back onto the bed. He goes to take my shoes off but puts my leg up on his shoulder instead. "No, Dré…. Food… Don't Start!" I fight to wiggle myself out of his grasp.

"I'm just joking but seriously you don't need shoes, they'll be here shortly."

"Shortly?" I question noticing his bulge.

"Yes, shortly." His eyes pointing downward. Our eyes lock. I nibble on my bottom lip while reaching for his belt. As I get his pants loose there's a knock at the door.

"Ughh. Damn!" We laugh in unison.

"One second!" Dré calls out.

"I'll be out in a second." I tell him while standing to fix my dress.

"No doubt, take your time baby.

125

Dinner starts with a wine tasting, André asking me to select the wine for the evening. I oblige and select the Petrus Pomerol, a smoky red that would pair elegantly with the lamb chops that were a part of the main entrée. I'm prepared to enjoy the finest cuisine tonight. The chef, I learn, is the top chef in Mulancia. His name, Westley Frunmasno. He's a native to Mulancia and lives up to every word of praise.

The first bite melts in my mouth. Whipped chèvre tucked into warm fig, drizzled with mulled honey. It tastes like being wanted on purpose. André's really pulling out all the stops. I'm pleased to see this part of him. The guy I fell for. A spontaneous passionate lover boy who is full of surprises and thought-provoking gifts. He has returned to me and I'm in awe. This past week has felt like a dream. But I'd dreamed before and still woken up alone to a disappointing reality.

We move through each course like we have nowhere else to be, like the world outside this bungalow doesn't exist. He listens while I talk, nods when I tell stories I'd already told before. And when he laughs, it's not out of obligation.

He reaches for my hand between the second and third course. Just holding it, no ulterior motive just being present. Like he's trying to memorize the feel of me.

"I know I've messed up," he says quietly. "But I want us to build something different this time. No more almosts."

I don't say anything. Not because I don't want to believe him but because part of me already does.

After dinner, he plays a song he says reminds him of me. Something soft and vintage, the kind of song you slow dance to, barefoot in kitchens you don't own yet.

And that's exactly what we do. Right there in front of the fire pit. My head on his chest. His hands on my hips. It feels like the beginning of something. But I can't tell if it's the beginning, or just a beautifully wrapped ending.

Later that night – after dessert, more kisses, and one too many glasses of red, I find myself alone on the patio. Dré had gone in to shower. Said he'd be right back. The waves whisper across the black sand, and the moon looks too big to be real.

I stare at the water and whisper to no one in particular, "Don't disappear." Unsure if I mean him or me.

The Invite

Yari

Days were still speeding past me. It was hard to wake up and face the realization that I only had one day left in paradise. The two weeks had felt like hours and here I was on the last slice of this piece of heaven André had gifted me.

I rolled over to find the spot where André had fallen asleep the night before empty. My attention went straight from the bedside to the view of the beach through the mirror in the corner of the en-suite, allowing me to ignore the growls of my stomach. I mustered up the strength to rise from the bed so I would be closer to the salt air that breezed into the space.

My eyes had never beheld such a beautiful sight. I watched as locals melded with the tourists along the black sand beach. The seabirds whistling notes to match the serene sounds of nature. I didn't want this to end.

I'm jerked out of my thoughts by the sound of notifications going off on my phone. It had been on do not disturb since leaving

Cream after my run in with Cynthia. I forgot I had turned my notification back on last night to check in with Arias. I make my way towards the nightstand to check it but to my surprise the it isn't there. Instead, there's a note addressed to me.

Yari,
My absence is not in vain.
There's a breakfast platter arriving for you any second now.
André

A millisecond after reading the note there's a knock at the door causing a smile to spread across my face. I guess that's breakfast.

I grabbed my phone to check the notification before opening the door. As I reach for the handle, I open an email. It's an anniversary dinner invite.

"Be so fucking for real," I whisper to myself, tossing my phone on the chaise lounge and opening the door. I'm not in the head space to entertain any stupidity.

A gentleman dressed in a black and gold bellboy uniform stands in the doorway next to a cart topped with an elaborate breakfast spread fit for royalty. Heart shaped mini waffles, fresh berries, home fries, turkey bacon, sausage links and locally sourced orange blossom syrup.

"Miss, for you," he says, presenting me with a serving tray that holds another note.

Indulge in your favorites.
Once you're done,

head into the closet,
but take your time.
No need to rush!

My cheeks flush and my heart melts. He's really showing me all his cards. I can't wrap my mind around why he's choosing to pull out all the stops now. What had triggered him to see the value in nurturing what we were building?

I shake those thoughts from my mind. This wasn't about overthinking or doubting, this was about receiving what I had always deserved.

I sit at the table where the bellboy had left the cart. Fixing my plate and, following instructions, I indulge, making sure not to rush for whatever was awaiting me in the closet.

I scroll aimlessly through my social media feeds while finishing the last of what I can enjoy from the platter. Pictures and videos of the afterparty for *Quest's* latest concert at Cream were everywhere. This was going to be great publicity. The number of people from out of town that would be checking Cream for the hottest kickbacks would give us a large enough following to look into opening other locations soon.

I took the initiative to clear the table and discard what little was left from the platter. I didn't care to leave it for the housekeepers; I just wasn't like that.

Once I was finished, I practically skipped to the closet. Opening the French doors to reveal what was inside, I couldn't stop the tears from falling. My vision, now blurred, could barely take in the thousands of ivory roses, wrong color but still my favorite. I stepped inside the walk-in to find a white jumbo-sized box wrapped with a champagne gold bow on the marble floor, and another note dangling from the chandelier. I knew the note was meant to be read before I opened the box.

You are beautiful. No matter what you wear.
That doesn't mean I won't spoil you a little.
It's time to get dressed. There will be a car waiting for
you in an hour.
I'll see you soon!

I kneel down to the box, lifting its lid. Inside was a ton of
rose petals covering two separate smaller boxes. The first box held
a beautiful, ivory Chantilly lace flare romper from the boutique
brand Briniao. The second box, a pair of Ferragamo Zelie kitten
heeled leather mules.

The outfit's a little revealing for my taste but I wasn't going
to let that discount his efforts. The look was gorgeous; I just wasn't
sure I could do it justice.

I do my best to shrug off my doubt and get ready, by taking
a shower and doing some light make up. I can't be sure what the
occasion is so I needed to prepare for anything. He hadn't given
me many clues in the direction of what he had up his sleeve, and
although I usually didn't like surprises I wasn't too bothered by
this one.

Out the door and down the stone driveway I found my car
waiting, a gentleman holding the door for me.

"Yari?" he inquires.

"Yes," I answer with a blush and a smile. The excitement was
starting to settle in, I was ready to see my man. André had made
my morning thoughtfully beautiful, and I wanted to thank him for
gifting me mindfulness and peace.

The driver kept looking at me through his rearview-mirror
and I could tell he knew what was going on by the smirk on his
face. We drive for some time before he slows the car pulling to the
side of a winding road.

Panic finds a home inside my chest, my breathing picking up.

I don't know where I am or who this man is.

He turns around to face me, "Miss for you." The pepper and citrus notes of his cologne tap dance into the backseat as he hands me a matte black box with a lace bow. Inside another note, this one matte black to match the box, and laid atop a piece of fabric. I read it to see what comes next.

As you cruise through the hills of Mulancia,
Know that you are safe with me,
I would never put you in harm's way.
Slip on this blindfold, once your driver gives you the signal.
Trust Me Baby, it will be worth it.

I look up at the driver, his eyes hold a warm yet mischievous twinkle that speak for him. I find myself sinking into the plush leather and becoming slightly more comfortable.

"Ok Sir, I'm ready!"

With my permission he steers back on to the road and we continue on our way. Mulancia is breathtaking. Every blink a snapshot of beauty. I was convinced André had taken me to the Islands of Heaven. Nothing was chaotic, time seemed to standstill, all was calm and right in the world, effortless perfection, like Heaven.

Just as my nerves began to ease, I noticed the driver's eyes again, trying to catch my attention.

"It's time."

I took a deep breath and lifted the fabric from the box, fingers brushing its softness before I laid it in my lap.

I hesitated.

I wanted to believe this was real.

Last time I let André blindfold me, my nostrils burned from the cheap clash of sweet citrus and sour berries, lies wrapped in luxury.

I wanted this change to mean care. The type that was so precious it had to be locked away for safekeeping. And maybe, just maybe, I had cracked the code, and proved love could return where silence once lived.

But I'd mistaken roses for truth before. And quiet for kindness.

I wasn't about to get ahead of myself. Not this time.

I tie the blindfold over my eyes, and my breathing grows shallow. Each inhale sharper than the last, as I work to give my trust legs. I still have no idea what André is planning but I make the decision to believe him anyway.

After what feels like forever, the car begins to slow again.

We must have arrived at our destination. I hear my door open and I hesitate when I feel a hand brush mine. The pepper and citrus are replaced by something dark, warm, woodsy, and familiar.

"Dré! Baby, what are you doing?" I wonder aloud.

He assists me out of the town car, then his hand caresses my chin, saying, "Trust me!"

We walked a few steps forward before stopping. "Watch your step," he warns just as my steps went from cushioned grass to hard flooring. He releases my hand and steps directly in front of me.

"Remove your blindfold, but keep your eyes closed," he instructs me, and I oblige. "Do you trust me?"

I laugh, "Clearly, I do,"

He chuckles, "Hold on to me."

I reach for his waist, exclaiming, "I got you!"

"Where are we?" I ask, my question laced with anticipation.

"Keep your eyes closed."

I hear a loud motor startup, then what sounds like a door closing, as I feel the temperature rise around us.

"Dré, I don't like this."

"Yari, trust me," he says, strapping something heavy to my body, then he goes silent.

"Dré?"

"I'm right here."

"Ok," I reply, my hands now shaky. I didn't know how much longer I could just 'trust' him.

Moments later he speaks. "Open your eyes."

I blink my eyes open a few times taking in my surroundings and finally understanding where we were.

"DRÉ! OH MY GOSH DRÉ!!! A HOT AIR BALLOON!"

Dozens of other balloons surround us. I was inside a Getty image. I reach out to hug him, kissing all over his face. I loved hot air balloons. I always had.

The other balloons float in place suspended like lanterns in a still sky. The sun dips behind the volcanoes, and in that moment, even the air felt like it was holding its breath.

I remember mentioning my love for hot air balloons to him months ago when we went to the fair during the summer. I didn't realize he was listening. I had never been in one before but the International Hot Air Balloon Festival had been on my bucket list because I'd wanted to experience a moment exactly like this.

I was smiling from ear to ear drinking in the beauty of this experience. I was a long way from home; I had just landed in my imagination. I had been living in a daydream the entire two weeks I had been away. This felt too good to be true. At least for me.

I felt André approaching me from behind, he began kissing my neck.

"Baby I never want you to feel like you are not heard. I pay attention, I listen, I care, I love you. I want you to know that. Even if I get busy working and I'm tied up with whatever. I promise that for as long as I'm able, I'll have your best interests at heart. I'm not perfect, I can be selfish and inconsiderate, I'll get some things wrong. But I will always choose you, and us. I want this for however long you'll have me."

I turn to face him, our eyes meeting. "Dré, I …."

He places his finger on my lips. "Just answer one thing for me."

I wait for him to continue, but instead he turns me around and points. One by one the other balloons drop banners from their baskets.

Will…You…Marry…Me?

"DRÉ!!!!"

"Yari, I don't need years to know you're the woman for me. We are one and the same. Go Getters. Lovers. We are a power couple. I wanna share all the parts of me with you. Will you?" My eyes trace his face for any uncertainties. I don't find a single one. "Yes…. Yes…. YES, DRÉ! YES!!" I wrap my arms around him as he kisses me deeply. "I love you Dré."

He places a fat round solitaire diamond ring on my finger, yelling, "SHE SAID YES!!!!!"

The people in the surrounding balloons, cheer as we are lowered to the field below.

Once I was safely back on the ground, I squeal to get out the basket so I could take a second to admire the ring that was now on my finger. This proposal was everything I could have ever asked for. André had me blushing from the time he picked me up from the airport 'til this very moment. Nothing could bring me down from this high.

I never expected him to choose me in this way. All my doubts, about my minor weight gain or busy schedule just disappeared from my internal conversations. Of course 'We would make a great power couple.'

We watched as the bannered balloons slowly came down from the sky. I wanted to thank the people he had hired to help with this special moment. As they floated to the ground, I soon realized these weren't just perfect strangers.

The last balloon landed, all the doors opened, and the tears started rolling down my face. My mom, dad, sister, Naveah, and Imani exited from one balloon. A few of my cousins, my aunt, and uncle came from the next. André's mom and dad from the third and other family members came from the last.

"You thought of everything… How did y'all get here?" I ask, hugging my mom as Naveah and Imani drool over my ring.

"Hey baby girl, André flew us all in last night," my dad responds while kissing me on my cheek.

"Dré, what in the world? You're so sneaky, I don't like it, but I'm so glad you all were brought here to share this with us."

The atmosphere is filled with hugs and smiles with everyone congratulating us on our engagement.

"I can't wait for you to be my daughter in law," André's mom assures me as she smooths out the hem of my romper.

"Ok everybody, let's head down the hill to the town cars, they are taking us over to where we will be having dinner," André announces and everyone proceeds toward the line of black town cars awaiting our arrival.

As the sun melts behind the hills and the last balloon drifts to the grass, I stand in the middle of the field, savoring a moment I never thought I'd be chosen for. A proposal and a public, intentional, all-eyes-on-me acknowledgment of love.

My ring catches the last streaks of golden sunlight as we walk toward the town cars, laughter echoing across the hills.

I didn't know what tomorrow would hold, but tonight? I believed in all that it was. It was a choice. It was the future. It was a version of love that shows up when things are easy and stays when they get hard.

Before slipping into the lead car, I turn to the field for one last glance. Our family's laughter harmonizing with the purple and orange hues piercing the sky.

The fairytale Dré was feeding me, the most romantic happily ever after a girl could ask for.

With a faint smirk, I whisper, "Don't disappear."

Just then, the driver clears his throat, his hand poised on the door. "Madam, whenever you're ready."

I smile, nodding, "I'm ready."

The door closes with a soft thud and a hush descends. Even the island knew not to disturb this feeling.

The Corner Pocket

Jarell

Even the post-workout shower isn't helping. I hadn't felt this level of agony in a long time. I feel damn near sick to my stomach.

I haven't heard from Yari in what feels like months. Even though it was my fault for her disinterest in communicating, I wanted more than anything for her to say something. A joke. Sarcasm. Instead, she has only given me silence. A gift I didn't know would be so heavy and empty. Her absence teaching me the hard lessons of recuperation during moments that had been taken for granted. Yari only wanted me to notice my spiral, so this time I could save myself from it. It had always been my stubbornness that landed me in the ring, going toe to toe with my pride. That was always my downfall. Unable to be vulnerable long enough to heal, or honest enough with myself about my quick retreat to self-destruction as a way to cope with anything I wasn't brave enough to confront. I want to reach out or just show up at her place, but I have no idea what mindset she's in. I guess I'll just link up with

X and Cam instead. It'll help level my head and I need to talk to someone about what I'm dealing with.

I pull out my phone to send a group text. Not knowing what else to send I opted for the bat signal with the words:

Jarell [12:33 PM]: Suede in 30?

My notifications go off instantly. Of course, X is the first to respond.

X [12:34 PM]: Hell Yeah, I'll head that way now!

Shortly after Cam sent over his confirmation

Cam [12:35 PM]: Yep!

I stand from the couch to get dressed. As I enter my closet another notification comes through. Someone just responded to the invite I sent out last week.

Yari? She's coming? I scroll through my email to find her response. She responded Maybe? She also requested a plus one? I don't even care if she comes with someone, I just want her there. I approve her request as quickly as possible, with the hope that it would persuade her to change her maybe to yes.

I toss my phone onto the bed. I need to throw on some clothes, I can't link up in my briefs. Grabbing the first fit I can find, dark gray sweatpants and a hoodie with a fresh white tee and some J's, I get dressed. Suede was on the other side of town; I needed at least 20 minutes to get there. With my phone in hand, I grab my keys and head out.

Arriving at Suede felt normal. Me and the fellas used to link here at least once a week or so. It had been forever since we got together, and on a bat signal at that. Tonight, I needed my boys, I needed to stop running from my problems. As I pulled up, I see Cam stepping out of his ride. He was always on time; it was me and X who always ran late. With a smirk on my face, I whipped into the spot next to his and hopped out.

"Yo Yo!" He greets me.

"What up man?" I extended my hand to dap him up as he walked around to my side of the car.

"Where's yo boy?" He asked, shaking his head.

"Ay yo you know how we do. I'm surprised I even pulled up on time."

We laughed.

"Naw cause for whatever reason y'all don't believe in time."

I throw my hands up. I can't even stunt with him knowing he's speaking straight facts. "Listen, time can be a conceptual thing, you feel me? Technically we all on different clocks anyway."

He pushes me back slightly, forcing me to catch myself.

"Naw don't give me that 'time is a theory bullshit.'"

The both of us bust out laughing, that is until the weight of the elephant waiting to be addressed came and sat right in between us as the silence quickly grew thick.

"Man, are you ok? I know you called us out but how are you? Like mentally and shit! What's going on?" Cam is now leaning against his car waiting on my response.

The only problem is, I don't know what I'm feeling – if I'm ok or if I wanted to gloss over everything and simply say I'm working through it. I had no time to try and feed Cam bullshit because he noticed my hesitation immediately.

"Look man, I didn't cut my evening of planning a surprise for my shorty early for you to bring no bullshit to me, if we gon' kick it tonight Imma need you to be honest with not only me but yourself."

His stance is firm and I know I can't get a lie past him so I just tell him the truth, "My girl, she on some fuck shit, I can't go into details but I'm hoping that once I surprise her, she'll be back to her regular program and it will be good."

He nodded, "I feel you on that, you know they trip from time to time, it's really just in their DNA, nothing they can do about it. They are built to crash out sometime."

I just nod, thankful I dodged going into too many details. I really want to just get inside and kick it. My head has been all over the place lately.

"So, what about Yari? Ya'll good?" Cam asks me as he locks his car door and throws his head in the direction of X walking up behind me.

"Man, I wish I knew, I haven't spoken to her in weeks. She hasn't responded to any of my texts or returned any of my calls. I don't know how I'm getting back in her good graces, but I need to figure that out." I salute X as he approaches and the three of us walk towards the entrance of Suede.

The doors open and the smell of high-quality ganja and top-shelf whisky kicks its way up my nostrils. I pull my membership card from my wallet, flashing it at security so I could get to the festivities. Once inside, I see the place is even more suave than I remembered. The walls are covered in a smoky-gray diamond textured wallpaper that pairs nicely with the bourbon brown leather sectional seats placed throughout the lounge, along the original hardwood that's aged to perfection. It's low key a vibe.

Tonight, we opt for our own private room. All the private rooms have their own exclusive bar and cabinet humidor. Using my membership card, I unlock our private room and head straight over to the bartender.

"What we doing, shots?" X asks, hyped as hell about the selection of cigars as he scanned through the cabinets along the wall.

"I'm cool with shots," Cam says, already throwing back a

shot of Hennessy Gold.

"Naw," I say, turning towards the bartender. "I want an old fashioned."

"AN OLD FASHIONED?" Cam questions, already downing his third shot as he sets up the pool table.

I grab my drink from the bartender and step over to where the pool table is. "Yes, an old fashioned." I sip the golden amber liquor before placing my glass on one of the chest high tables. "Spare me man you know what's up!"

"And what's that? What's up?" X asks, joining us with three fresh cut cigars in hand.

"He miss Yari's ass" Cam answers before I can say a word.

I know he's speaking the truth once again. I do miss her. Probably more than I will ever admit. I wouldn't go for an old fashioned in normal circumstances, but it reminds me of her. It's her favorite 'slow sip'. That's what she called it. I could hear her explaining it to me years ago, "My grandfather always said you would appreciate the craftsmanship of a whiskey cocktail, but only if you sip slow." I peered into the distance, remembering her smile when she pondered the advice given to her by her grandfather. In this very moment I agreed, the full body of the drink can't be appreciated if you don't take your time. Every drop sinks you deeper like you're riding theta waves. The type that allows for deep internal focus. The kind that allows you to sort out your thoughts and helps you connect to your intuition.

"Hey, Earth to Jarell!" X claps in front my face pulls me back into reality. "Damn man, You feenin like that?" He questions.

"Right, man just hit her up. She probably ain't even mad anymore." Cam tries to reassure me while he struggles to round up the balls for another game.

"Naw, I ain't trippin man. Roll Up" I finish off my old fashioned and sit the cigar he had given me moments earlier down. Tonight called for something a little more special.

"Say no more," X replies, and Cam begins jigging in celebration of the ceremony of relaxation we were about to embark on.

"Ms. Bartender lady," I start, before looking at her name badge. "Trina, can we get another round of shots please ma'am?"

"Sure!" She replies, her voice a pretty as her smile.

I feel my body straining to respond. Although she's bad as fuck, I'm not feeding into it. Tonight isn't about that. I have enough women problems as is, I'm not about to add to the equation before I got the chance to subtract.

"Yo Jarell you called us here, so you do the honors then, tell us what's going on," X says, handing me a perfectly rolled spliff. I proceed to flick the lighter, igniting the end of the blunt while inhaling. The burning herbal sensation fills me. I hold onto it, like my sanity depends on it. Then pass it off to Cam before exhaling.

"I've been all over the place lately." I admit, for the first time since that night I saw Q. But the thing that gave me the courage to use the bat signal was Yari. I hadn't spoken to her for so long, I was starting to feel off balance. I can't think of a way to ensure she'll allow me to apologize. She really wants nothing to do with me. I disrespected her. Throwing money in her face was crazy even if I was on one. She never deserved that. I'd replayed that scene on the cameras more times than I could count. Her wiping tears while wiping my counters. That was the part I couldn't let go of.

Cam passes the blunt to X to complete the first rotation. "You telling us like we don't know that shit," he says, speaking around the thick smoke that filled his lungs.

"I need y'all help to figure out how to get this shit with Yari straight." I inhale, confessing without mentioning why everything was falling apart in the first place. "Look at this shit!" I open my phone to the video footage of me disrespecting Yari. "Listen to me man, I damn near called her a bitch." I throw my phone on the sofa as I begin pacing.

"Aye man, you gotta stop feeling sorry for yourself, you know better than to bring that energy to her. She don't wanna hear that shit man." Cam states, throwing his hands up before grabbing the blunt from X. He reaches over to hand me my phone and taps the sofa for me to sit.

"Listen dog, you just need to man up and face her. Let her know you wanna talk or some shit. Women love when we just tell they ass how we feeling. Ain't no secret to how you need to handle this man. Just be straight up. Simple." X shrugged taking my turn in rotation.

"I agree with X man. He's a fucking idiot sometimes but right now he's speaking facts. Just reach out." Cam agrees as he sets up for a round of pool.

"Ya'll right but shit, I sent an invitation to this dinner and she never responded."

"So you think you gone be able to disrespect Yari and she just gon' show up? What would be her reason for wanting to support yo disrespectful ass?" X asks while laughing.

Him and Cam are now in a full roasting session about my audacity. I can't take the heat from it tonight though. "Okay, Okay. Real shit though, I'm going to try and reach out."

"Cool, so about this invite..." X starts, I quickly cut him off changing the subject.

"Man, just be there!" I say.

"Whoa whoa okay calm down no need to pull out any money to tip me. Imma be there." He responds, always finding a way to joke about any and everything.

"WOW! That's crazy, you coming at me like that on a bat signal.? To soon man!" I remind him of the distress I'm in.

Cam shakes his head. "We'll be there man."

"Bet! Stop thirsting on that drink and come get this ass whooping." I call over to X. His eyebrows raise. "Ms. Bar Lady.... Trina right?" He pauses for a moment then continues, "Yeah, Trina

144

run us another round tray of shots, let me school these clowns."

She winks, "You got it baby."

The boys are laughing, the shots are coming, and I try to laugh with them. But I couldn't manage to outdrink what I'd done.

Brunch At Poochioani's

Yari

Touching back down in Roseville brought on a level of anxiety I'd never known was present before. Nothing felt the same, and I wasn't ready to get back to reality just yet. My mini vacation had transformed me from a girlfriend to a fiancé and I was loving every minute of the unexpected bliss I had been gifted.

I'd never felt more love from André than I had these past two weeks. He'd pulled out all the stops.

I had to leave him behind so he could handle some business related to a partnership with some brokers from Mulancia. I wasn't sweating it though I knew when he got back, we would continue the journey towards our forever.

Naveah and Imani had dedicated their return to setting up a cozy girl's night at my loft. On the plane, I was instructed not to return home until I got a text saying I could. I loved themed surprises especially from my girls, so I obliged them.

Arriving in Hollins Square, a neighborhood located in the

heart of the city, I stepped out of the town car they'd forced me into when we'd landed. The Square had never seemed so festive. To be fair, I rarely visited this part of the city this close to the holidays.

I was dressed fall comfortable in a pumpkin-colored cable knit sweater set, my sage green trench puffer vest bouncing against my heels as I stepped onto the sidewalk. The air was crisp, clean, and smelled like apples were somewhere nearby.

I immediately noticed my favorite restaurant, Poochioani's. Although I didn't frequent this area, I always sent Arias here for my lunch or when I needed catering for an event. My cousin, Poochi, owned the place. Although she and I didn't speak as often as we used to, we respected each other's hustle. Our parents were close so naturally we were too. We never really let ourselves drift too far apart, that was until Vince, and all the low-down shit he was doing at CAKES came into our lives.

Shaking off my reservations, I start toward Poochioani's front door.

The bell above the door jingles and I notice the hostess quickly approaching me with a menu.

"Hi, Welcome to Poochioani's," she greets me. "How many will be joining your party this afternoon?"

I smirk and wave at Poochi standing proudly in the corner.

"A booth for two!" she calls out as she begins walking up to the hostess station. "Hey Tempest," she addresses the hostess, "we have nothing booked in the private hall for the next few hours. Would you mind closing it off for me?" She reaches for my hand, "And I'll accompany this lovely lady over to her booth!"

I hold and give Poochi's hand a gentle squeeze as we head towards the private dining hall. I hear Tempest calling out to the back of house informing them of the private luncheon Poochi just arranged.

"Baby, look at you! You are GLOWING!" she gushes,

looking me up and down. "What's his name and what is this on your hand?" she probes, dramatically pretending my ring weighs as much as a boulder as she lifts my hand to her face. "My goodness," she breathes out on a laugh, lifting my arm higher, inviting me to spin. I oblige, giggling and blushing. "You know Imma call momma as soon as we get all caught up."

"Yes Pooch, I know. I've been good," I respond trying to contain my blush that wouldn't subside.

"Sit and do tell. I wanna hear all about the young man that put that chunk of coal on your finger. Has auntie Kora met him? Details please."

Within seconds of us sitting the waitress appears and my excitement settles enough for me to order a cherry rose Martini and Poochi her signature Poochberry Punch. It's like a luxurious Kool-Aid but, according to her, it's crafted with much more skill and way less sugar, faucet water, and paper packets. I pretended to believe her. There was no doubt that her punch was the shit though. Every other customer that came in was ordering it with their meal, so it was obvious she was doing something right.

"Okay, his name is André. We've been dating for almost eight months now, and he proposed on our mini vacation," I flash my ring squealing. I was so excited to start the next chapter of my life with André.

"That's amazing girl! I'm so happy for you. Let me know how I can help, in anyway. I got you."

"Just promise you'll provide all the food for the bridal shower. That would be a big help. I'll give you Imani and Nevaeh's contact information, they're taking the reins on all things wedding."

She hands me her phone just as our drinks arrive at the table. "I can do that. I'm actually surprised I didn't have to reach out to you for Jarell's dinner this weekend. Must be because you were busy on vacation."

My eyes roll before I can speak. "Yeah, I was busy vacationing, busy living, busy becoming a fiancé. I don't know what Jarell has going on and to be honest its none of my concern."

Her brows form question marks across her forehead. "None of your concern? Okay; wow, what's going on there?"

My eyes find the ceiling as I shrug. I wasn't interested in speaking about what had happened between Jarell and I two weeks ago. To me it was old, and I was past it. I hadn't decided if I would be attending his little 'anniversary dinner' but it was whatever at this point. I wanted to focus on catching up with my cousin and getting into some bomb ass brunch food. I begin to respond when the waitress, who I now know is Amber, interrupts us.

"Thank you, Amber. You're right on time!" I say excitedly, feeling Poochi's eyes monitoring my body language. Her lips press together, letting me know she wasn't buying my lack of interest but wasn't going to push the topic.

"Great, I'm glad to hear that, what will you ladies be having?"

"I'll be having the lobster and andouille stuffed waffles with rosemary honey butter and agave. Oh, and a side of shrimp and grits," I rattle off.

"Yes ma'am."

Poochi's fingers crawl their way over the top of my menu pulling it down so I can see her eyes stretch to the size of quarters. "You want that full-sized, Yari?" she asks me.

"No, a half-size, please. I won't finish all that. But I can't come here and not get your shrimp and grits that would be disrespecting my soul."

"Oh okay, I was about to say..." Her side eye hits hard.

"Look girl, I was busy. Mulancia owes me nothing. All the exercise I got while there..." I wink, and Poochi giggles.

"Yeah, I bet."

Amber waits patiently blushing and trying not to laugh at our commentary.

"Ok Amber, I'm going to have the breakfast bruschetta trio. Sub the ham for turkey, and no fig halves; just fig jam on the side."

"Ok, perfect. And for the table would you ladies like fresh berries or croissant minis?"

In unison we choose fresh berries, and Amber whisks away with our menus; leaving to put our order in.

"So, you gonna tell me what's going on with you and Jarell? Or we moving past that?"

I could have sworn Poochi was going to leave that alone.

"I'll say this, Jarell needs to get his shit together. I think it's best he handles that in whatever way he needs to for himself. That's it."

She knew there was more, but she shrugs and we continue catching up for the next fifteen to twenty minutes before our food arrives at the table.

"Oh my goodness, y'all give a beautiful presentation Pooch. This looks absolutely amazing," I praise, my mouth watering as a steaming plate is placed in front of me.

"I forgot that this is your first time dining-in; in a while. After the renovations and expansion, I wanted everything to be top tier. I hired an in-house chef who curated a lot of our new entrees and even gave us a custom bar menu. I'm so content."

I reach for her hands "Yes, girl. You should be. The place looks beautiful. When you said you was getting out that club and never turning back, I didn't know you meant like this," my arms spread wide, gesturing to the space and emphasizing my words.

"After Vince started being possessive and wanting to manipulate and try and man handle me, I was done with that club and him. His snake ass tried to pull a fast one on me though. When I opened these doors five years ago, he was sending someone to keep an eye on me."

I paused mid bite at her words. "What you mean man handle?

And he was sending someone to keep eyes on you? WHAT THE HELL, POOCH?!"

She looks over her shoulder then leans forward, shushing me as Amber returns to the table with a second round of drinks. "Here you are ladies."

"Thanks Amber," Poochi smiles wide, waiting for her to leave the room before continuing in a hushed voice, "You know how long I been covering this up? Five years. Wigs. High bangs. Strategic lighting. But you family, so Imma show you why you don't look back once you walk away. You see this?" Pushing her sandy brown and black curly bangs out of her face, she points to a scar on the side of her face near her right temple.

"Yeah, is that from him?" I question.

She nods, "A month after I left him, he pulled up and wanted to push up on me. I never saw him as the 'I don't take no for an answer type of dude' but he sure showed me that night. Some women get baby pictures. I got this. A mark that says I didn't die loving the wrong man," she says, a faraway look in her eye.

"Anyway, I have this on the side of my head to reminds me every time I go to wash my face, leave the first time." I watch as her eyes moisten and her cheeks flush. "I'm surprised you've never had any 'visitors' at Cream. He was sending some youngin' in here every day dressed in a suit and tie. He would only order coffee and watch the door for at least three hours. When he got ready to leave he would leave a blue face on the counter and a half drunken cup of Joe. Who pays one hundred dollars for a cup of coffee? I knew Vince had something to do with that shit. But as soon as he started hooking up with Cynthia all that stopped. I'm grateful the bitch took his ass off my radar. He was beginning to make me contemplate leaving the city."

My eyes widen at that. "You never told me any of this Pooch, why? I'm family, we're family. That's dangerous and the type of secrets you don't keep. I've never noticed anyone like that at

Cream....but I did see Cynthia recently."

Pooch energy transforms from sadness to barely controlled anger. "Saw her or 'ran' into her?"

"I saw her. I didn't know she owned The Cheeky Boutique down on Scottsden Ave. I was in there a few days before André and I flew out. She came off nice and sweet. That is, until I invited her to hang out at Cream."

Poochi squints and I watch disgust wash over her face. "Ok and why the fuck would you do that?"

"I know; I know. But she and I use to run together back before CAKES was dirty. I didn't even know she was with Vince while you and him still had a thing going."

"Listen Yari, people change when money is involved. I seen a switch in the best of them. You lost her as a friend the minute Vince's slime ass swiped that black card. The fucking second he started making those pathetic ass promises wrapped in golden tickets to abandoned factories, she was no longer your friend."

"I just wish things would have gone differently. We were never suppose to get caught up in the club's dirt. We went into CAKES to stack money and move along. She definitely forgot the move along part."

"Sure, did. And now the place is pretty much a whorehouse compared to what it was back when I used to dance. I had the girls on a tight leash you hear me?" She sips on her house Cosmopolitan, which has hints of lime and apricots. "Them bitches made they money and got the fuck out. When them newbies rolled around, I got them into shape, but it was something about when Cynthia started getting involved. Shit just changed."

"Yeah, it damn sure did."

"Look, I ain't telling you what to do or who the hang out with. But Yari baby, watch your back. I don't trust that bitch. She still fucking with Vince?"

I nod finishing the last sip of my old fashioned.

"Then yeah; keep that bitch far enough so you can see her. Get to close and you're bound to get burned. Trust me," she lifts her shirt showing me a burn mark on her side.

"What the fuck, Pooch?"

"Like I said Yari, be careful. We family, no secrets"

I'd never seen Poochi flinch before. Never seen her face wear fear like it belonged there.

But those scars? They told me everything I hadn't asked. Whole chapters written in those marks.

And the fact that she trusted me enough to show them, that meant more than brunch or bloodlines.

"If shit goes left," she continues, "it's one call and you know the fam will clear that whole fucking club out. Bitches included."

"Yeah, I know."

I reach out to touch her burn mark.

"Girl it's ok, I told the tattoo artist just give me feathers, wings, something wild. I want beauty growing where he tried to put shame, I'm just thankful to be alive."

"Yeah, I feel you, Pooch."

Amber walks over with a cheesecake sampler flight for us to indulge in.

"Thank you, Amber," I call out starting to feel the tipsiness kicking in as the other ladies around her help clear the table.

"I'm so happy you came in house today for brunch. It's so good seeing you cousin."

"Yes, same it's been so good seeing you too. I have to make time to hang out more often."

"Mmm hmm, Yeah, right."

We laugh and finish our dessert.

The text telling me to get back to the loft had come through while we'd been talking. The city didn't look the same walking out as it did walking in. I kissed Poochi's cheek, promising I'd come by again soon. But the truth was, I wasn't sure what I was walking back into. Only that the real world didn't wait for fairy tales.

Rooftop Remedies

Yari

I didn't know how to re-enter life. Not after a dreamy vacation with a diamond on top. Not when my feet still felt like they were hovering somewhere above Roseville. Being engaged to Andre' felt unreal. The proposal had explained all his absent moments and canceled plans. I would have never guessed he was ready for the next step in our relationship.

The elevator doors close behind me and I lean into the silence. My mind is all over the place. I can't stop thinking about what Poochi had finally spoken out loud.

With Vince out the picture, I have high hopes she won't give up on her chance to find a genuine man. She deserves that much. It was never okay for a man to assault a woman. Especially under the notion that she wasn't interested in entertaining his bull shit any longer.

The sound of an alert from my phone snaps me out of my thoughts. It was a reminder from the invite Jarell had sent me. I'd responded *Maybe* when I was in Mulancia.

Now, as my finger hovered over the notification; I wondered, should I go? Is this the time to showcase my not giving a fuck? Or was I supposed to support him in a time that I know hasn't been the easiest for him? My finger wavers back and forth as the questions in my head bounce. Without making a selection the elevator comes to a halt, reminding me I don't have to make a decision right now.

I pull down the elevator's metal gate so it could transport me to my private level; which was located on the 12th floor. I wait for the large metal doors to close behind me.

The sun was beginning to set casting its purple and orange rays to tint the walls. The colors reminded me of peace, of joy, of the freedom to give myself credit.

In the past few weeks, I've focused on my own happiness. I never realized how much of that I had given up. It wasn't until I got away that I was able to recenter and see the true problem. I needed to set boundaries, something I sucked at. But it was about time I became more acquainted with doing just that. If Jarell had taught me anything in these past few weeks; it was that when you set boundaries you create room for peace; and I loved that for me.

My cheeks begin to shift up as a smile appears on my face once I stop in front of my door a few steps later. These chicas had out done themselves. I was greeted by a ton of white, cream, gold, and silver balloons. A few fancier ones shaped like diamond rings and another bunch of gold with silver letters that spelled, "It's A Fiancé." How they'd managed to do all of this in three hours, I would never know. There was a cream and gold foil envelope attached to the balloon floating near the front door next to my monstera. I instantly begin giggling as I open it. Inside the note has instructions for me.

It's not only a fiance;

It's an entrepreneur;
It's a best friend;
It's you;
It's time to give you your flowers;
It's time to remind you to let your hair down;
It's time to remind you you're enough;
You have always been enough!
It's time you let us love on you a little!
Ring the bell when you're ready!

My eyes find the skylight windows as I fan away the tears. I have to use the sleeve of my sweater to wipe away the few that started to fall. I was starting to feel that type of overstimulated I was so unfamiliar with.

I was used to helping everyone. Used to being everything for everybody. When the bottom falls out from under me, I always just pick those pieces up myself; and put them back together with my just in case shit hits the fan glue I kept in my purse, inside of my emergency pull yourself together kit.

My girls wanted to celebrate me, and tonight I wasn't going to push it away, or deny wanting and needing it. I'm in my "I'm enough!" era. Words of affirmation? Not needed. Validation? Unnecessary. Tonight, I was going to leave the doubt and anxiety of if I was who I wanted to be behind me. It's time to celebrate who I was, and who I am!

Pressing the doorbell, I hear shushing and music coming from inside. The door slowly opens. I walked in, placing my tote down on the entry sideboard, the whole time, my jaw resting on the floor.

I couldn't believe my eyes; my entire loft was being swallowed in hundreds of balloons. Wavy gold streamers covered the large warehouse windows.

Arias and Sasha are walking over to me carrying a two-tier cake big enough to share with possibly everyone in the loft building. There was even a huge plush pillow fort that was created around my coffee table in the middle of the floor.

"If y'all are here who's at Cream handling…"

Sasha doesn't let me finish. "Don't worry, the girls are fine, it's Soulful Sunday, everybody is relaxing and vibin'."

I throw out a mean side eye at that.

"It's fine boss lady I promise, I have my ears all over the place. I got X handling everything security and we will be leaving to head back shortly," Arias cuts in, knowing how I feel about business before pleasure. I mean; I wanted to celebrate but not to only have to be disrupted with bullshit later.

"Okay, I trust you ladies have it covered." My side eye rounds and falls back center to land on Imani and Nevaeh running over to hug me, one on each side. I feel Nevaeh pull away and head towards the bar cart as Imani instructs me while tipping my head back. "Come on Yari girl, no stressin' tonight."

"Open up girl!" Nevaeh calls while walking back towards me.

A smile paints across my face before I open my mouth giving myself permission to drive the boat. The peppery vanilla notes of Asombroso La Rosa Reposado Tequila fill my throat and I peel off my vest, allowing the proof to warm my body instead. Down comes my bun and my shoes are kicked to the side as the five of us make our way to the fort.

"You know; I suggest we start the night off with a drunken Never Have I Ever!!!" Imani cheers; shaking her tits, trying to hype us up. The loft fills with laughter as she jumps up to grab a tray of already prepped jello shots. "Ok, the rules are simple; if you've never done it no shot; but if you have, then… its a shot; drunkest lose but most sober has to do something they've never done. I'm going first. Never have I ever…kissed a stranger!"

The room grew quiet as Imani finished her turn, everyone's eyes roamed around the circle. Seconds later everyone but me reached for a jello shot as our laughter climbed up the exposed brick.

"Y'all are some freak ass heffas," I say, shaking my head knowing they would get me back for never experiencing that.

We each take turns, sharing all our nevers and at some point forgetting the point of the game.

"Okay, okay, I'm next, then we need to get going!" Sasha says, standing to emphasize how her and Arias need to head out. "Never have I ever... had chocolates and flowers delivered to me, in... let's just say, a special way."

Arias giggles at the confusion on my face as she crawls over to blindfold me. I don't know what they have up their sleeves, but I choosing to actively not think too much about all the what ifs. Tonight was only getting started, I wasn't going to ruin it with worrying. Once the blindfold was secure I heard a door open.

"Boss lady, once the music starts you can remove your blindfold." I could tell Arias was now behind me.

"I have a delivery for Yari," a voice I don't recognize says. Seconds later the beat drops to Ginuwine's Pony.

As instructed, I remove my blindfold to sight of a beautiful dark chocolate brother. His body, sculpted to perfection; oiled and glistening. He's dressed in a black bow tie and basically nothing else. A golden jockstrap holds his girth like a holster custom fitted for a knockout sized treat.

"For you!" He announces, placing his hands at his waist. There was a beautiful arrangement of thornless red roses I thought he was holding until I realized they were nicely arranged and held together by a satin ribbon attached to his jockstrap. His eyes meet mine, and I can't help but blush.

He moves to stand over me. "Oh baby; you're blushing," he says, with a sultry baritone, smooth like expensive whiskey. His pearly whites glistening, his scent addictive.

"Aren't you going to smell the roses?" He questions, placing his leg up on the coffee table to give me an open invitation to his full package.

Normally, I wouldn't even be tempted but I honestly wanted to be closer. I couldn't fathom why though. Dré had been amazing. In the past month I had been on cloud nine like never before. He was finally making me feel wanted. Yet, I wanted all of the attention Mr.Bow Tie was offering. He was bringing out a hidden part of fantasies I had never disclosed to anyone, not even myself.

I lean closer, my eyes never leaving his. I could hear the encouraging cat calls from Imani and Nevaeh. The scent of my favorite flower and *him* combined to make my panties wet.

His hands cup my chin and tilt my head up to him; as he begins to bend down to me. His soft lips meet mine. I'm shocked, but I don't pull back. He takes that as an invite to continue, and our tongues start to swim passionately.

He scoops me up off the floor and my legs wrap his torso, my arms wrap his neck, and my ass held firm in his tight grip hovering above the bouquet. The heat radiating from him sends a pulse through me, a slow ache blooming as warmth spills between my thighs. My body answered before I can think, the silk between my legs now damp as his grip softens. The ribbon slipping loose as he draws me down his body, his tongue still tangled with mine, never leaving my mouth.

Once I'm securely back on the floor, we finally part ways. He plants one final kiss on my cheek and picks up a few rose from the scattered bouquet on the hardwood. Gripping them he hands them over to me.

"Never have I ever had the pleasure," he states, but I'm speechless.

He gives me a final once over and heads toward the front door, grabbing a duffle bag I hadn't even noticed. Once the door closes behind him I pretend to faint as Arias and Nevaeh hit me with pillows. Sasha and Imani giggle and fan themselves.

"GIRL...I was not expecting all of that!" Sasha says.

"Neither was I! Who are you and what have you done with our Yari?" Imani asks.

"That was freshman year Yari, that was CAKES Yari, that was not OUR YARI! BAYBEEE!" Nevaeh claims.

"We have to get up out of here, Imma see if I can catch Mr. Chocolate," Sasha says, scrambling for her shoes.

The laughter doesn't subside until Arias and Sasha are gone. Now alone, me, Imani, and Nevaeh gather in the kitchen for wine and cake.

"Thanks, y'all, I appreciate y'all doing this for me tonight." I say, holding back the emotions I'm sure they know I'm feeling.

"Girl you're welcome, you deserve rest and relaxation," Nevaeh reminds me.

"Yes, and a little naughtiness here and there." We all laughed as Imani mimicked a fake make out with herself.

"I got something to help us top this evening off old school style." Nevaeh mentions, sliding across the floor in her fuzzy socks to reach inside her purse. She retrieves a metal container, and I immediately know where this is going. "Y'all remember our rooftop remedy sessions back in college?" She asks.

"Yeah, when we thought those frat boy problems were the biggest problems we would ever have." I reminisce.

"Yes, I remember. What was that asshole name..." She wonders aloud.

"LAMONT!" Nevaeh and I remind her.

"Girl, he was all we heard about." Nevaeh called her out grabbing her sweater. We follow suit.

"Yeah, I know girl. I was so crazy over that." Imani admits biting her finger.

"Ewww... don't fucking start." I laugh, slipping on a pair of fuzzy socks of my own, and putting on my Uggs. I grab my keys and open the door, as Nevaeh grabs the bottle of champagne from the ice bucket on my bar top. "To the roof we go!"

Using the stairwell, we make it up to the rooftop. Because of the private floor concept my building has, the roof is all mine. I had designed it to feel like a little oasis. Plants covered and wrapped along the circumference of the roof, encapsulating the bohemian outdoor furniture I paired with bamboo flooring and turf grass.

"Damn girl, you redid this whole roof!" Nevaeh mentions while plopping down on the outdoor beanbag next to the succulent wall.

"So, we burning this green or not?" Imani asks; now cradled next to me on the couch under the wooden pergola my dad and Jarell custom built this past summer. The fairy lights that draped the pergola twinkled against the industrial windows that peep down through the ceiling into my bedroom en-suite.

"Yes, we're burning, there's no mistaking that." I reassure her.

"Hey Yari, didn't your dad and Jarell build this?" Imani asks, admiring the craftsmanship of the pergola.

"Yeah, they did." I respond, trying to not give away any inkling of the fact Jarell and I were not on speaking terms.

"What's going on with y'all, Yari. Every time his name is mentioned you get this look on your face like you lost your best friend?" Nevaeh notices, and I concentrate on holding back the tears that are threatening to fall at her words.

"I believe I have. I haven't spoken to y'all about how I feel but I'm just jaded by his actions. I can't be the brunt of his blows while he figures out what needs to happen for him." I finally admit to them. Having a safe space to say what I've been feeling for almost a month feels good. I don't want to burden them with drama about Jarell but I knew they didn't see it as a burden.

"So, I'm assuming that means you won't be going to his

dinner party Thursday night?" Nevaeh questions, while pulling out a blunt perfectly rolled in pink paper. Her lighter sparks as she sets the mood.

"I'm not sure still. If I go, he's probably going to want to talk to me and I haven't seen or spoken to him in almost a month now." I say, grabbing the blunt and inhaling my rotation. This was the perfect time to indulge in some gardening. I had multiple weeds to pull, and my favorite group of gardeners.

"A month?" They question in unison.

"What do you mean a month, Yari?" Imani asks. "So, he doesn't know about your engagement or anything?" Her question continues, reminding me that I haven't felt the urge to share the news with him.

I don't know if the news was worth sharing with him, or if I was still battling with my own thoughts behind the engagement. He wasn't happy in his own situation in the relationship department. After how he had been acting I wasn't expecting him to show happiness for me.

I also wasn't sure if I was even sure. My engagement although exciting, was slightly confusing to me. Why now? For months we had been just going through the motions of what relationship was. We barely spent time with one another. He had become a different man and I for sure was evolving into a different woman. I just never saw it coming. Something about that didn't feel natural for a couple taking next steps. Maybe why the attention from Mr. Bow Tie felt quite refreshing. There were so many things up in the air. It's pretty ironic that Andre' asked me to marry him while we were in that very same position. Up in the air, in a balloon, with no certainty that we would ever find the ground again.

My mind continues to wander until I notice it's my rotation again. "No, he knows nothing." I pull in the herbal remedy hand off to Imani.

"I think you should at least consider it. You guys are peanut butter and jelly. It don't make sense one without the other." Nevaeh says.

My laughter chokes me, the green obviously starting to work in my system. "I'll think about it, but you know what?" I stand holding the bottle of champagne Nevaeh had sat on the round table that centered us.

"What?" Imani says, laughing for no reason and trying to stand too.

"Tonight we toast!" I say knowing my words are coming out slower than I actually thought they should.

"Tonight we toast." Nevaeh agrees, slowly standing and clipping the blunt.

"Toast to what girl? What you talking bout?" Imani ask, still trying to help plant her feet in the turf.

"Girl, stand up." I command.

Finally finding her ground Imani joins us.

"A toast to these rooftop remedies, to us continuing and growing our friendship, and these next steps we all are taking to continue… Growing, glowing, and remembering who the hell we are."

The silence after my words, as loud as it was, turns into laughter as we share group hug and continue our night relaxing and reminiscing.

Interlude

Soft Glow

The loft is quiet again. The kind of quiet that waits, soft, heavy, breathing slow. A few balloons brushed the ceiling, their strings tangled like leftover joy. The faint scent of cake and citrus perfume lingered in the air, and the fairy lights along the window still twinkled low.

I move through the room barefoot, brushing a stray rose petal from the counter. The memory of my laughter was caught somewhere in the walls. The echo of Nevaeh's smile, the warmth of Imani's hug, the shimmer of champagne. Each echo hung in the air like blessings that hadn't quite settled.

The night air slipped through the slightly cracked window, carrying a whisper of faint smoke, sweet wine, and the sound of women remembering who they were. I smile as it passes over my skin.

I think about how easy it is to capture joy when you're with people, but how hard it is to hold it when you're alone. Maybe that's why God gives us nights like this, so we can practice keeping joy when the music stops.

My eyes lift toward the lights again, their small bulbs reflecting in the windowpane. They remind me of Mulancia's sunsets, those pink-orange skies that promised warmth even after the day went dark. My grandmother used to say, *"The light don't leave you, baby. It just moves so you can see it from somewhere new."*

I smiled. Maybe that's what tonight was, light moving. The proof that healing didn't always roar; sometimes it hummed softly in the corners of your home, wrapped in laughter and leftover lipstick stains.

I poured the last bit of champagne into a glass and held it up to the window. A cheers to joy, to friendship, to staying soft when life gets hard. My reflection stares back, mascara smudged, curls wild, but my eyes were bright again. Not perfect, just present.

"Keep the light," I whisper to myself. "Even when the room is empty."

Then I turn off the fairy lights, leaving one strand still glowing. Not for company, but as a reminder that peace had finally found its way in. Soft and glowing.

Food For Thought

Jarell

The alarm blares beyond a volume that my head can tolerate. Today was Thursday and even though I needed to get my day started, mustering the energy wasn't in the cards for me just yet. Everything needed to be in its perfect place for the anniversary dinner party tonight. I had cars picking up Q's family from the airport. They were due to arrive around 4 o'clock.

Q hadn't answered my text from two nights ago. I assume because she's upset with me. I guess that was to be expected. I hadn't been communicating with her much since I'd sent her away. That's probably why she'd told me she had extended her trip. Which gave me time to handle dinner party arrangements here and put the final touches on her surprise.

I wasn't in any rush to leave my bed so I grabbed my phone from the nightstand and sunk deeper underneath the lightweight goose feather duvet, a housewarming gift from Yari.

"You can't be laying on pre-teen comforter sets in this damn house," she'd said.

I smirk at the memory. She always keeps me together. She balances me. Not having any contact with her for the past three weeks left me feeling empty. With every waking hour it just seems like I'm forgetting something. My mind runs rampant, wondering if she feels the emptiness from my absence too. I slowly drift back to sleep.

I must have laid in bed for at least two more hours because when I wake up again, it's early afternoon.

Opening my phone and toggling over to my RSVP list. I had eight confirmed guests from the eleven invites I'd sent. Nevaeh, Imani, Cam, Both of Q's parents, one of her sisters, Stephanie, and her twin brother, Quincy. X hadn't even opened his invite, and Yari was listed as a maybe. I had even offered her a plus one and she still wasn't biting. I know I'd fucked up, but I never expected her to cut me off to this extent. A message notification from X dinged from my phone as soon as I was about to toss it across the bed. He bet not be on no bullshit.

X [12:15 PM]: Yo, Yo!!!

Jarell [12:16 PM]: What's up fool?

X [12:18 PM]: Get yo ass over to the gym, we bout to shoot around for a bit before class...

Jarell [12:21 PM]: Who the fuck you talking to? And why the fuck you ain't RSVP for tonight?

X [12:26 PM]:I did when I told yo ass I would be there the other night

Jarell [12:28 PM]: Open yo damn email
and accept the damn invite

X [12:30 PM]: Yeah, whatever. I'm doing it
now....You coming through or what?

Jarell [12:31 PM]: Yeah give me like
thirty

X [12:31 PM]: I'ma give yo ass fifteen,
don't prolong the ass whooping my guy

Jarel [12:33 PM]: Man, whatever I'll be
there

X [12:33 PM]: Alright, bet!

I take a quick shower, throwing on some sweats and a white T-shirt. Trying my best to keep my head as clear as possible. After noticing that Yari hadn't confirmed her attendance to the dinner, I'd run through a million and one scenarios over and over in my mind. I need her there.

I head out the door to meet up with the fellas. Knowing those clowns will keep me levelheaded until I'm getting ready for tonight.

When I arrive at FLEXD, it's pretty packed out. I pull into my spot up front but notice a car parked deeper into the parking deck I hadn't expected to see. Yari's cream-colored G-Wagon with gold accents stuck out like a bruised pinky.

I jog inside to see if I can find her. As the doors close behind me, my eyes scan the front lobby. No sight of her. My head hangs low between my shoulders as disappointment begins to creep up on me. Just as I walk through the main training area of the gym, I hear her laugh. It comes from one of the yoga studio suites near the private club member entrance.

My head swivels in the direction of her laughter. I can tell she isn't alone, because of how hard she's laughing. The secondary laugh flows from the hallway. Suddenly, Imani waltzes through the doors with her back to me, still talking to Yari. They share conversation and laughter until Yari's eyes land on me. Her smile freezes and her face stiffens.

"Girl, what you looking at?" Imani questions, as she turns to see me standing, watching, waiting, hoping for a chance to try and fix everything.

I want to apologize; I want to beg for her forgiveness. What I'd done was fucked up. I had crossed a line that led to the end of the beautiful friendship we'd held onto for so many years. I was careless with her, I hadn't realized how much she meant to me until she'd been gone. I'd taken our connection for granted because I hadn't worked to earn it. Look at where that got me.

Dropping my gym bag to the floor, I plead, "Yari? Can we talk? Please?" taking a step towards her.

She looks away from me, shaking her head. "Naw; I have things to do," she states very matter-of-factly, about to follow Imani to the exit.

Without thinking I blurt, "Yari, I'm sorry! I mean, I apologize. I know you don't like the word sorry. I just want you there. No, I need you there. I love you, Yari. Please!"

She turns towards me, squinting her eyes, tear ducts filled with her salty Atlantic waters. I could see her heart shattering. I could hear her hurt plain in her voice.

"I have to go. Good luck, Jarell," she replies as she swings her yoga bag over her shoulder to head out the door.

That's when I spot a ring on her finger. "Yari….YARI!" I call after her as she hurries to catch up with Imani. I run after her, only to see her pulling out of her parking spot and speeding out of the garage. Just then my phone rings.

"WHAT!" I answer loudly, panting.

"AYE YO, WHAT THE HELL WRONG WITH YOU?!" X barks back at me.

"My bad, man. I'm here, but I gotta go handle some shit."

"Yeah you go do that cause I don't know who the fuck you talking to like that my guy."

"I gotta catch ya'll later man."

"Alright, Bet!"

I run back inside to grab my gym bag, then jump in my ride.

Did she get engaged? Or was that ring a symbol of another broken promise? Had our lives really changed that much in three weeks? Did I just confess to loving her? I would never have admitted that outright, or out loud for that matter.

I had to regain some level of self-control. I needed to know what was going on with her. Her eyes looked like she was going through some type of internal battle with herself. I've seen that look from her before.

I sped down Halsted Street, my heart racing. I was panicking. So many questions ran through my mind as I arrived at the industrial buildings that cornered South Halsted and Main.

Using the spare key fob in my glove box, I whipped into the private side of the parking deck to Yari's building. Shortly after I'd found my way up to the top floor. I pondered if I should knock but instincts took over and I inserted my key letting myself in instead.

The scent of eucalyptus, pomegranate, and French berries filled the air of her loft. Steam danced along the hardwood as the sound of a shower running met my ears. I stay near the front door, waiting.

As I stood there, my heart started to soften, my eyes getting heavy with regret. Regret for allowing this to transpire.

Suddenly the stroking thumps of water subside, and my heart begins racing again. The door to her bedroom opens and she steps out into the living room with her body wrapped in a towel.

"Yari, please talk to me," I beg, approaching her slowly.

She turns and I notice the tears rolling down her cheeks, the tremble in her voice as she asks, "Jarell, why are you here?"

I step closer, attempting to wipe her tears from her face but she leans away.

"Baby girl, I don't know how to fix this. How to fix us. You mean so much to me. You're not okay, I can see it in your eyes. What is this?" I question grabbing her hand and staring into her eyes to make sure her answer is legit.

"It's none of *your* business! What are you doing here? You wanna apologize now? You should've been here apologizing a long time ago. The locks haven't changed, Jarell. No, you know what? That shit should've never have happened. You should've never spoken to me like that. But you wanna talk now, so let's talk. Let's talk about how I have always been by your side. I've always made sure you were good, Jay. I was so caught up making sure you were good, I didn't leave time for myself." She stops abruptly, her tears continuing to fall. My heart has jumped out of my chest and draped itself across my shoulders, and all I can do is watch as she wears a hole in her hardwood.

She was absolutely right.

"Yari, I've been miserable these past three weeks. I fucked up. I took you for granted. I didn't realize until you drew lines with me that the love I was expecting to feel in my relationship, I was already getting from you. I want our friendship. I want to show you that I value you. I never meant to hurt you, or disrespect you. Yari, please."

She wipes tears from her eyes and walks to the front door. "Jarell, my heart broke once I came to the realization that I was just the safe space for you to dump your garbage without being charged. I can't always be everything for everybody. I have to do what's best for me," she says, finally turning to me.

"So, that's what's best for you?" I point to her hand. "Yari, do you even believe that yourself? Two months ago he was cancelling on you and not showing up for dinner dates. Not to mention the 'slut candy' you smelled on his couch pillows. You're really going to marry this clown? You deserve better than him baby girl, come on now," I plead, watching her look down at her hands.

I step a bit closer. Now standing directly in front of her. Using my hand to gently lift her head waiting for her eyes to meet mine, I continue, "This is not what you truly want, we both know it. If you want me out of your life, fine. But I can't promise that I'm going to leave without first making sure you don't make stupid decisions. Why would you want this with him? He hasn't shown you anything that deserves you saying yes to this."

I go to grab her hand once more, but this time she snatches it from me. Her eyes now squinted, and her jaw clenched.

"I don't need no fucking speech right now, Jarell. I have no appetite for your food for thought. If you want to apologize, that's cool, apology accepted. But if you wanna play real friend, chop it up, and keep me around just so I can continue be your safe space, you're wasting your time."

She walks over to the kitchen island, retrieving two hundred-dollar bills from her wallet. "Here, send me the invoice for any other billable hours I've accrued throughout our friendship. Just make sure you subtract your garbage dumping fees." She spits, throwing the money at me, and grabbing the door to open it.

"Yari, I deserve that. I do, but please listen, I just want you to do what makes the most sense for you. I truly am apologetic for disrespecting you. You don't have to come to the dinner tonight if you were still considering it. I won't take up anymore of your space."

Reaching into my pocket to remove my spare key and fob, I place them and the money she'd thrown at me moments earlier on the sideboard near her front door.

Turning to her, "If you need me, I'll be around. I'm always here for you baby girl," I kiss her cheek and walk out.

I hear the door slam behind finalizing what I already knew.

I'd just lost my heart, my Yari.

The RSVP

Yari

The slam of the door doesn't bury Jarell's truth…it amplifies it. And the feeling that lingers with me afterwards cuts deeper than his absence.

I had allowed myself to be wooed by things that just didn't match up. I'm not crazy and I know Jarell has my best interest at heart. I had spent many days crying over André's shortcomings, but I want to give us a chance to be better. Maybe getting engaged isn't the way to do that but I definitely appreciated the gesture. André's finally taking steps in the right direction. Why would I shut down his grand gestures?

I wipe the last tear from my cheek when my phone's notification draws my attention over to the coffee table.

Arias had sent me a message asking if I want her to oversee Cream while Jarell's dinner party took place upstairs. She said I was on the guest list, and she wants to get ahead of any planning that needed to happen for the evening. I don't blame her. After months of meetings and negotiations, Cream was chosen as the venue for The Ballers Bachelors Ball. It's tonight, at the same time as Jarell's party. The Roseville Lions had won the Southeastern Conference and were heading to the Rose Bowl. The Rose Bowl is the Southeast's version of the Super Bowl. It's a sports tradition with all the minor teams in the Southeast. This bag could not be fumbled, all puns intended. There will be players not only hailing from the Roseville Lions but surrounding cities as well. I need tonight to go flawlessly.

I shot Arias a text informing her that my attendance at Jarell's party was still up in the air and I would let her know within the hour. I want to take him up on the offer to have a plus one. It's the only way I would dare step foot into an anniversary dinner party for a relationship that's more on the rocks than mine. I don't understand the reason for the dinner anyway. Maybe the two of them had patched things up while I was gone on my little baecation? Or maybe he finally spoken to her?

He seemed like he had come to a resolution of some sort in the past three weeks. I'm not going to pry at his mindset or his reasoning for why this dinner is so damn important. But I had known Jarell for what seem liked forever now and I know he didn't just let that shit go.

I pace back and forth from the kitchen to the living room, wondering if I should go to that damn dinner. I pick up my phone and decide to call André so I could put a cap on whether or not I would be going. He answers on the third ring, sounding out of breath.

"Ummm did I get you at a bad time?" His voice muffled by the noisy background.

"Naw... I'm just..." Movement muffled his phones mic causing a short pause of silence before his voice came back "I'm just wrapping up my workout...what's up? You good?"

Him knowing something might be wrong caused me to

blush and I giggled a little. "Yeah, everything's fine. Are you busy tonight? I was invited to this dinner party at Cream, and I need my plus one."

I hear his breathing come back to normal and his voice become clearer through the phone.

"I'll be your plus one anytime girl, you know that. What should I wear?"

I'm happy to know he'd be on my arm. I just want to show that my decisions to say yes, was a step into the right direction. Even if there's nothing to prove to Jarell, I still want to make sure he sees that I can make decisions with my head and not always my heart. "Just know I'm wearing a black dress. Match me, that'll be cute."

He chuckles "I can do that. What time should I pick you up?"

I look at the digital clock on the stove. It was 3:52. The dinner was due to start at 8:00. "8:00, I don't want to arrive early."

"A late arrival, fashionable or purposeful?"

"Both, I'll be ready by then; that's cool?"

"You got it, future Mrs."

My face is aching by how much he has me blushing. I hang up the phone and waltz over to my bar to fix me a Neon Bourbon Cosmopolitan. "Alexa play my Brown Bag Whiskey playlist." She obliges.

I allow my head to fall back, as the horns blare through the speakers around the loft. Allowing my mind to settle on the night ahead and the image I want to project at this party. I dance across the floor into my bedroom to search for the perfect dress for the occasion. I settle on one of the designer dresses I bought from a small boutique while in Mulancia. An off the shoulder, body contouring, black, velvet dress. It's very classic, knee length, with a hidden kick slit, and buttons down the entire back. I decide to pair it with my Kate Max Christian Louboutin's to add to the classic look.

I shuffle around in my closet for something to lounge in.
I take tiny sips of my drink as I grab a pair of chocolate brown
biker shorts and a crisp white baby tee. I prance around my loft,
swinging my hips and enjoying the vibes.

Jarell

I arrive back at my crib, filled with frustration. I had gotten
confirmation that Q's parents were settled into their hotel, and
she would be getting ready soon for our dinner. I toss my keys
across the kitchen counter and poured myself a double shot
before retreating to my bedroom. My phone rings, catching me
completely off guard and pulling me get out my thoughts long
enough to reach down into my pockets and answer.

"Yo!" I answer the call I realize is from Cameron.

"Yo, she responded." His words sat there, because I couldn't
draw a connection solid enough to know what he's speaking on.

"Who responded? I need you to speak in complete sentences
man. I'm all over the place." I admit to him.

He responds with a chuckle. "Naw, man I'm talking 'bout yo
girl Yari. She responded! It looks like she responded to the invite."

I slide the call onto speaker and my fingers busied themselves
to pull up the invitation RSVP bulletin. "Oh shit man, she's
coming." I confirm letting out an open-mouthed sigh. I didn't think
she would even care to show after out little exchange earlier.

A FaceTime request from Cam's simple ass comes through
my line. I open the camera. "What fool?!"

"Damn yo! The way you sighed just now and went silent I
had to make sure you was alright... I mean if she wouldn't have
come, you think you would make it?" He teases.

"Chill man, I ain't fooling up wit yo stupid ass right now.
You figured out what you wearing?"

"Yeah, I mean probably. You know I've been kicking it with Nevaeh low key since Open Mic Night a few weeks ago."

"What? Hell naw I ain't know that. When did you tell me that? You ain't told me fool. That's what's up. How's it going?"

"Man, look she on her grown woman shit and I love that shit man. We coming together tonight, so I'm wearing navy blue and blush pink." He chuckles.

"Oh word! Cam that's what's up man. Hopefully she turn your ass into an honest man."

He stops mid fold of the blunt he was rolling. "Man chill, I been an honest man. Talk to that clown X about honesty."

"Speaking of his ass I'm bout to add him….hold on" I toggle on my screen to add Xavier to the call.

"Yo, Yo what up?" X answers the FaceTime blowing smoke into the camera.

"Wow, the disrespect," I call out while taking a sip from the bourbon that sat warm in my glass on the nightstand.

"You see this mother fucker?" Cam asks, finally firing up his blunt.

"I'm just trying to get my head together for this fucking dinner. I got two sets of guys securing Cream tonight. One inside and one outside. I need my nerves calm in case things get out of pocket." X admits as he put the remaining part of his blunt out.

"You got mad pressure on you tonight man."

He nods, "Hell yeah the Rose Bowl brings out the Southeast's biggest ballers, hoochies, and gangstas. We gotta be up on security this weekend for sure. Cream bout to be on the map for sure after the Bachelors Ball. Yari knows it too. When we spoke about her plans for expanding and the things she wants to do with technology and Cream as a whole, she bout to do the damn thing. I'm excited to watch this shit blow up for her. She works hard as hell. I'm just happy to be apart of it all." He says while rubbing his hands together as if he just got word of a major lick.

"I'm happy for the both of you." I say, hoping to change the subject from Yari but the attempt wasn't as successful as I'd hoped.

"Come to think of it, why you having your dinner on the same night as the ball? She won't be able to enjoy all the flowers tonight would bring her." Cam asks, plugging up his iron.

"I booked it tonight almost a month ago. She said it was cool, I don't think she was expecting to be selected as the venue. And when I offered to change locations, she said that would be ridiculous." I explain.

X nods "I definitely agree; this way she can be in house for the ball and still at the dinner. I mean the private event quarters overlooks the entire lounge. So shit, honestly it works out even though they are on the same day."

"You got a point" Cam says.

We spend about another thirty minutes on the phone – just shooting the shit, chopping it up and cracking jokes. Once we ended our call, I glance down at my Tissot, only to notice it was nearing 6:40. I roam into my master bath so I can start getting ready.

Yari

After stepping out of the steamy shower, I allow my body to air dry for a little as I sat at my vanity, ready to start my makeup. It was 7:00. I had about 45 minutes before I knew Andre would be heading upstairs to sweep me off my feet and into his arms for this anniversary dinner. My skin was flawless. I had been keeping my cortisol levels low and drinking plenty of water. This was the first time I would be wearing make up in months. I want to be as feminine as possible tonight. Before starting, I wrap my towel around me, mist my face, neck, and chest with rose water and lit my Magnolia Hills French Kiss candle. "Alexa, play my 90's Fine playlist!"

The thing about me is I sometimes, most times, need to set the ambiance for me to stay motivated to leave the house. I don't know if it's tied to my nerves or if I'm just trying to match the vibe I'm on tonight. Grabbing my flat Kabuki foundation brush, I step straight into my 90's Fine. Contouring, blending, and dusting my face calms my nerves with every stroke of my brush – helping me settle down for the night.

My finished look is a natural beat and a sultry ombré red matte lip that match the bottom of the shoes I had selected earlier.

I walk over to the clothing rack next to the full body, glassless mirror in the corner of my bedroom. Dropping my towel to my feet, I stand there, giving myself time to admire the body I had been so dismissive of. She really is beautiful. My eyes trace the curves of my body as I hook my lace strapless bra and slide on my high waisted panties. I proceed to roll on my sheer pantyhose before stepping into my dress and slipping my shoes on. Rubbing my collarbones with the perfume that sat on the corner of my vanity. I begin to dance along to the playlist while the notes of sheer musk, vanilla, davana, orchids, and hints of cherries melted into my skin. Tilting my head forward, I gather my fresh blow out into a fancy messy bun leaving some of my hair loose so I can curl it. I bop my head and rock my hips along to Sybil's "Don't Make Me Over" as I put the final touches on my look, when the doorbell rang. I give myself one final look over before heading to the front door to greet my man.

André stands there, his eyes slightly hazy and peering through my soul. He carries a small arrangement of wildflowers. The thick scent of cognac and sandalwood blows kisses at my nostrils, sending alerts to my feminine parts of the precautions that need to be taken. I give my eyes permission to take in the sight of him. This is mine. He's dressed in a black on charcoal grey pinstripe suit with a black button down. He had left the top three buttons undone to show off his jewelry.

"My oh my! Damn girl you look like fine fucking art on a custom canvas," he compliments.

My cheeks flush as he grabs my waist, pulling me close enough to slip his tongue down my throat. He frees his other hand, dropping those wildflowers to the floor so he could grip my round ass.

"Andre' we have to go." I moan through our dancing tongues trying to wiggle away from his grip.

"I want you now!" He admits. I want so bad to give in, but I know if I allow us to take it there I wouldn't be going anywhere.

"Dré please! I want you too baby, but I know we won't be leaving if we get started right now." I confess, finally slipping from his grip.

"Baby come on, look at him, you want me to go to dinner with your people like this?" My eyes fall to the bulky bulge he was showcasing.

Biting my lips. "Huhmm…no I can't let you go like that."

He grabs himself like it was paining him.

"I'll take care of him, then we can go." I don't wanna deny him and I would get the pleasure of control and release while he would get the pleasure of release and ecstasy. It's really a win-win. Besides, control tastes better than confusion anyway.

He walks in and kicks the door close behind him. I grab his hand and lead him over to the kitchen island.

"Stand right here… and don't move." I command while pointing to the spot I want him in. I take a quick second to unfasten him, then tug at his pant legs. He caresses my cheek as I curtsey never allowing my eyes to leave his. "Keep your eyes on me," I whisper, before kissing him, leaving traces of my lipstick on his thigh. Maybe if I give him more of this version of me, the one he seems to want at this very moment, I won't have to feel like I'm slipping.

I part my lips, and allow my tongue to cradle his arrival. With anticipation trembling through me as I look up at him. Giving him the perfect place to land, I can hear his breath stutter, and the room narrows to the space between us. The rise and fall, the wanting. I move closer, taking all of him in slow, steady rhythm, guided by instinct more than thought. Our eyes lock, neither of us daring to look away. The sound of his breath, the taste of his skin, the weight of his need, it's all I can feel, all I can answer. I feel André's right hand cradle the back of my head. I use the gesture as a gentle invitation to let him take some of his control back. Using my shin, I release my left stiletto then reach for my right one with my hand as I ease myself into a kneel; allowing my head to fall back into the cradle of his palm.

"Ugh…you feel incredible," he breathes, voice rough with hunger. His words send a tremor through me, making me ache for more. The soft sounds escaping my throat only urge him on, his touch deepening and my body drips while finding a southern heartbeat. And I honestly don't mind. I'm busy devouring him as if he was food, damn near eating him at this point. I'm not just turned on, I'm determined. I slip a hand beneath the silk, chasing the pulse that's already racing as I watch Dré's body tense up from my slurps. His left hand grabs my right boob and he began fondling my nipple. Matching his rhythm, I tickle and caress his body, regaining only a slither of my control. It's all I need to help him release. It works. Shortly after he announces his final landing, he leaves the traces of his journey across my boobs. I notice him carefully aiming it away from my face and dress. "That's very mindful of you." I say, taking the hand he offers to help me stand.

"I don't want us to be too late. That would be way too much cleanup." He has a point, it's was already fifteen past eight. After I freshen up, we wouldn't get to the dinner until after 8:40.

"You got a point, take a towel from the guest bathroom so you can wipe off and freshen up. I need to reorganize what we disturbed and almost destroyed." André smiles and heads toward the guest bathroom. I turn back toward the mirror, touch up my lips, and smooth the hem of my dress.

The dress is on, so is the mask.

Dinner Is Served

Jarell

I pull up to Cream about twenty minutes shy of eight. I spot Tony standing guard at the front door.

"Aye Tony, what's up man?" I greet him dapping him up.

"Yo, Yo! What up Jarell! You good fam?…You got your dinner party tonight, right?" He asks while unlatching the velvet rope that separated the lines from the door.

I nod and step forward. "Yeah, got a little surprise for my lady. She will be arriving shortly with her family." I say, going over tonight's plans.

"Cool, cool I got you! Poochi is already upstairs setting you up. Enjoy your evening and the celebration. After 15 years of marriage, I can tell you youngblood, anniversaries are important. Make them memorable."

A forced smile spreads across my face. "Oh, tonight will definitely be memorable." He nods dapping me up once more before I retreat inside.

The servers are moving around the lounge getting last minute things in order for the Baller Bachelors Ball. Yari had the place decorated to perfection. It had her touch in every detail. From the drapes along the windows to the centerpieces that sit on every table. I'm so proud of her and everything she's done. I only wish we weren't in such a weird space so we could celebrate this moment. My hope is that she'll be willing to have a different conversation with me by the end of the night. I just want her forgiveness and to get back to where our friendship was.

I finish looking around the room and head towards the elevator. I step left then right to move around the Satin Dolls that are lining the hall. I wasn't expecting that. Their whispers and small chatter cause me to shake my head as I walk straight into Arias.

"What you smiling for? Boy, ain't nobody checking for you."

My eyebrows raise immediately as I press the button for the elevator. "Is that right? I can't tell," I state, looking down at her hard nipples. The door of the elevator opens and I step in.

"Boy, please! I just came from outside, it's cold."

I chuckle, "Yeah, sure," I call out as the doors close.

As the elevator arrives, I smell Poochi's food before the doors even open. My stomach grumbles in anticipation for any and everything on the menu. I walk past the glass wall that leads into the room. She decorated the place beautifully. Blush pink satin drapes along the back wall with hints of gold. It picks up the shimmer from the new golden crystal chandelier Yari has in the center of the room. A twenty-foot-long dining table, dressed in a blush pink table cover with custom gold runner and an extraordinary centerpiece on the table. There are flowers and candles everywhere. I asked Poochi to cover the floor in petals, and that's just what she did.

Poochi is in the front corner of the room hanging small polaroids of us from strings she had hidden throughout the room.

She spots me and begins climbing down from the ladder she was on.

"Jarell, you're here.." She says, slightly out of breath. "What do you think?" She asks, presenting the room to me with her hands held up like Vanna White.

All I could do is laugh. "Yeah, Poochi, you did your fucking thing. I appreciate you for putting all this together with such short notice." I lean in to give her a hug.

"No problem, Jarell. I've known you forever now, your family. Let me show you the food selection."

She grabs my hand and walks me over to the table in the back of the room. One by one she flips the golden domes to reveal the menu of the night.

"I have a private bartender here KaTrina. She gon' hold you down, make sure the champagne is flowing. She will also be able to do some custom cocktails by request as well."

I smile at KaTrina. She's the same bartender from Suede. She blushes and turns to prep her ice buckets. "Everything looks amazing. Thank you again Poochi."

She smiles, pinching her face together and holding her hands to her heart in joy of my approval.

"You're welcome. There will be three servers assisting me tonight…We won't start serving until everyone is seated but no worries, the food will remain fresh and hot." I nod in agreement.

"I'm going to go freshen up and get dressed I will see you shortly. I have a host that will walk your guests from the elevator to their assigned seats."

"Ok, I guess that's what these are for," I state, grabbing the small place cards from the table.

"Yes, I positioned everyone based on your instructions, so everything should be the way you want. If you wanna change anyone's place, feel free, and I can let my hostess know."

With a smile and nod I assure her that everything is perfect.

"Perfect, go ahead and get freshened up Poochi. I'll take it from here." With that she turns and scurries out of the room.

"It's time!" I voice, noticing the flash of an alarm on my phone flickering to alert me of the time. Just then a text came through from Q.

Q [8:15 PM]: Baby, the driver said we're
fifteen minutes away.

I send her a thumbs up in response when I hear the elevator ding. The hostess floats past the glass wall, escorting Cameron and Nevaeh into the room. "I knew y'all would be first," I say, greeting Cam with a dap and Nevaeh with a hug.

"You know me man, time is money," Cam says, taking a step back and sizing me up.

"Ok, ok you clean up nice for a little gym rat."

"WOW! Gym rat? You on bullshit tonight, ok, ok remember that," Nevaeh giggles and I quickly look in her direction. "It's like that Veah? You get with this clown and now everything funny huh? Big ass head."

She places her hands on her hips. "Don't go there Jarell, you know your fucking noggin is in Guinness Records dude don't even play."

"Ok. Vaeh I see you picked your side...that's cool. Naw, but seriously I appreciate you guys for coming. Y'all can take your seats, Ms. KaTrina will be over shortly for your drink order." I turn to give the nod of approval to Trina so she knew she could approach.

"Wait ain't that ole girl from?..."

"Yep, that's her." I watch Nevaeh's eyes scan KaTrina as she walks over to greet them.

"From where?" She questions.

"She was a bartender for us at Suede. Nothing special just a familiar face."

Her eyes roll, "Yeah, ok."

"Nevaeh it's nothing like that."

"I'm not sweating it. I know it could never be anything but nothing. Cameron knows not to play with me like that."

Cameron reaches over and grabs her face, "You damn right. I'm all yours, baby." He proceeds to tongue kiss her right in front of me and now KaTrina, who just made it over to us.

"Eww, y'all get a room."

"We would have had one man, but we RSVP'd for this damn dinner." I couldn't do nothing but laugh.

As I walk away Xzavier walks into the room.

"Ayo, ya boy is here!" His hands spread wide like he just completed a victory lap.

"Yo, find you seat and sit in it." Cameron instructs him.

"You know he don't know how to act." Imani calls out, walking in behind him.

"You can't take his ass nowhere."

"Why everybody gotta get on my tip all the time? Damn, let me rest."

An uproar of laughter spreads throughout the room when the elevator dinged once more. My heart skips a beat, immediately knowing who must be next to enter the room.

Yari

I turn the water off and dry my hands, making sure not to forget to put my ring back on my finger. She's the main character I want center stage tonight. André and I were taking steps in the right direction. Our intimacy had catapulted to new levels. He's been staring at me as if he couldn't stop and doing things to my body that he never had throughout our entire relationship. I freshen up my lipstick and glance at the time, 8:10 PM, we need to head out. I walked back into the kitchen to find Dré awaiting my arrival.

He walks over to me and smiles. "Hey, you...Are you ready?" He asks, kissing my cheek.

"Yes, I'm ready. Let's actually make it out the door this time."

He laughed, "Sure, we can do that," he says, grabbing my hand and leading me out the door.

We get to Cream twenty minutes later, after getting stopped at every light on the way there. I'm anxious to say the least. I stare out the window as we get closer to the building, eyes scanning the line that was trailing from the front door. I'm damn proud of the things I'm accomplishing. This line is proof that I know what I'm doing and that I am making sound and solid decisions. I look at Dré as he drives us around so he can park. The night sky twinkling off his diamonds.

"Thank you for accompanying me tonight." I say, placing my hand upon his as he opened my door to help me out of the car.

"The pleasure is all mine baby. Glad you asked." He flashes me a smile, locking the car and escorting me to the entrance of Cream.

"Hey Tony." I greet him as he opens the ropes to let us in.

"Hey there, Yari, I think everyone's waiting on you." He reaches to give me a hug while nodding at Dré.

"Ok, thank you. Tell Rachael I said call me so we can link up for drinks soon." He gives me a thumbs up as the door closes behind us.

"You ready?" I ask Dré. Before he can answer me, his phone rings.

"Dré! You know you gone have to silence that thing during dinner."

He nods, "Yes, baby I know but I need to take this, I'll be right up. Go ahead without me."

My face scrunches, but before I can give any rebuttal Dré answers his phone and walks over to the bar in the main lounge. I can admit I'm annoyed but I'm running to late to hash things out now. I hurry down the hallway towards the private elevator.

Jarell

With my head dropped in-between my shoulders and my eyes squeezed closed, I wait with anticipation. I can hear the heels clicking towards me paired with the buzz of her excitement. I stand, slowly licking my lips and swallowing every word I want to utter.

Q appears dressed in the gold and glittery spaghetti-strap trumpet style gown and fur shrug I had one of the boutique's stylists pick out for her. Her hair is straightened and appears to have fresh highlights. I hadn't laid eyes on her since I left for my business trip. I feel my eyes watering and my throat stiffen as my blood threatens to boil. She was my everything. I was working so hard to give her the life I thought she deserved. I spent countless hours praying for the chance to break the curses I lived through. I hoped to break those curses with her. She was always so genuine and kind. Her heart big enough to love the world. I never saw her in the same light as her family.

They follow her in like her retinue. Her father, Pastor Eugene Landsin Esquire, bold and proud in all his judgement of all things 'ungodly.' More of a puppet master than a Priest. Her mother, First Lady Gwendolyn Landsin, the bougie puppeteer. Telling me I need to make sure her daughter never wants for a thing. I smirk at the thought of all she had lost in the process of her greed. That need to have her cake and eat it too caused her to outgrow her seat in first class. Her sister, Stephanie, I should have fucked her when she came to town for Homecoming and was drunk and horny. Up in CAKES, feening for me to take her down, asking if I wanted to get a private room and everything. Talking bout, "My sister don't deserve you, you need a woman like me". I never spoke on the situation and chalked it up as her being drunk and talking out her head. Her brother, Quincy, a fake-ass secret dough boy. Only pushing weed and barely got the clientele to really consider himself a weed man. Supply super mid and his gear is trash. Working at a car wash, talking bout, "he going back to school for business." Really wish he would get an identity and a real job.

A bunch of phonies and I should had taken all the red flag seriously, now look at me. A single tear rolled down my cheek. I quickly wiped it away and cleared my throat.

"Thank you guys for coming." I say as I shake the hand of her father.

"Absolutely, son. I figured it would be worth the trip," he replies, patting me on the shoulder.

"Jarell, baby its beautiful in here!" Q says, tip-toeing to reach me for a kiss. I throw my cheek down to meet her lips. I can feel her confusion as she plants a half-assed kiss on my cheek and quickly sits down in the seat I had pulled out for her.

"Stephanie, Quincy, First Lady Gwendolyn nice to see you all again. Please take your seats." I offer as KaTrina brings their champagne flutes over to the table.

"We have one more guest expected to arrive everyone, but in the meantime KaTrina has a round of lemon drops for the table," Poochi says as she steps inside the room.

"LEMON DROPS? What we gone do with Lemon drops. Hey Trina, baby can I have a shot of your best tequila? What's the best you got girl?" X asks, trying to flirt while looking serious.

KaTrina smiles, placing the last champagne flute down in front of Stephanie.

"I have a luxurious Komos Rosa…" She starts walking over to X's seat and squats down beside him.

"And what's that?" He chokes out, not expecting her to drop down so close to him.

I chuckle. "He's out of control."

"It's a beautiful blush tequila, inspired by Mediterranean wine making. Aged in old French wine barrels. It's soft and round with dark berries and cocoa. Would you like to taste it?" I can tell her response to his question had my boy X dissolving. I watch as his eyes met hers and the room becomes slightly warmer from the heat of their connection.

"Ahem" Pastor Eugene clears his throat. I chuckle glancing at Cameron as he holds in his laughter.

"Let's all be civil." His raspy voice breaks the ties that were sure to knot.

"Ugh, yeah, I'll try some thanks." X answers Katrina as she stands. He rocks in the seat to adjust his self and Cameron and I bust out in laughter.

It's almost 8:50 and there was no sign of Yari. I wasn't sure if she actually would show but I was about ready to have Poochi start the dinner service. While everyone continues chatting, I stand to excuse myself from the table so I can find Poochi.

"Hey Poochi, have you heard from Yari?" I ask, with hopes she had.

"No Jarell, I haven't…I could give her a call…" She starts but gets cut off by a familiar voice coming from behind us.

"No need, I'm here."

It's her. She's dressed in an off the shoulder velvet dress, she paired it with a fur shawl. It wraps her curves beautifully. Her hair is effortlessly flawless. She even wore make up. I feel like I couldn't catch my breath since she stepped into the room.

She steps towards Poochi and gives her a hug and a kiss on the cheek.

"Jarell," she says, looking me dead in my eyes. I watch as she walks around me to head into the room.

"What was that?" Poochi asks me.

"A deep misunderstanding. We can start the dinner service now Poochi." I respond, lips tight as I re-enter the room.

Yari

The elevator was stuck on the top floor. Looks like they've locked it from running. I looked down the hall to see if André was headed my way. Realizing he's MIA, I opt for the stairs instead. I figure it would give me time to cool down. I don't want him to slide back into old patterns. I would be sure to have that conversation at some other time. Tonight though, I just want to show that I made a decision I can stand behind. I know we have things to work on, but I don't feel like it was impossible to smooth things over.

I reach the top step slightly winded, making a mental note to get back to the gym so I can stay on track. I can hear music playing lightly in the background and a little talking and laughter. Grabbing the door handle, I slowly walk down the small hallway to finish gathering myself. I take a second to shoot André a text.

Yari [8:55 PM]: Take the stairs, elevator
locked!

The volume of the music gets slightly louder as I reach the doorway that leads to the top floor. I can hear Jarell and Poochi conversing. I quickly greet her, acknowledge him, and head towards the private room. Walking in gives me goosebumps. Poochi really did her thing. The room has transformed and been elevated to another level. Even though the occasion isn't anything special in my opinion, I know based on the ambience Q would feel the opposite.

I spot her first, she was glowing and smiling from ear to ear.

That smile quickly wiped away once she locks eyes with me as Imani makes my presence known.

She stood and pranced over to me grabbing my hand to show me off. "YES MA'AM!! Fashionably late and it was well worth the wait."

I'm now blushing from all the eyes on me. "Thank you, not too much!" I giggle, walking over to the table to find my name card. I'm seated next to Nevaeh towards the opposite side of the table from where Q is seated. Thank God, I think as my eyes can't stop themselves from rolling at the sight of her.

She glances down at her phone before standing to excuse herself from the table. Jarell walks back into the room after exchanging a few words with her as she heads toward the elevator.

"She's going to the ladies room." Jarell announces to the table as he sits.

"And why would we care?" I mumbled only to feel a nudge from Nevaeh as she used her hand to shield her whisper to me.

"Yari, play nice."

I smirk "I would if she was a better human." I respond under my breath while scrolling through my text messages. Dré had sent a screenshot of a quote from some deal he was working to close, with the caption 'One step closer.' He's in the middle of negotiating a partnership with an investment brokerage. If the deal landed by Spring, we would apparently be the youngest and richest newlyweds in the city. I feel proud of him. The hard work he had been putting in was starting to pay off. Although I don't need his financial support, if felt good to know he would be able to support our new life together without any support from his daddy.

"You have any requests?" I hear faintly from the bartender, bringing me back into the room. I watch as she places the prettiest old fashioned down in front me. It was smoked with a perfectly curled blood orange peel and a single Luxardo Maraschino Cherry. The aroma of the bourbon lifts to my nostrils, giving me goosebumps again and I feel my mouth begin to water.

My eyes peer over at Jarell as he raises his glass in my direction and nods before taking a sip of his own old fashioned. I shyly smile lifting the smoky lowball and sipping my drink.

"I'm glad to see everyone is here." Poochi says, winking at me and signaling for her servers. "I know the guest of honor stepped away but we are going to start serving."

The sounds of plates clinking in the background as they begin placing our meals and making their rotation around to everyone. Jarell really pulled out all the stops. Maybe he had done some soul-searching and maturing in the last few weeks. I watch as he converses with Xavier, who's seated next to Jarell.

"Excuse me" I hear from behind me as Q shuffles back into the room. She seemed antsy and rushed. The girl was always all over the place. What did Jarell see in this charity case? I love a good project from time to time but something about her just never sat right with me. My level of irritation slowly rises and I wish the night would hurry up and end already.

Jarell

Everyone waits patiently as Poochi and her crew finish serving our plates. Bits of laughter and conversation sprinkled throughout the room. I watch as Poochi speaks to Yari before placing an extra plate down in front of the empty seat next to her.

"Attention everyone. Pastor Landsin? Would you mind doing the honor of gracing this meal?" I asked him.

"Why sure son." His raspy baritone echoes as the room grows quiet. It always amazed me how quickly black folks got quiet when it was time to pray.

"All heads bowed, all eyes closed." He starts and I hear shuffles from Yari's end of the table. I peek my left eye open as some dude hurries in and sits quickly, kissing her cheek and preparing for grace. I close my eyes to center myself. That's him. So, she took me up on that plus one after all. I thought she wouldn't, but here he is. The lame that now wants to marry her and build a life with her. I'm surprised he even had time to show. I didn't expect to ever see him show up for her.

"Amen" I hear, echoed throughout the room.

"Amen." I say, rising my head to get a better look at this clown.

"Yo, who is this cat?" X asked getting my attention.

"That Yari's fiancé."

"Fiancé?"

"Since when?"

"Man, I don't know. But she's 'in love' from what I know."

"Yeah, sure." He shakes his head. His disapproval said a lot. X was the President of the Fuck Boy Committee. If anybody knows a fuck boy, it's him.

The evening creeps along, everyone chatting and enjoying their meals. I watch Q smiling, blushing, and giggling as she chats with her sister.

"Excuse me everyone." I call across the table, clinking my champagne flute. "I would like to propose a toast." Everyone's eyes slowly turn in my direction as they gather their glasses.

"Qiana Gwendolyn Landsin, the woman I have grown to love over the past two years. You are very special indeed. I spent a lot of time planning every part of this moment. The mini vacation I sent you on to Raynol's Island was preperation for tonight. I wanted it to be perfect for you. It was always meant to lead up to this very moment. Us all here at this celebration tonight. An amazing friend of mine told me I needed to get my shit together and figure out what I wanted and what I wanted to do. I believe I've done just that tonight. If you all would join me." I invite raising my glass and reaching down to grab Q's chin. "To you, Qiana."

I pull out a remote from my jacket pocket that controlled the projector functions in the room. Clicking the down arrow. I watch as the screen floated down from the ceiling into the room and pressed play.

Yari

Proud was an understatement for what I was of Jarell. I don't agree with him going out of his way, but he seems to have come to terms with everything. I watch as the projector comes down and the lights dim even lower than before. The soft music playing in the background changes to audio of the video.

Digital polaroids of different photos of them were falling onto the backdrop of the video. Each picture zooming into a memory of the two of them enjoying life together. A photo of Jarell's 2nd Annual Health & Wellness Cookout popped onto the screen. It was when they first met. A cute little snapshot of them taking wheatgrass shots flashed across the screen. The pictures and moments keep rolling. A clip of Jarell and Q from our ski trip last winter and then photos from the same trip. They were bundled up on a bench across from the slopes with hot chocolate smiling from ear to ear, Jarell's eyes glued to the camera.

I remember when we all took that trip, I was the one who took the picture. Cameron was standing near the slopes sign and Xavier had fallen on the ground with one of his skis flying up in the air. I was trying to capture the moment, and there they were in the background laughing. Imani and Nevaeh had to be somewhere nearby.

The next clip caught me completely off guard. Jarell was strolling through a jewelry store and talking with a jeweler. There on the screen was a sketch of a beautiful diamond ring. He inserted clips of him and the jeweler talking design details. The process of the diamond sourcing and the stages of making the ring.

Everyone at the table slowly went back to sipping their drinks and nibbling on their food. Q's mom and sister awed at every photo. It was becoming almost too much. I took a sip of water and went back to my food.

"Baby I'm going to run to the restroom. I'll be right back." André says, kissing my cheek and getting up to leave the table. I watch as he leaves the room.

"Girl, I can feel the steam coming from your panties. Calm down." Nevaeh whispers in my ear.

"Girl…." I laugh, crossing my legs. "It's almost time to go."

"This is cute though, you think this is what I think it is?" She asks me, nodding towards the projector.

"Yeah, I think we are smack dab in the middle of a proposal."

"I love proposals." She admits, slightly pouting.

"Oh, don't worry, I see how boo'd up you and Cameron are. I give it less than a year." I say, making her blush.

Suddenly I think I hear a faint moan. Confusion wipes across Imani and Nevaeh's faces as I scan the table, realizing it was short-lived and everyone was still chatting. Q's eyes catch mine, and she gives me a fake close-lipped smile, causing me to squint then sigh before going back to my conversation. Imani had convinced Cameron to switch seats with her for a little. She missed us.

"Girl you see how packed it is out there?" Imani asks as the three of us look down. The soundproof glass kept the vibes of downstairs away, but the view of the festivities was unobstructed.

"Yes, I'm really excited about what this will do for business."

Another moan echoed through the room. My head snaps up. "What the hell? Ya'll heard that?" I asked my girls.

"I thought I was tripping." Imani says, motioning the bartender to run us another round.

Moments later our drinks arrive. More moans. I look over at Jarell and he's deep in a conversation with X while holding Q's hand. She's in awe watching the video that's still playing. Her mom and sister behind her with the same looks on their faces. Her dad and brother eating a second serving of Poochi's Cajun sausage fagioli soup. It was paired with her Caribbean stew chicken, seasoned to perfection. If I wasn't dressed so sexy tonight I would be knuckles deep in another serving. Then more moans, this time louder.

"What was that?" I hear Q's mom ask. I assume this is her first time hearing it.

"Gwendolyn, you need to put the wine down, that's enough." Q's dad says, slurping on his soup and smacking his lips.

"Eugene I'm not drunk, I heard something just now."

"You heard your mouth yapping with all that awing. You over doing it Gwendolyn."

Fanning her face with her hands, she rolls her eyes and takes another sip of her red wine. "I know what I heard." She says.

I know she isn't crazy because we heard it too.

Jarell

I was talking to X when the sounds from the video started to prick my ears. It was almost time for my surprise. Q's hand was warm and clutched in my palm as the last memory started on the screen. A clip of our vacation this past spring arrived on the projector. I turn my head to watch as we splash around on the beach in the Thailand heat. Then static interrupts the scene, showcasing distorted flashes of the scenes from the night she broke our commitment.

Back and forth I watch as the projector toggles from glimpses of the Thailand trip to her entertaining another man. The audio from Thailand slows and the moans from her escapade get louder and louder. The air in the room grows thick. I feel her pull her hand from me as the sound of knives and forks hit the fine china. A glass shattered on the ground at the back of the room. "YES...YES..." Her moans muffled, but louder as I got the audio from the video enhanced. I fix my jacket and stand at the table.

"Oh my Lord!" Her mother cries out. "What is this?"

Q is silent and flustered. She's realizing that she had been found out.

"Jarell what the hell is going on?" Her sister Stephanie questions as everyone eyes glued themselves to the screen.

"Turn it off, Jarell!!" Q commands.

I look her in her eyes, watching tears fall from her face.

"Is that y'all?" Imani asked standing.

My eyes roam the table then glue themselves on Yari. She's watching with her dinner napkin covering her mouth.

"Eugene!!! Do something." He was smacking on his food so much he never noticed the video that was playing in front him. A playback of his daughter giving head to another man.

"Gwendolyn, what you yelling about woman?" He asks, while sucking on a chicken bone.

I wondered if that's where Q had gotten her skills. Suddenly it disappears as he looked over at his wife and up at the screen. He begins heaving and choking.

"Oh My Lord, Quincy help your father!" First Lady Gwendolyn shouts! Scooting back from her seat, she tries to stand before tripping and falling on his dinner napkin, pulling some of the tablecloth with her.

"JARELL TURN IT OFF!!!!" Q yells running over to her father. I stand there. Saying nothing and doing nothing.

"You know what? This right here is a real party." X says sipping from his drink as he stands from the table.

"You can't do this Jarell...this isn't okay." Her sister pleads.

Seconds later Yari's plus one walks into the room. His jacket now open and his jewelry on full display. I squint looking a little closer; feeling the heat rise in the back of my neck. I look from the screen to him and to the screen again. It clicks in my head why he looked so damn familiar.

"IT WAS YOU!" I shout across the table. Just then an angle of the Q and her mystery lover boy flash onto the screen. The pendent from his necklace painted across the screen and his side profile front and center. My eyes fell to Yari, all I could feel was anger and regret as I watch her entire reality turn to a nightmare right before her eyes.

Shifting my focus, I walk over to her end of the table. She stands slowly from her seat. Her tears cutting lines through her foundation as they drip down the curve of her cheeks.

"Guess you were right." She whispers with a tight lip smile then grabbing her things to leave.

"Yari, I'm sorry I didn't know." Her cinnamon eyes were burnt red and saddened as she stares through me.

The dude I now know Is André walks over and grabs her hand. She snatches her hand from him and smacks him hard enough to make his face red.

"I deserve that baby." He says through clenched teeth, grabbing her hand once more. "I can explain, it's not what it looks like baby."

My face twists in disgust as I start to speak but was cut off by Yari's words. "André, I may be crying, but these tears aren't for you." She says, pulling her hand back. "I'm mourning the death of something that was so much more special to me." She finishes, looking me up and down before throwing her shawl over her shoulder and walking out of the room. Imani follows behind her.

X makes eye contact with me as he stands at the door, giving me a nod. He had read my mind.

"Listen man, she never told me she had a man," he says to me, throwing his hands up to surrender, and backing up, with a smug ass smirk on his face. My blood had boiled over causing heat to flow down my arms as I clinched my fist and reared back to land a mean punch to his pretty fucking face. His body falls limp onto the floor.

"Well, that didn't take long." I hear X say from the door. I hover over André. Watching him with disgust, as he slowly tries to get his shit together. Blood leaking from his mouth, but he remains slumped on the floor. Cameron rushes over to my side.

"Man he ain't worth it. Let's just go." He attempts to pull me away but my body is stuck here.

"Yo, have you lost your fucking mind? You think this shit funny?" I hear Quincy's bitch ass shuffling to get across the room from behind me. I turn to face the direction he's coming from, ready to lay his ass out next to André cemetery style if need be.

"Look here my dude, stay in a child's place. Aren't you the baby brother or some shit?" Cameron asks, stepping in-between us. "This grown man business, that shit yo sister pulled was lame as fuck. She got caught now she gon' have to deal with the embarrassment." He continues.

I spot Q's sister walking over towards us.

"Hey bitch, watch it!" Nevaeh calls out walking over to grab Cameron from between me and Quincy.

"Jarell, I can't believe you! How could you stoop so low?" Stephanie cries out.

"Your tramp ass sister goes lower." Nevaeh addresses her.

"Who are you calling a tramp?" Q says, now standing. "Jarell ain't all Peaches and Cream, Lollipops and Rainbows. He has his fucking flaws too. As concerned as he was for that stupid bitch who ran out of here crying, he shouldn't even care that I was fucking Dré."

She has some fucking nerves.

"Qiana Gwendolyn Landsin, watch your mouth young lady. You were not raised like this." Her mother says, finally getting her father back into his seat.

"Yeah okay, sure mom. Everyone has secrets. Probably even you." Q says rolling her eyes.

"You watch your mouth talking to your mother that way." Her father's voice was now lower and weakened by his choking from earlier.

"I'm not the one committing crimes. Revenge porn is a real thing." Q says, staring at me.

"Not when you're in my house with another man. That's trespassing."

"Oh, you got some fucking nerve. You think you gon' get away with this shit?" Q asks, finally having the balls to stand in front of me.

"I wanna know what made you believe you had gotten away with it?"

She turns to walk away from me but gets intercepted by Nevaeh's face hovering over her shoulder and whispering in her ear, "You're lucky I'm more concerned with Yari than to stay and play fist, palm, kick with your stupid fucking face. If I were you, I would leave out the back, so I don't have to do the walk of shame through the entire club." The smirk on Nevaeh's face speaks of a detail we must have all missed. I follow her finger, pointed towards the soundproof glass walls that pointed into the downstairs festivities. Everyone within sight of the private suite have their eyes glued to the projector.

The sound of loud banging on the door cause everyone's attention to focus on the door as X opens it to find Arias and Tony bickering.

"Why the hell y'all banging on the damn door like the police for?" X questions.

"All the audio is crossed with the damn projector." Arias steps over André and shuffled over to the backside of the projector pulling the cord from the wall.

"Tony lower the wall shades please." She demands. Tony

slowly steps into the room and flips open a panel near the door frame to lower the panels. "Jarell! What the fuck is going on in here? This is against every policy for any private events we have ever had." She shouts. "The way Yari just walked pass me, mascara running and her head hung low. Have you lost your fucking mind?" She questions, looking directly into my eyes, then takes a second to pan over the room and take inventory of the situation. Even though Tony had lowered the panels, it was too late. The truth had already seen the light.

Mascara & Mirrors

Yari

The silence after a storm is never really silent. It hums. Not out loud, but beneath your skin. In the pit of your stomach. Somewhere between your jaw and your pulse. That's where it lives.

My heels hit the tile fast like I am trying to run a marathon, but I don't care. I just needed air, or space, or something that didn't feel like the shame crawling down the back of my neck.

I close the bathroom door behind me slowly, pressing my back against it, needing something solid to hold me up. The sounds of the party disappeared the moment I stepped inside, but the scene keeps replaying in my head like a song I don't want stuck on repeat. The moans. The screen. The look in Jarell's eyes. The way André said, "I deserve that" like his betrayal was poetic.

I'm not crying anymore. Not now. Instead, I stare into the mirror. My lipstick is still perfect. Red, rich, unbothered. A cruel joke. My mascara though… that was the traitor. It had streaked and smudged in ways that told the truth. I look like someone who had been cracked open in public.

I reach for a paper towel and turn on the faucet. Cold water. I need cold. I let it run over my hands, feeling the sting. Dabbing at the corners of my eyes, I try not to wipe too much. I want to look whole again. But the mirror knew better. It was catching all my micro-expressions. The twitch of my jaw. The forced exhale. The quiet swallow of disappointment.

Then a knock on the bathroom door startles me.

"Yari... it's me." Imani's voice is soft, barely there. Like she knew I couldn't take anymore right now.

I unlock the door and pull it open, stepping aside to let her in. She closes the door behind her and wraps her arms around me without asking. I let her. I needed the anchor.

"You good?" she asks with her face buried against my hair.

"No."

She nods like she expected that answer. Like it was okay to not be okay in front of her. That makes the tears fall again. Slower this time. Tired tears. I'm emotionally exhausted.

Imani pulls back and leans against the counter next to me. She doesn't fill the space with advice or empty affirmations. She just lets it breathe.

"Nevaeh's outside losing her damn mind. Cameron's tryna calm her down before she tries swinging on Q. Again."

I almost smile.

Almost.

"I don't wanna go back out there," I admit.

"You don't have to. But I do think you should come back to yourself, wherever that is right now."

I look in the mirror again.

"Can you tell me who that even is anymore?"

Imani doesn't answer. She didn't need to. Because the truth is, I wasn't sure either.

I splash more water on my face. Not to fix the makeup. That

part was a lost cause. I just needed to feel something that wasn't boiling from the inside. I dry my hands on a towel and sit down on the chair that accented the private bathroom suite.

"Did he know?" I ask, without looking up.

Imani sits across from me on the closed toilet seat, her legs crossed at the ankle. "You mean Dré?"

I nod.

She sighs, "I don't think so... but when he walked in, and that video was playing... I don't know. It felt like God drew the blinds to reveal and unmask *everybody*." She shakes her head with disgust while staring up at the ceiling.

"And snatched the rug right from up under me! I feel like I damn near cracked my head on the marble floor." I admit.

I look down at my hands. They're trembling. Sweaty, achy, and weak from having to hold the weight of this ring after the levels of shame it carried.

I didn't even look back. Couldn't. I had walked away looking strong, like the salt under the rug was guarding me from choices that could shatter everything. Maybe that's why God decided to pull that very rug from under me. I stay seated putting the entire picture together piece by piece.

"He looked right at me," I say, "When it ended. Like he was waiting for me to say something. Like I was supposed to comfort *him* after what I saw. After what *everyone* saw."

Imani's eyes narrow, "Girl, don't you dare carry his shame. That was *his* mess. Not yours."

"Yeah," I whisper, "but the whole room saw me fall with him."

She reaches out and holds my hand.

"No. They saw you rise from that fall. And slap the dog shit out of him in six-inch Louboutin's. In front of God and Q's father."

I huff a short, tired laugh. "You saw that?"

"Everybody did. That slap was generational. My great-grandma felt that thump in her urn."

I finally smile, weak but genuine. Imani knew how to make grief flinch. The silence folds back in, gentler this time.

"I feel empty," I confess. "Like... I've been pouring from a pot with no water. Loving from a place that's cracked and leaking, but I kept pretending it was enough."

Imani rubs my knuckles. "That's because you've been surviving. Not living."

I swallow, "And I thought love was supposed to fix that."

She pauses, "Yari... Love don't fix broken. It just shows you where it lives."

I let her words sit in my chest for a moment. They're heavy, but they fit. Like grief and truth stitched from the same cloth. I stand up slowly and turn back towards the mirror.

"What you see now?" Imani asks behind me.

I stare hard. Past the mascara stains. Past the smudged lip. Past the false calm.

"A woman who's finally stopped lying to herself."

She nods, "Good. Now let's go."

Imani stands with me and I take one last peek at myself in the gold framed mirror over the pedestal sink, before giving Imani the nod of approval. And then I open the door.

Crossing the tiled floors as if my reputation depended on it. I don't want anyone to snap pictures of me looking like this. And now that I know the entire lounge had seen and heard the unraveling of a private dinner party gone wrong, I couldn't face that music yet. Not like this.

Head down as I strut across the parking deck, I hear my name from behind, causing me to double step trot to get to my truck. I can't face the music tonight. Then again, "Yari!" I hear a female's voice echoing against the cold concrete corridors. Familiar. Warm. Safe. I slow my stride as the voice gets closer.

"Yari!"

It's Nevaeh. Her voice Is soft but firm. The kind of voice that could hold me up before I even knew I was falling.

I stop walking but don't turn around. A moment passes. Then I feel her presence beside me. She doesn't rush, doesn't reach. Just stands there for a beat, like she is letting me breathe. Then, gently, her fingers move to fix the back of my dress, smoothing a wrinkle near my shoulder. Like a sister would. Like a stylist. Like someone who knew exactly what it meant to want to hold yourself together.

"You good?" she asks, eyes scanning mine. Not for lies, but for limits.

I take a shallow inhale of the cool night air.

"I'm... standing." My voice cracks but doesn't break. "Then that's enough," she says. "For tonight, that's more than enough."

Behind her, Cameron approaches slowly, hands in his pockets, eyes soft with something I wasn't expecting. Understanding. Not pity. Just quiet recognition.

"Whatever you need, Yari... just say it," he offers. "We'll make sure you get home safe."

His tone is calm. No jokes. No extra. Just presence. And in that moment, I am grateful for his stillness.

"Imani's getting the car," Nevaeh adds, brushing a strand of hair away from my cheek. "Cameron's going to drive you home, and we'll be right there by your side, okay?"

I nod, swallowing hard.

Cameron steps slightly to the side, giving me space, but not distance.

"You ain't gotta explain nothing to nobody," he says, "not tonight."

Something inside me loosens. Just a little.

Nevaeh leans in and kisses the air near my cheek. A gesture of grace more than affection. Then she turns toward Cameron, her hand briefly brushing his as they walk to my truck while Imani pulls it around the side of the building.

Cameron opens the back door and reaches for Nevaeh's hand, this time fully, helping her up into the truck. Then he turns to me.

"Yari, come on, sis. I got you."

I take his hand as he helps me in, then waits for Imani to climb in before closing the door and jogging around to the driver's side.

"You ready, babe?" Imani asks as Cameron shut the door.

"No," I say honestly, "but I gotta go. Like now."

She loops her arm through mine without saying another word. Nevaeh leans her head against mine, and together, they cradle me with warmth as Cameron pulls out of the lot toward my loft.

The ride back to my place is a type of quiet that lingers in the air when something cracks wide open and no one's ready to speak on it.

Imani breaks the silence but only for a second. "You think he planned that whole night just to hurt her?"

I don't answer right away. I wasn't sure how. Before I can I hear a heavy sigh from the front seat.

"This shit is so insane. I don't know what's going through his head. He never told us what the dinner was. Shit caught us off guard too."

I try clearing my throat to fight my voicelessness.

"I think he wanted to finally be heard," I say. "And maybe he needed her to feel what it was like to be embarrassed for loving the wrong person." I'm trying to make sense of Jarell's actions. I want to protect him from judgement. I'd seen how this mess had caused him to fall apart the night he'd found out. I'd watched him ache and wither. I knew the extent of his feelings. I just wanted to protect him. I needed to protect him.

Imani turns to look at me. "But you were the one who ended up humiliated."

I nod slowly, "I know."

My eyes stay on the window, my reflection faint in the glass. Mascara and mirrors.

It's funny how we only see these types of scenes in movies, or in music videos. But to be living in this moment right now, felt like an out of body experience. I want to pinch myself to make sure this was real but the sting of my tears made sure I wasn't confused about what I was feeling. My new reality.

Cameron, surprisingly gentle behind the wheel, glances at me in the rear view mirror every so often like he is watching for signs of me shattering.

Nevaeh uses her hand as a brush, softly massaging the headache she must've sensed was blooming behind my eyes. No words. Just presence. And honestly, it meant more than anything else could've.

As we pull into the roundabout outside my building, the air inside the car shifts.

"You sure you don't want us to walk you up?" Cameron asks, putting the car in park. His voice was soft but grounded. The kind of voice that knows when to lower itself out of respect for someone else's dignity.

"I'll go up with her," Imani offers, already unbuckling her seatbelt.

Nevaeh opens her door but pauses. "You need anything, like anything at all, you call. Don't try to be cute and brave."

That makes me smirk. "Cute and brave is my middle name."

She leans back into the car, pressing her forehead to mine. "I know. That's why I'm saying it."

Her eyes didn't leave mine until I nodded. Satisfied, she slides out, giving my arm one last squeeze, and loops her own through Cameron's as they wait for me to climb out of the car and Imani to escort me upstairs.

In the elevator, Imani stands beside me, unusually quiet. She doesn't fill the space with small talk or sarcasm. She just looks at me, like she understood what it meant to lose your footing while smiling in stilettos.

When we reach my floor, I unlock the door with a sigh that comes from somewhere deep in my soul.

The loft's lights blink on low, dim, golden, still. I kick off my shoes, wincing as the silence wraps around me like a wet blanket.

"You want me to crash here tonight?" Imani asks, slipping off her heels. "The couch is big enough. I can stay close if you need."

I shake my head, even as I keep walking farther inside. "Nah. Thank you though. I just... I need a second to be with myself."

She doesn't argue. Just nods, walking over, and wrapping me in a hug that felt like solid ground.

"I love you, Yari. For real. Call me if the walls start talking." Her voice is light, her eyes steely.

"I will," I whisper into her shoulder, suddenly afraid that if I say anything else, I'd break again.

She grabs her heels and lets herself out, pulling the door closed softly behind her.

Standing in the middle of the living room. Still in the velvet dress. Still in these damn pantyhose. Still wearing the ultimate lie, this ring.

The silence was different now, loud, accusing, echoing. The loft was still, still like silence had weight to it. Still like every object in the room knew not to hold their breath.

I catch sight of myself in one of my mirrors. The gloss had vanished from my lips. The liner faded from my waterline. My mascara had betrayed me. Streaking down my cheeks like vines of grief.

I don't wipe them instead I sit down on the floor in front of the couch and tucked my legs underneath me. For a moment, I just stare at my hands, the weight of everything finally seeping through the cracks.

The ring.
The video.
The slap.
The silence.

The soft hum of the refrigerator is the only sound left behind after Imani closed the door and whispered, "Call if you change your mind."

I said no, of course.

Because the night already felt like too much. Because saying yes to comfort felt like defeat. Because admitting you need someone when you're used to being needed... cuts different.

Peeling off the dress I lay it across the velvet chaise and wander into the kitchen pouring myself a glass of wine, the same red from the dinner. I'm not even sure why I brought the bottle home. Maybe part of me didn't want to let go of what *almost* was.

I stood at the island, letting the chilled glass sweat against my palm. My reflection in the microwave catches my eye. Smudged mascara. Eyes still wet.

The same mouth that told André he didn't matter with a smack across his stupid face... still trembling from telling Jarell, indirectly, that *this*, whatever we were, meant more than I was ready to admit.

The wine tastes too luxurious for what I'm currently feeling. I wanted a burn. I open the cabinet and grab one of my depression glass lowballs. It's so fitting for tonight. The pink royal lace design instantly reminds me of my childhood. Back when life was simpler.

I had a way of crawling back into nostalgia, like it was one of those fully decorated cribs that could comfort me when the world turned into a big meany.

I try sipping slow. Try being a lady. But I end up taking gulps instead.

As the bourbon burns the back of my throat, the tears start

to dry. Then another gulp. Anger begins crawling to the surface of my grief. And just like that, I can hear my granny's voice, clear as ever:

"He only gulps that stuff down when his heart and mind done got tired. Any other time, he pulls up a chair and keeps it company."

She used to fuss from time to time when my grandfather was stressed or heartbroken and she had no fix for it. But she'd allow him grace. Quiet grace. Sitting in the corner chair watching her soaps, waiting patiently until he drank enough to drop the chaos and finally find his peace in a pillow.

I stare at my phone on the counter. My chest feeling both swollen and hollow. The kind of ache that live in the muscle, but belongs to the memory.

I think of how Nevaeh hugged me before we parted ways, just tight enough. How Cameron hadn't said much, just placed a steadying hand at the small of her back as she got into the car.

How Imani had offered to stay without prying, just presence, no pressure.

And how alone didn't feel empowering tonight. Just... hollow.

It was too much. Too much for one body to carry.

So, I reach for my phone, and I do the thing I swore I wouldn't need to do tonight. Imma call my girls.

I stare at the screen. No missed calls. No texts. Just that blurry photo of the three of us. Me, Nevaeh, and Imani at the Cream grand opening. Smiling. Drunk off laughter and cocktails. I had set it as my background a week ago, not knowing tonight I'd need it like medicine.

The line rang once before I propped the phone up on the counter.

"Yo?" Nevaeh answers first, her voice already alert.

"I know it's late..." I begin, trying not to cry again. "I... I don't want to be by myself," I say, not even trying to sound strong anymore.

"You want us to come?" Nevaeh interrupts softly, no questions in her tone, just understanding.

I swallow the lump forming in my throat as my emotions continue to force themselves to the surface.

"Yeah."

Then Imani chimes in from the background, "We're already in the car, be there soon." She confirms.

Before the call even ends, the tears return, but this time, they're different. Softer. Not sharp like grief, but thick like healing. I didn't know what I would say when they got here.

If we would talk. If we would just lay around on throw pillows and pick at leftover charcuterie and cry over romcoms.

I didn't need to know.

They were coming.

And for tonight, that was enough.

And for the first time all night...

I exhaled.

♪ ♪ ♪

I wanted a quick shower. I needed to try and remove tonight off my skin. That's exactly what I did.

My face was clean, stripped of all traces of warpaint. Yet the ache behind my eyes throbbed like it had unfinished business.

An oversized tee, no bra, and hair pulled into a pineapple. The kind of outfit you wear when your heart has nothing left to prove. The kind of outfit I need right now.

I throw on my favorite oversized hoodie noting that it still carried faint notes of Jarell's cologne from the last time he'd borrowed it to grab coffee from Bubbles, the cute coffee shop on the corner.

The knock at the door isn't loud, more like a heartbeat. I pull it open to find both women standing there in sweatpants, bonnets, without any judgement in sight. They came back with slippers this time.

Nevaeh had wrapped her braids into a loose pineapple and changed into a hoodie that said *Soft Doesn't Mean Stupid*. Imani wore fuzzy socks with sloths on them and a sleep shirt from our college days *Monroe Belle University* printed across the front in cracked indigo letters. Neither of them say anything. They just walk in because we all knew the rules were different this time.

Smiles creep across their faces.

"What?" I ask, concerned about what the smiles were meant.

Nevaeh reveals what she's been hiding behind her back.

"I brought ice cream and cookies," she says, holding up a pint of Marabello's *Bourbon Vanilla* ice cream and a paper bag from UnTamed Cookies like they're sacred. "And Imani brought the dumb ass card deck."

Imani steps in front of her. "We brought what the Lord would've wanted," she says a she raises it up, already smirking. *Healing Cards for the Emotionally Exhausted.* A gag gift turned ritual.

I settle back into the couch between them. "Y'all really came back."

"Of course we did."

"We always do."

The silence that follows isn't heavy like before. Its layered. Honest. Full of things we didn't need to explain. I let myself lean into it, not the silence, but the presence.

"First card," Imani says, shuffling. "And don't roll your eyes, Yari."

"I'm not," I say, even though I was.

She flips it over.

What are you pretending not to know?

Nevaeh snorts, "Oh this deck messy tonight."

I exhale a quiet laugh, a real laugh. I look at the card. Then at them.

"I'm pretending not to know that I've been grieving Jarell... even while I was saying yes to André."

Imani doesn't flinch. "Say more."

I wiped the back of my hand against my cheek. "I think I wanted André to become the answer so bad, I ignored how often he made me the afterthought. I let the ring become proof of something I didn't really feel."

"And Jarell?" Nevaeh asks, already knowing the answer.

I close my eyes. "He's been my mirror... and the reason I kept wiping it down, hoping I'd see something different. Even when we weren't right, we were *real*. And now..."

"You don't know how to hold that kind of ache."

"Exactly."

The card game had turned into storytelling, and the storytelling turned into silence again. This time, it was warm. Imani lays across the rug with a blanket and a half-eaten cookie on her chest. Nevaeh curls her legs under her and reaches for my hand.

"Whatever you do next, Yari... do it from your center. Not your shame."

I nod, a single tear tracing my jaw.

"I just want to come back to myself," I whisper.

"You already are," Nevaeh says. "Every time you tell the truth, you're home."

"Say less or say everything," Imani offers, curling beside her and handing over a warm oatmeal cookie. "Whatever you got in you."

I took a slow bite and let the sugar melt on my tongue.

I let out a long breath, my eyes filling again, but the tears stayed put.

"I let him walk me to the edge," I finally say, "and then I jumped…Thinking love would catch me."

"And?" Imani asks gently, settling on the ottoman, her hand resting over my foot.

"It didn't. Not love. Just… gravity."

We sit like that. Three women. Still, soft, and sacred. Nothing rushed. Nothing demanded.

Eventually the wine is poured.

The playlist is low.

A candle flickers.

And I rest my head against Nevaeh's shoulder like a child finally letting herself be held.

And before I know it, I had finally fallen asleep in the softness of being seen. No mirrors. No mascara. Just me. Still breathing, finally home.

The Apology Tour

Yari

The morning settled heavy. Not the kind that creeps in quietly, but the kind that settles on your chest before you open your eyes. The kind that tastes like yesterday's mascara, and unfelt dread.

I didn't check my phone, even as I heard it buzzing across the room. Blowing up with headlines, mentions, and calls I wasn't ready to answer. Instead, I reach for the folded up napkin on the coffee table with Nevaeh's handwriting scribbled across it.

We got you. Breathe first. Don't try to fix it all before breakfast.

I fold the napkin back up slowly, like it might tear if I moved too fast. That note held more truth than anything in my inbox ever could. I pressed the paper to my lips like a prayer.

My grandmother's voice drifted up from memory, "Quiet is where the Holy Ghost does its best mending, baby. Let it work."

So, I moved slowly, with intention. My body wanted to lie down again, but shame wouldn't let me rest. The weight sitting atop my ribs was too heavy. I didn't want to be needed today. Besides, there was no time for that now. Not when Cream was bleeding in the press, not when shame still leeched out of my pores like sweat. I moved through the loft in silence my mind clouded with fog. No playlist, no candles, no selfcare ambience. The quiet matched the hollowness I felt inside.

Catching my reflection in the bathroom mirror I wasn't surprised that I looked feral. One streak of mascara still beneath my left eye, lips faded to a bruised red.
I rinsed my face with water so cold it felt like penance. The water ran black for a moment, then pink, then clear. I watched all the versions of me swirling down the drain.

I almost cried again at the sight. Almost. But the tears dried up with the heat of humiliation.

I wrapped myself in a towel and stepped into the living space.

The hum of the silence propping me up.

The silence was suspenseful, waiting for me to acknowledge the weight in my chest, and suddenly it's too damn loud.

My grandmother would've said, "Silence got memory, baby. It knows what you trying to forget."

I wanted Jazz, in all of its moodiness.

I needed it.

Like a feen in an alley filled with dumpsters searching for just a piece of something that could ease the pain of silence.

"Alexa, play my," I pause to think what music would soothe me.

"I'm sorry, I didn't get that," comes her interjection into my thoughts. Clearly, I was taking too long for her. She was always ready. For a split second, I envied the simplicity of her existence.

"Alexa, play my Martini's and Lowballs playlist...please!"

Seconds later my entire loft was drenched in Billie Holiday's "Good Morning Heartache". I closed my eyes, my head falling back as the sting of F major and D minor became a thousand tiny hair strand thin needles pricking my skin causing goosebumps to blaze a trail down my body. Her voice washed over me as I slowly turned with the melody to face the kitchen.

The cocktail from last night was still on the counter.

Neon pink.

Unfinished.

Mocking me.

I poured it down the sink, watching the pink swirl down the drain. Like I was baptizing the shame out of my countertop, or giving it its own offering. A sacrifice to its deity.

I made tea without thought. Sat on the floor instead of the couch. Still not checking my phone. Still not wanting to know what the world was saying.

I decided to check my emails on my laptop instead. The first subject line punched me in the chest: *Regarding Last Night's Incident at Cream.*

The second: *Cancellation Confirmation.*

The third: *Press Request – Statement from Owner.*

I couldn't even read the actual messages. I just closed the laptop, saying to myself, "Not yet. not before breakfast!"

The title **Owner** carried an accusation this morning. Owner of what? Chaos, spectacle, my own public humiliation?

Before I could spiral further, Arias called. Her voice, normally bright as summer, was laced with winter steel today.

"Yari, what happened?" she asked, getting straight to the point.

I sighed, "Which part?"

"SE Talent and Echelon Media were there. They're calling last night '*The Creammax*'. They want to spin this thing and turn it into some kind of coined term. Like it was some kind of porno premier. I'm not having it girl. You know I got your back. Get over here now! I'm ready to go nuclear PR. But you gotta let me know, are we saving this or shutting it down?"

"We're not shutting down anything," I say. "Not ever."

"Ok but you don't have to carry this yourself."

"Actually, yes I do," I reply. And I meant it. Because the truth was, I'd been carrying this place in my chest for so long it felt like lungs. And if Cream stopped breathing, I was sure I would too.

"Then breathe and get to Cream. I'm sending a town car. You got 8 minutes," she hangs up.

Breakfast would have to wait.

Needing to get ready quick I decided to throw on a jogger set so I could be comfy. I had no idea what I was walking into, but I wanted to be prepared for it.

The moment I stepped out of my building, the bubble of stillness I'd found myself in this morning popped. The city outside felt louder than ever. Hungry for the drama waiting to see if I'd survive, or if it would eat me alive.

Taking a seat in the car Arias had sent, I turn my face to the window. I'm not feeding any appetites right now.

Cream's doors groaned like they hurt to open.

"My poor baby took a beating too," I state before walking in. The lights weren't even fully up. The morning sun had just begun to bruise the sky with its rays, and Cream looked like it had seen war.

Empty wine glasses were scattered everywhere with lipstick ghosts around their rims, staged like evidence in a crime scene. Floral arrangement slightly off-center, the faint scent of rose-wood candle wax mixed with the sour stink of Cabernet clinging to the velvet banquettes.

A napkin with *RESERVED FOR ROSEBOWL* laid crumpled

on the dancefloor, mocking me.

I walked the perimeter. Ran my fingers across each table's edge as if they were rosary beads.

I continue through to the lounge; memories clung to its every corner.

It looked like the room was harboring secrets. And it was. This was the scene of the crime after all.

I stood in its center, hands on my hips, trying not to replay every moment of the night before.

The screen lowering.

The gasps.

The slap.

The silence.

The way my name had immediately felt like it didn't belong to me anymore. Like Yari Gervais had somehow become obsolete, and only the owner remained.

Then I checked my phone.

My feed confirmed everything. A shaky phone video of the private suite, projector screen dropping, a blurred tangle of moans and shouts.

Hashtag **#CreamClimax** already at eightysix thousand mentions.

Geri Stone's name, the premier wedding and bridal planner for my elite clientele, appeared in a notification, her message sugarsweet and terrifying.

> Geri Stone [9:22 AM]: Hey love! Hope
> all's well. Shall we postpone next week's
> Bridal Society Brunch until the dust
> settles?

Even kindness cut.

Mentions.

DMs.

Everything was quickly unraveling. I felt so exposed, and I wasn't even in the video.

For a millisecond I worried about how this could be affecting Q. Jarell had gone too damn far with this dinner. I got his intention, but this was messy.

I scrolled further.

A polite text from another business partner.

> Velvet Magazine [9:30 AM]: Morning Yari,
> just checking in. Should we hold off on
> this week's feature?

Translation: We don't want your smoke on our feed.

Another from

The Alumni Gala's Vice President Renee – Hope all's well. Let us know if we need to reschedule the event planning meeting.

Even the kindness stung.

A ping sounds, an email from SE Scene Magazine. A Reminder. A Request for a quote 'from the owner'.

I almost laughed. The title meant something different now.

Ping!

Text from Auntie Regina in Louisiana:

> Auntie Regina [9:35 AM]: Baby, y'all
> alright up there? You need me to drive in
> and throw a shoe?

Love can be loud.

I tucked the phone away. Let the shame gnaw at me a little longer. Let it scrape and claw a few more pieces of me away before I starved it for good.

The sound of heels clicking against the flooring reach my

ears. Out of place to me, unfamiliar. Arias never wore heels. She hated them. That's how I knew she was ready for war.

She strode in dressed headtotoe in funeral black, Manolo stilettos sharp enough to slice gossip open.

"Hey Boss Lady! Security's posted outside," she says, not stopping to take a breath she continues, "I got some staff on the way. They'll have to check-in TSA style. That includes phone lockboxes, and full pat down. We also have NDA refreshers to sign. No more leaks, and no more home movies. We're officially Fort Knox. Cameron and Xavier are already in the back with Tony and the boys."

She hands me a coffee. Black, no sugar, no nonsense.

"You still got the juice," she says. "Don't let this shrink you. And as Lovita Alizay Jenkins would say to Regina—You my Shero."

Despite myself, I smile. A broken one, but it counts.

"Not you quoting the Steve Harvey Show this early in the morning," I quip halfheartedly.

"Desperate times."

"Is that why you call me Boss Lady?"

"Yes, and because I wanted me a little 90's secretary haircut back in the day."

"Back in the day when? Girl you are 25."

"And? Listen Boss Lady, I joke around, but I ain't the only one who thinks highly of you. We won't let this get ahead of you." She points to a clipboard sitting at a table near us. "Let's make a plan!"

I nod, taking a seat where she had set up my makeshift desk.

The lights flicker as Cream's soul begins to stir. Staff appeared moving quietly, the ones who were loyal, the ones Arias knew wouldn't sell out for a story.

Just as Arias and I were getting started with the planning. The front door opened, hissing this time. The air chilled.

"I'm sorry, we're clo-" my words catch in my throat.

CeCe slithered in like she never left. Bodycon dress, trench coat, and intentions masked behind a foxfaced grin. She surveys the chaos like an HGTV host assessing demo potential.

"How did you get in here and *why* are you here Cynthia?" I ask finding my voice again.

"Wow," she purrs, "is that how you speak to a paying customer?"

My eyes squint at her tone. "Y'all cleaned up quick. Or maybe the dust was always part of the décor."

I say nothing, Arias stiffens beside me.

"Heard your private screening went viral," CeCe continued, tracing a finger along the bar top. "If you need PR help, I've got a crisis team. Real discreet. Real fast." She says as her eyes drag across the floor. "But if it's too far gone, what's Cream worth? I'm picturing it could be a really cute sixlevel parking deck. Real communityforward," she finishes, laughing maliciously. Mapping her hands across the room as if she was a visionary.

"Cynthia you're nothing but a snake in stilettos. Cream's not for sale," I say.

"Everything's for sale when your trauma's trending. Pride leads to foreclosure and the only thing that can save you from that is a pretty price tag," she snaps, flicking imaginary lint from her sleeve.

Arias steps forward, pointing, "Door's that way."

CeCe winks, "Hit me when humility sets in."

Her heels click softer on the way out. Even smugness respects sacred ground.

I let the silence settle in her wake, taste metal on my tongue. Not today, Yari. I can't go to jail right now. I remind myself.

"What the hell was that?" Arias asks as the door closed behind CeCe.

"Doesn't matter. Let her plot. We've got bigger storms," I

respond walking over to grab a broom from the corner of the room.

The door swings open with ease the next time it opens, and I look up to find Cameron walking in. He gives me a slight smile as he walks over.

"It's all good sis, we got you! I brought some help," he reassured me giving me a hug. His energy is light, fresh, steady. He rolls up his sleeves and starts cleaning without another word. I couldn't help but smile as I looked around for the help he brought.

And there *he* is. Standing cautiously off to the side looking as if his heart was about to beat out of his chest.

Jarell.

Xavier waves him through. Cameron I'm going to kill you, I think as I see him looking between Jarell and I before leaving the area to give us space.

Jarell approaches me with the caution of a zookeeper approaching an agitated lion.

"I'm not here to fix it," he starts, "I just wanted you to know I see what I did. And I'm so sorry Yari."

I look at him, eyes tired.

"Sorry doesn't undo public ruin. Nor does it make up for the threats of skeletons."

"I know. But I didn't want to stay quiet. Not again. Wait… What?" He paused.

"Jarell, don't," I cut in before he can continue.

His hands raise in surrender.

I don't cry, I don't yell, I just nod as I say, "Go help Cameron."

And he does.

Not even 30 minutes passed before the front doors swing open again. The footsteps that follow tapping across the floor with entitlement. André.

Holding a single white rose. Looking like a man who thought apologies were transactions.

"Arias, is there anyone securing the building?" I yell out bringing attention to André's presence.

"I just wanted to check on you," he says.

"You brought a flower to a burial," I say, stepping aside.

He walks further into the space slowly, taking in the half-lit room, the staff moving like shadows behind us. I see the moment he spots Cameron and Jarell behind me.

"Baby I didn't expect it to go down like that," he says, placing the rose on the bar like it was a peace offering. "My final apology. I never wanted to hurt you, and I will never hurt you again."

"Oh, I know you won't," I spit.

"Baby you know that wasn't the whole story. That video... it didn't show everything."

"It showed enough," I say, my eyebrows reaching the chandeliers as my gaze clung to the floor near his feet.

He sighs, "I didn't mean for you to be embarrassed. You're still my-"

"No," I cut him off, the word hanging in the air, a steeltipped knife between us. My head now up gaze shifting to the crown molding in the corner of the room. "Absolutely not! You're kidding right?"

He hesitates.

"You don't get to call me that," I say, voice low but strong. "You broke us long before that video. The ring didn't change that. Even if I wanted to pretend like it did."

"I just thought maybe we could talk. Figure out a way forward baby. You know I love you," he professes.

I nod, smiling and picking up the rose.

Crooking a finger at him to follow me.

I feel the silent judgement of our audience floating through the room.

I also feel Andre's smug satisfaction at my shift.

"Follow me baby," I say, taking his hand and stepping slowly across the room.

I walk right over to the trash can near the lobby, taking a second to face him and find his eyes. Then...I drop the rose in. It's *thump* echoes as it hits the bottom. I stand still, eyes locked on his. Allowing my silence to speak first.

Then, "Goodbye, Andre."

Later, Arias and I sit near the bar with her laptop open and a spreadsheet on the counter. Names, strategies, a column labeled 'Priority Outreach'. I was overstimulated.

"We'll hit RoseBowl first. Then SE Scene. Then the bridal partners. When do you want to get started?"

I didn't answer.

Instead, I stood. Observed the lounge, the body I'd helped heal. The tables had been reset. Candles replaced. The light was beginning to shift through the windows.

Then I pulled out my phone and took a photo of the space. Still imperfect, still recovering, but upright.

Opening Instagram, I type,

My grandmother used to say, "Baby, if the house falls, you don't apologize for the bricks. You gather what's still standing, and you build again."
I'm building.
#CreamStillRising

I hit post.

Then I walked back over to Arias, picked up the plan from the table, and ripped it in half.

Arias blinked, "Wait, what are you-"

"No more apology tour," I say. "No more explaining grief to

people who weren't in the room."

Imani and Nevaeh stepped through the vestibule then.
Dressed in hoodies and fleece joggers, eyes soft with pride. They
didn't need dialogue, their presence more than enough.

I tossed the torn plan into the trash, covering André's rose.

"I'm not asking to be forgiven," I tell the room. "I'm
choosing to be free."

And in that moment, the weight that had been clinging to my
name slid off my shoulders like a coat I never needed to wear.

This wasn't a comeback. It was a rebirth.

And this time?

The only tour I was taking…was back to myself.

Later, after the staff had left and Arias had double, and triple
checked that the doors were secured, my girls and I stretch across
the velvet booths. Nevaeh and Imani bust out some UnTamed's
lovely lemon cookies, Marabello cookiebutter ice cream, and the
cheap house wine that never makes it to the premium list.

Through the skylights we watch the sky violetover into night.
Nevaeh cues up a 90s R&B playlist and dares me to rest my head
in her lap. I do.

"You know," Imani says, "every headline ends up in archives.
Meanwhile, legacy? That's God's press release. It don't expire."

I smile against the cushion, eyes wet, but peaceful.

"I think we should have a rooftop remedy here at Cream,"
Imani continues, grabbing the wireless speaker and heading
towards the elevator that leads to the roof from the back of the
building. We laugh standing from the booth to follow her.

"Wait up," Arias calls.

Nevaeh stand reaching back for my hand, "Come On!"

I exhale with a genuine smile, and grab her hand. "Ok, I'm
coming."

Cream smelled like sage and bleach, and second chances.

Tomorrow, we'd mop the floors again, buff the tables, restock the topshelf bourbon.

Tomorrow, the RoseBowl Committee would get their statement. Short, honest, unshaken.

Tomorrow, my name would still be mine.

But tonight?

Tonight, I'd let silence cradle me, let the candlelight kiss my corners, let Nevaeh's fingers braid a loose twist in my hair, let Imani hum an offkey gospel riff.

And for the first time since the screen dropped. I started to believed again that a house could fall and still be sacred.

The Cabin Knows

Jarell

The gravel popped beneath the truck tires as Cameron turned off
the main road onto the cabin's long driveway. Pines, tall and silent,
reaching toward a gloomy sky that couldn't decide if it wanted to
rain or shine.

I sat in the back seat, arms folded, jaw tight. I hadn't said
much since we hit the two-hour mark of the drive. Just watched
the woods roll past like they owed me answers. I was annoyed,
frustrated, and hurt. Everything had crumbled so quickly and
completely. And I felt so fucking stupid for letting it happen.

"You mad at the road or yourself?" Xavier asks from the
passenger seat, glancing back at me.

Could he hear my thoughts? I wouldn't put it past him to
have some innate mind reading ability.

I don't respond, he can read mind to figure it out.

Cameron smirks, "Don't worry. He'll talk once the bourbon
kicks in. Or the fish start biting."

"As much doing he's done lately his ass is tired of doing by now fo sho," Xavier teases, checking to see if he can get a response out of me.

The truck comes to a stop. The cabin looked the same as it always did, rough. Wood-framed, a porch swing hanging off rusted chains, and years of soot blackening its chimney.

"You told me we were going to reset," I mutter, "Nobody said nothing about an intervention."

"This ain't an intervention," Cameron says, popping the door open. "It's an invitation to shut the hell up, sit down, and face the silence. Maybe say what you need to clear your mind."

"Yeah, get that stick out yo ass and that crooked S off your chest," Xavier pouts with his arms crossed mimicking me as he heads toward the cabin.

I slowly get out the car. I wasn't in the mood for this. I want silence alright, but I wanted it in my own home. Especially If I was gonna have to tolerate these two for the weekend.

Inside the cabin, the air smelled like cedar and stories that don't get told twice.

Cameron threw a couple of logs in the fireplace while Xavier unloaded groceries onto the counter.

I just stood in the doorway not wanting to step any further inside in case the past decided to jump out and bite me.

"You not gone say nothing?" Xavier asks.

"I said yes to the ride. I didn't say I was ready to talk," I responded regretting even being here.

"Man," Cam chuckled, "you showed your whole heart on a damn projector screen, but you quiet now?"

I shoot my eyes toward him with what I hope is a dangerous warning for him to stop.

"That's not what that was," I say finally, low.

"Then what was it?" Xavier presses.

I rub my face, "It was everything I should've said…when I

still had the right to say it."

Cam walks over from the fireplace, "Look you can feel how you want man. Like I said this ain't no intervention. But we not doing a pity party. You wanna speak, do that shit with your whole chest."

"Right! If you would've told us about this shit we wouldn't be here like this," Xavier chimes in, closing the freezer. "We would be at the strip club celebrating your newfound singleness with some thick cigars and even thicker broads, you feel me?" he chuckled, reaching to dap me. I left his arm extended as I walked past him down the hall to the bedrooms.

"Damn, you not gone keep dissing me man. I'm trying to be supportive while you recover from heartbreak," I hear him call out after me.

"Aye man chill out, give him time," Cam whispers, right as I slammed my bedroom door.

I toss my duffle on the bed and almost instantly noticed some sort of paper sticking out the side pocket. Confusion washes over my face and I wonder for a split second how it got there before locking the door and grabbing it from the pocket.

It's a note from Yari. I started to read it only to notice it was aged. The crinkling of the paper's corners revealed the truth of a date months back. The anniversary of my mom's passing. I showed up at her place because being home with all my grief was too dangerous. I was drowning in Vodka and out of my mind; I never noticed it.

I sit down on the edge of the bed, paper trembling slightly in my hand. The ink had smudged a little at the edges. Like it had been held by someone with sweaty palms or too many thoughts.

Her handwriting was neat and controlled in a way that told me she was going to use every word, every letter, to get her point across in a conversation she knew I might never be ready to have.

Hey You,

I wasn't planning to write this, but there are some things that won't let me rest and you're one of them.

Not because I need answers.
But because I need peace.

I can feel you slipping, Jarell.
And it's not the loud kind of leaving, it's that slow fade, the one where memories stay but the spirit goes missing.

My throat tightens at her words.

I fold the letter closed before I even finish it. Couldn't read the rest. Not yet.

She wrote it when we were still…whatever we were. It was a mirror I hadn't earned the right to stand in front of. Not now, not after everything.

Leaning forward, elbows on my knees, I clutch the letter to me. It's evidence. Of what, I wasn't sure. That I mattered? That she had noticed when I started disappearing? That even when I didn't ask for it she had tried to stay close because she knew I needed her.

Outside the door, I could hear Xavier talking shit again. Something about fishing lines, and mermaid booty. Cam laughed low, steady, a heartbeat in the background.

And for the first time since we got here, I wanted to join them.

Not to talk.

Just to be.

Because the cabin knew. It always did.

That afternoon we went fishing. Well, Cameron and Xavier fished and set up a line for me. I sat on the edge of the dock, legs dangling, letting the cold-water lap against my ankles and remind me what it felt like to be human.

The wind was soft. The lake waves whispered. The Birds did their thing. Nobody rushed me.

And then Cam, out of nowhere, "You ever grieve someone who's still alive?"

I look over at him.

"That's what watching her walk out felt like," Cam adds. "I watched you grieve her while she was still standing in front of you."

I closed my eyes. Hoping they would not betray me right now. Not when I'd finally found some peace.

"I thought the truth would fix how I felt. I didn't think she would get caught in the crossfire," I say, dropping my head.

"No," Xavier interjects, "you thought exposing the truth would free you and force Yari to feel what you never had the balls to say. We all know you love that woman."

My head falls even further.

"She deserved better," I mutter.

"She still does," Cam say, casting his line. "And you know better. Ya'll been cool since grade school man. You could have admitted that shit at any time. Be honest with yourself, man."

"Yeah," I couldn't even defend myself. I hop up from the edge of the dock. "You ever was afraid to swim even though you knew how?" I ask looking up at the stars forming against the top of the distant trees.

"Bro! What?" Xavier bursts out, slapping the back of my calf.

"Yep, you just lost me man," Cam says reeling his line closer.

"Ok I'm saying, like you know how to swim right. You've swam in pools, lakes, maybe even in some rough rivers too. But the ocean... the ocean terrifies you," I try explaining.

X squints and slowly nods his head, "Sure!"

I chuckle; he had no clue what I meant. "Anyway, Yari is the ocean. She terrifies me because her rip current can pull me in and under, even when though I swore I wouldn't get to close," I pause, watching my breath curl into the night air. "With her, it's not about knowing how to swim. It's about knowing you might drown and choosing to jump in anyway."

Cam looks up from his reel, quieter now.

"I've been doing laps in shallow water my whole life. Playing it safe. Holding my breath. With Yari... I wouldn't be able to touch the bottom. And that made me panic."

Xavier whistled low, "Damn."

Shrugging, "She makes me feel everything I buried. And instead of learning to float, I dragged us both under," I finish, finally feeling my tears arrive. This time I wasn't avoiding them.

Xavier was the first to grab me, Cam followed shortly after.

"I don't know how to fix it man. I fucked up bad. I put her in jeopardy of losing everything. Including her mind. All because I couldn't admit I was scared." My head hung low as my brothers breathed life over me. A few seconds later I felt Xavier tap us out of the huddle. I exhaled.

Just then the line Cam and X set up for me started pulling.

"Ooh shit.... Grab it!" Xavier shouts. I reach over and spin the reel, drawing the line in closer. "Ain't that some shit.... this dude ain't even want to fish and he out here catching," X continued.

"Must be the only fish swimming today," Cam joked as I pulled a pretty bass up to dock.

Xavier snapped a selfie of us with the fish. Grabbing the line and bringing the fish up to his face, "Listen you pretty fucker you. Yo ass is lucky we got burgers to put on the grill."

I unhook it, tossing it back.

"Your threat is the reason no other fish are out here tonight," Cam says, packing up the cooler.

We all laugh and finish gathering our stake out.

As the night continues to creep through the space between the trees, we decide to light a fire.

Bourbon makes its way around in gift shop mugs. The heat of it isn't enough to burn the pain off, but it sure helped soften its edges.

I was starting to feel again.

"I loved her before I even knew what I was doing," I say, "before André, or Cream. Before Anything. And I kept waiting for her to choose me. But she couldn't because I never really asked her to."

Xavier leans back in his rocking chair, "We've all been there, bruh. Loving from the shadows. Talking loud but never saying nothing."

I nod at that, "And then I lost my mom... and my trust. And I started thinking love needed proof. So, I planned a performance instead of a conversation. I just thought she would see in and she would know that it's been her this whole time."

Cam shook his head, "You gave her a funeral when she needed a confession. That dinner almost killed her man."

Silence stretched between them. Honest. Unforgiving.

"I don't know how to come back from that," I admit.

"You don't," Xavier says. "You come back to *yourself*. And maybe, God willing, you earn the right to sit across from her again one day. That's it."

I stare at the fire. The flames crackling in agreement with his words.

"I don't want to be him," I say. "My stepfather. He made my mom beg for things he could've given freely."

Cam met my eyes, "Then stop withholding from yourself too. Start by forgiving who you were when you didn't know better."

"Yeah," I sit up staring into the fire then lifting my mug, "Cheers to that."

"All we need now is some big booty mermaids to get the party started and cap the night off right," Xavier wiggles his eyebrows, dancing in his chair.

"Speak for yourself. Nevaeh would kill me," Cameron says matter-of-factly skipping no beats.

I laugh, "My boy's in love."

"Yeah he is," X laughs. "Cheers to that," he says as he stands. "I'm bout to FaceTime Trina fine ass. See if she'll show me a titty or something."

The cabin roars with laughter as Xavier disappears down the hall.

Later that night, I stand outside on the porch alone. The sky above the lake was velvet and starless. The kind of black that just swallows you whole.

I pull out my phone just to scroll through my photo roll.

I stop on a picture of Yari on her birthday two years ago. She's laughing, wearing a silk dress, wine in hand, eyes closed. I hadn't been the one to take it, but I'd been the one who'd never stopped staring at it.

"I see you now," I whispered into the night.

No reply came.

But the cabin knew.

On Sunday afternoon our weekend comes to an end. As we're preparing to head back to the city, Cameron and I took turns loading the truck. He stopped me mid stride "Hey man, you gone be alright?"

I ponder for a beat then gave him a close lip smile as I shrugged my shoulder. "I got to be alright. The damage is done... now I have to face the consequences." I admit. Shortly after X walks out.

"Yeah, yeah, yeah...chill with all that sappy shit. Hold yo head up and handle yo business." X states while hopping into the passenger seat and rolling down the window. "Let's hit the road yo!" I look over at Cam as he shrugged and walk around to the driver side. I take one last look back at the cabin as I open the backseat door and nod my final salute.

The gravel crunched under the tires as Cameron's truck rolled back into the city.

No music, just wind. I sat in the passenger seat this time,

elbows on my knees, eyes focused on nothing in particular. Roseville came into view like it always did; fast, loud, and distracting.

But I wasn't distracted. I was present now. I had faced something in those woods I hadn't had words for before.

Not grief. Because grief was what happened *after* you lost something.

Not shame. Because shame was the *belief* that you were inherently flawed most time without repair.

It was guilt. Because guilt was the *remorse* of my actions. Yari deserved my public plea for forgiveness.

What I felt now was… stillness. And somewhere beneath it, the slow hum of regret began to transform into responsibility. I knew I needed to man up and make things right. With genuine words and not performative actions. Yari wasn't the kind of woman who wanted performance.

Cam and X dropped me off outside my place.

"You good?" Cameron asks me.

"No," I answer, "but I'm here."

"That's enough," Xavier says, fist bumping me once before they drove off.

I stand on the curb for a moment before walking up to the door. I don't text her. Don't check her socials. Just let the night hold me.

Responsibility.

Interlude

Stay Anyway

The gray morning makes the silence feel louder. Pines line the road, still dripping from last night's rain, and steam curls from the lid of my coffee cup. The air feels clean, but heavy, like it knows what I'm about to drive toward.

I sit in my car, the cabin in the rearview, but my mind's already miles away. I rub my hands together, feeling the weight of everything I haven't said. Yari had always been my safe space. The one person who saw me beyond the gym owner, beyond the man carrying grief.

But today, I want to be her safe space too. I think about the way she smiled when I used to bring her breakfast-for-dinner, the salt on the rim of her margarita glass, the sweetness of strawberries we always shared. Simple things. But it was those simple things that made me feel closer to her, like maybe I could bridge that distance between our friendship and love.

I take a deep breath, feeling the fear of what might happen

if I crossed that line, but knowing either way, I had to show up for her. "Just give me courage," I whisper, a small prayer that doesn't ask for much. Not to win her, but to be steady. To be what she could lean on if the world tilted again.

I know she might not open the door, I fear what might happen if she does. I also remembered where she kept her spare key. Tucked inside the little terracotta pot beside her aloe plant on the front shelf. She told me once, laughing, that she never hid it too well, because she never wanted to live a life nobody could reach her in.

I smile at the thought, the gift of knowing her. And maybe this morning, I don't need her to invite me in. Maybe I just need to show up, anyway.

I put the car in drive, heading toward her place. The closer I got to her street, the slower I drive. Morning light is spilling through the blinds of every window but hers. I can see the outline of her balcony. The same one where we'd once sat too long, talking about everything and nothing all at once.

I don't know what waits on the other side of her door. But I know I'll be there. To show her that I can be the one to stay anyway.

Salt & Strawberries

Yari

The loft hadn't moved, but something inside me had shifted.

It was quiet. Not the sacred quiet my grandmother used to speak of, but the kind that pressed against you and made you feel as if cotton had been stuffed in your ears. Everything felt muted. Like the volume of the world had been turned down low and someone had forgotten to turn it back up.

The sunlight bled through the curtains, just enough to remind me that time was still passing.

I've been here for two days.

Same robe. Same couch. Same cup of tea sitting on the windowsill, long gone cold, half-sipped, the tea bag drowned in the steep.

I wrap a throw around my shoulders and pressing the warmth against my chest hoping it could undo something. My phone buzzes. I don't reach for it. I already knew who it was. Arias. Nevaeh. Maybe even Poochi.

Their messages sat unread in the group chat.

I wasn't hiding, I was a fly suspended in amber.

The fridge groans when I open it. The light hits me in an accusatory way, making me feel like a stranger in my own kitchen.

Three strawberries left in the produce drawer, softening but still red. I take them out. Let them sit on the counter and wait for them to tell me what to do.

My grandmother used to slice them slow, sprinkle sugar, and just a whisper of sea salt.

"Salt brings out the truth in sweetness," she used to say.

I wash them gently. Slice them carefully. Arrange them on a chipped ceramic plate, a somber ceremony. Sugar. Pinch of salt. Then nothing.

I don't eat. Just stare at them until my eyes water.

I realize the tears aren't just from staring too hard.

I'm grieving.

Grieving sweetness, grieving softness. Grieving how I used to reach for strawberries like they were joy in its edible form.

I wipe my cheek with the back of my hand and push the plate away.

Even sweetness spoils if you don't tend to it.

I leave the plate there and walk to the window, peeking just beneath the curtain. The city outside keeps moving. Joggers, traffic, a delivery guy arguing on speakerphone. I press my forehead to the glass to share my movement then closed my eyes; with hopes I could regain some stillness.

When I pull away, a faint smudge of mascara is left behind. I didn't bother to wipe it.

I lay down on the floor. Right in the sliver of light between the curtains. My breathing slows. I stare up at the ceiling and let silence cover me like a thin blanket.

Somewhere in the loft, Billie Holiday sings from a playlist I never forgot to turn off. Her voice hum faintly through the speakers, *"Good morning, heartache... sit down."*

I let it play.

Hours pass in seconds. Or maybe it's the other way around.

At some point, I pick up my phone.

Scroll to his name.

Jarell.

No new texts. No missed calls. Just the last message he sent.

> Jarell [2:11AM]: I didn't want this to
> touch you. I'm sorry it did.

I hover over the message. Press and hold. Copy. Reply. Delete. I don't make a choice.

I scroll a little further. Find an old voice note. A random one from months ago. He was teasing me about something, laughing between words like he had all the time in the world.

I press play.

His voice fills the room. Just loud enough to feel like he's somewhere nearby. His chuckle lands right in the center of my chest.

Like cotton my thoughts drown the noise of my surroundings and then the silence comes again.

I don't cry this time. Just press the phone to my stomach and close my eyes.

Suddenly there's a special kind of warmth radiating through the loft. I don't move I just drink it in.

Belonging.

Right here. Right now. This is enough.

As the recording came to an end, the scent of warm cedar and black cardamom slips into the room.

Familiar. Soft. Uniquely masculine.

The smell of comfort and calloused hands.

The inside of his hoodie late at night after a gym shower.

The curve of his neck when he buried his face in your hair to hug you without words. Because he knows they're unnecessary.

I don't open my eyes right away. I didn't need to.

I knew he was here. Not because he made noise. Jarell had always been light on his feet.

It was the energy shift. He arrived and the room exhaled, and so did I.

A single tear traces the valley of my sideburns until it finds the promise land of fibers in the rug beneath me.

The soul can see if you allow it to feel.

The word, allow, sits with me. I don't want to move yet. I wanted to *allow*. Give my soul the opportunity to feel the hurt it's been blind to longer than I would like to admit.

The gentle clink of a plate being moved from the counter. The shuffle of a trash bag being tied. The soft sounds of running water. He was cleaning. Not because he had to, but because he knew I hadn't.

I open my eyes, slow. Embracing the sun's attempt to dance with my eyelashes and across my cheeks.

From the floor, I can see the back of him in the kitchen. Hoodie sleeves rolled up to his forearms. Hair still slightly damp, like he'd showered and come straight here.

He moves like a memory and the present braided together. Deliberate, steady, protective.

He didn't ask me what was wrong. Didn't tell me to get up. Didn't try to fix me.

I didn't realize I'd drifted off until the scent of something new began to stir the air. Browned butter, thyme, and the warmth of something gently sweet.

Breakfast. My favorite meal.

I sit up slowly, the throw still draped over my shoulders, a shawl of grief and grace. Jarell had moved quietly, now standing at the stove with a cast iron skillet and the kind of focus that made everything feel sacred.

I don't say anything when he lights the candle near the stove. My favorite one, the one that smelled like sandalwood, roses, and rain.

I crawl my way over to the side of the couch, watching him, an artist in motion, floating effortlessly through my kitchen like it was his canvas. Spatula in hand like a paintbrush. The skillet his palette. Each flip, each stir, a masterful stroke painting the morning back to life.

Intentional.

Good cooking will bring you back to health. And this? This was medicine.

There were eggs. Soft-scrambled. Not too runny, not too stiff. Toast from the sourdough loaf he used to buy me from the market up the street because, in his words, "…you like that fancy shit." Crisped just enough to crunch at the edges but still bend in the middle. A little raspberry jam in a tiny ramekin.

Sliced strawberries on the side. Salt, and sugar, just right.

He plated everything like a man who knew healing wasn't grand. It was meant to be plated small. Bit by bit. Bite by bite.

He didn't say "eat." He didn't say "you need this." He just placed the plate on the coffee table, lighting a stick of incense, a habit he'd picked up from when I had migraines, and whispered, "Don't rush."

Then he picked up the remote. No words. No suggestion from me. Just instinct.

The TV blinked on. Low volume, soft light. An old episode of *Living Single* was already queued from the last time I needed background joy. Regine was fussing about rent. Maxine was eating someone's leftovers. And somehow, the laugh track didn't feel intrusive.

Jarell sat on the other end of the couch.

Just close enough for presence.

He doesn't look at me, didn't need to.

We eat in silence because sometimes healing sounds like breakfast and 90s reruns on volume 8.

After breakfast, I fall asleep again. This time, not from exhaustion but from ease.
Exhaustion drags you under.
Ease wraps around you and whispers, "You can rest now."

When I wake, the sun has shifted across the floorboards, tracing golden ribbons across the rug.

Jarell wasn't in sight, but his care lingered. The kitchen, clean. The plate I barely touched, quietly cleared. A note sits on the ottoman in his handwriting.

Run you a bath. Just let it help.

I stand, slower than I need to, and walk towards the bathroom.
It was already steamy. He hadn't just suggested it, he'd done it.

The lights were dim. A single candle flickered on the counter, the same sandalwood and rose I loved. A soft towel was folded neatly next to the sink. A clean robe, my slippers, and a glass of cucumber water sat beside the tub like it had always belonged there.

And the bath…

Lavender and pink sea salt spiraled in the water like galaxies. A few rose petals floated lazily on the surface. Arranged, in a pattern of their own choosing. The scent was floral and warm. Sacred.

I paused in the doorway, hand on the frame, unsure if I wanted to weep or exhale. Maybe both.

I stepped out of the robe, lowered myself into the water, and let my body sink. Let the tub hold me like it had been waiting.

Somewhere in the other room, Billie had been replaced by Coltrane, "Naima" maybe. Or "In a Sentimental Mood". I didn't know which. But the saxophone met the silence like a friend walking you home.

Steam kissed my collarbones. My breath evened and slowed, and for the first time in days, I remembered what it felt like to be cared for without question.

Not fixed.

Not rushed.

Not rearranged.

Just... seen.

I stayed in the water until the warmth faded and the candle burned low.

When I finally rise, the air outside the bathroom feels different, tended to. The kind of care you don't ask for, but feel in the bones. The kind that waits for you to return to yourself.

I wrap myself in the robe. Stepping out barefoot, I drape a towel over my shoulders, leaving my hair loose and damp. The scent of lavender clings to me, competing now with something heartier.

Butter. Citrus. A hint of roasted garlic. Dinner.

Jarell was back in the kitchen.

He moved quietly, like time belonged to him. Like he wasn't just cooking. He was stitching peace into the fabric of the evening.

He reaches into the fridge, pulled out fresh lemons, a piece of salmon, and that box of angel hair pasta I kept meaning to cook. He moved like he'd been in this kitchen before. Because he had. He's the one who used to refill the olive oil bottle.
The one who bought sea salt in a grinder because in his words "you deserve texture!"

I don't flinch when he turns down the playlist and lets the loft's brick walls hold the sounds of chopping, sizzling, and breath.

He'd already set the table. Just two plates, cloth napkins, and some cutlery. The low flame of the same candle he'd lit that morning. The strawberries I hadn't touched earlier were now washed and placed in a small bowl on the table. Salt and sugar perfectly balanced.

He was resetting the house. He was resetting me.

Not with grand gestures.

Just presence.

After a while, he looks over. Doesn't ask if I'm okay or permission to stay. He just meets my gaze, nods once, like he sees me, then goes back to slicing lemons.

I sink deeper into the couch, robe wrapped around me like armor undone, before rising to take my seat at the table.

For the first time in days, the silence doesn't feel heavy. It feels like rest. And the air smells like Jarell. Like something you forgot you missed until it's back… and the ache loosens.

When he finally seems close to being done, I get up and sit at the table. He sits across from me. He doesn't toast or offer a blessing. He just passes the plate. And I take it.

Not because I was ready to, but because he didn't need me to be. Because sometimes healing is a soft chair, warm food, and someone who doesn't need you to perform your pain. Just sit with it, and eat.

And I could finally taste what my grandmother meant. Salt doesn't ruin sweetness. It reveals it.

In the hush between us, with salt on my tongue and strawberries in reach. I remembered that healing doesn't ask for perfection or words. Just presence.

Sweet. Steady. Still.

Cracks in the Wallpaper

Yari

It had been quite a while since the loft smelled like browned butter and forgiveness.

Jarell hadn't been around when I woke up, but he hadn't completely disappeared either. The extra set of keys I left on the hook were gone. The dishes were done. The bath towel was folded back into the linen basket.

We hadn't spoken. No texts, no late-night voice notes. But I knew he'd been here. He gave me space, but not absence, and that was something.

I wasn't sure what we were yet, but I knew what we weren't anymore, angry. That was enough for now.

I spent most of my days floating. Not quite resting, not quite returning, just transitioning between movement and stillness. Between wanting to call him and finding comfort in letting the want be enough. Between grief and whatever lives after it.

So, when Poochi texted that she was stopping by and

bringing beignets, I didn't hesitate. She arrived with a pink pastry box, no makeup on, and mismatched earrings.

"You always look like a warning and a hug," I smile, letting her in.

"Good," she laughs, stepping over the threshold like she was checking the energy, "that means I'm consistent."

We set up shop on the couch. There were no words as she popped the box open and we reach for the warm fluffy dough in sync. Powdered sugar coated our fingers and the coffee table.

"You holding up?" she asks, after grabbing her second beignet.

"I'm... here," I shrug, dusting my fingers off before pulling my hair into a messy bun.

She nods slowly, eyes scanning the room looking for something unspoken.

"You ever notice how some things don't fall apart all at once? They just peel slow. And you don't even see the cracks in the wallpaper. Not 'til you've been still long enough to really notice."

I raise an eyebrow, "Is this about me or you?"

Poochi pops the last bite of pastry in her mouth and shrugs, "Both." She leans back, kicks off her slides, and sighs like the words had been waiting all day to come out. "Listen, I didn't tell you this before, 'cause you were already drowning in enough. But Vince, he's been seen around."

My breath catches. Vince was never seen unless he was up to something, waiting until he was on bullshit before showing his face to stir things up. He is addicted to power. And the thought of him brings the dough back up my throat.

"Where? Doing what?" I ask, my voice strained.

"Downtown of course. Talking to folks that he used to owe. Looking real comfortable."

"Comfortable?" I repeat.

Poochi's face hardens, "*Too* comfortable. Like the kind of

comfortable you get when you think people forgot, or forgave. I saw him outside the restaurant a few nights ago, late. He was standing under that busted streetlight near the back lot. Just... still. Like he was waiting on something or someone. Our eyes locked and my scars resurfaced. Yari, it felt like his pupils were committing arson. I can still feel the heat in my chest and the ash in my hair," she admits as tears fall to her cheeks. "He wasn't *alone.*"

That made me sit up.

"I didn't recognize the other man. He never turned around. Had on a ball cap, hands in his pockets, but" she pauses, "he moved like he knew power. Quiet, sharp, not new to it. Whoever he was, he knew how to stay unseen. Like he was trained for this." She shook off the unsettling memory.

"Anyways, it wasn't long. Vince looked right at me. Smiled like he didn't see me cry the last time he touched my skin. Then he walked off, and the other one went with him."

"You didn't see his face?" I ask.

She shook her head.

"No, but something about him felt familiar. Not in a way I could place. In a way I could feel. You know?"

I wrap the throw tighter around me.

"Why you think he coming back around?"

"I don't think, Yari. I know. He's up to something."

She reaches into her bag and pulls out a card – cream, embossed, linen stock, folded once. She opens it slowly.

To things we bury! May they stay buried.

"Where did you get this?" I ask, my stomach turning.

"One of your bartenders found it tucked behind the speaker booth. Said it looked older than the furniture. Like it'd been

waiting. Like it knew it would be found eventually. But baby…"
she places it on the table, her flat palm flat, "this is a message.
From someone who knows your fault lines."

I stare at the handwriting, Its Vince's.

My throat dries up, "Why now?"

"Because light makes shadows jealous," she says, locking
eyes with me, "And we been shining again."

I didn't respond. I couldn't.
The air felt charged.

We both sat still, the sugar-dusted silence stretching between
us.
Not wanting to move in case we disturbed someone watching.

The card sat on the table, ominously, like it already knew
what came next.

"I don't know what this means. But I know signs when I see
'em. And that one? That one's screaming." Poochi says, brushing
sugar from her lap and grabbing her bag. "Listen, if things shift. I
got people. Folks who don't flinch. You say the word; I'll call them
in."

"Pooch…" I start to say.

"Don't 'Pooch' me," she says, her tone soft but serious. "I
was wrong once. I won't be again."

As she opens the door to leave, a scent hits us. Sharp and
familiar.
Vetiver and black pepper. A scent I hadn't let myself remember,
until now.

She pauses, nose twitching, "You smell that?"

I nod, "It's him."

We stand in silence. The kind that's less quiet, and more
prophetic.

After she leaves, I walk to my bar, scanning it for the right
glass and go to make something to back me up from the cliff I was
standing on.

Textured rocks glass in hand; I fix myself a stiff Pins & Needles. One of the first signature cocktails I ever made for Cream. Bitterness and bloom in equal measure.

I add the ingredients to the shaker – slow, steady, intentional.

The velvet sting of warm apple brandy meets the bite of lemon and the depth of pomegranate molasses. Hints of rose and orange blossom soften the edges, while Creole bitters whisper something darker.

It's sweet, until it's not – floral, tangy, intriguing. It blooms, then it burns. You feel it where the truth lives, in the throat and just beneath the ribs.

I sit alone, glass in hand, card still open.
I stare at it, sipping slowly until the sun begins to lower.
And I hear my grandmother's voice, faint as gospel through an old church window, "The bloom is brief, baby. But the root remembers." Her voice fades, but the ache it leaves does not.

And I don't move. I can't. I just let the night sit next to me and take in the stillness of the loft. But not the kind of still that invites rest it's the kind that presses on your chest and asks, 'Are you sure?'

I'm not.

I look at the card again. Twelve words, one sentence.
But they echoed endlessly.

To things we bury! May they stay buried.

I trace my thumb over the edge. The ink had settled into the linen like it had been waiting. Like it hadn't been forgotten, just misplaced.

Then I saw it.

Across the room, near the baseboard, a hairline crack. The

floral wallpaper split like something beneath had pulled too hard and let go.

I stare at it longer than I mean to. I don't touch it. Just whisper, "I didn't even see you there."

Leaning in, I tilt my head to look at it more closely. A faint, but visible wound that won't heal.

"Everything that's pretty ain't whole," my grandmother used to say.

I built Cream like a poem. Intentionally curating a space full of soul. But now I couldn't stop wondering what I'd ignored while I was making it beautiful.

My phone buzzed on the counter with a name I don't want to see.
I don't answer, don't need to. Instead, I open a drawer and pull out the thick black notebook I use for the letters I never send.

Sitting at the kitchen island, I light a match, watch its flame grow, and light a candle before starting to write.

To the girl who thought silence meant safety...
You used to believe stillness was the same as peace.
But now you know! Stillness can also be waiting.
And what waits too long… rots.
You buried things thinking they'd dissolve.
But baby, roots don't disappear, they dig deeper.
Every name you didn't speak still lives in your chest.
Everything you forgave too quickly still hums under your skin.
You learned to smile through it.
Learned to host joy like a party, even when the walls inside you were peeling.
But now the wallpaper's bubbling.
And the cracks? They're starting to show.
It's okay. Let them.

Even a house with history can become a home again.
You just have to stop pretending the damage isn't there.

-Y

I close the notebook softly, don't sigh, don't cry. I just let it sit there. A small offering to the truth.

Then came the knock. Not frantic. Not loud. But just enough to say: *you're not done yet.*

I pad barefoot towards the door, unsure of who I hoped it would be.

When I open it, no one's there. Just a manila envelope with no return address.

The handwriting looks familiar, not Vince's. But someone close.

In slanted cursive across the top, it reads:

-Yari Gervais

I look down the empty hallway. I lift it cautiously, finding a polaroid inside from years ago.

It's me and my girls on Cream's opening weekend. The night we stayed late, drinking champagne and lighting too many candles.

Scrawled on the back in red ink:

You forgot who helped build this.
I didn't.

I stand still for a long time. Then, without thinking, I walk over to the mirror and place the photo up beside my reflection.

Me then. Me now. The smile hadn't changed., but the eyes... they'd stopped pretending. And that was something.

I slip the photo back in the envelope, folding the envelope in thirds, and tuck it into the drawer beneath the wine rack. The one no one checked but me.

I don't want to destroy it, not yet. Not until I understand the message inside the message.

I reach for my phone and dial Poochi's number. She answers on the second ring.

"You okay?"

"No," I whisper, "but I'm alert."

She pauses, "that mean what I think it means?"

"It means I need the locks changed at Cream, tonight."

"I'll call Javi and Dion. They'll handle it."

"And Pooch?"

"Yeah?"

"If you need to, check the drawer under my wine rack."

"Girl…"

"I'm not joking."

The silence on her end grew thick. Then I hear her anxiously fussing with her keys. "Noted. I'm already in the car."

Bloodhounds

Yari

It started with a knock that didn't wait. The kind that comes with a purpose.

Poochi stepped through my door like she'd never left. Phone in one hand, tension in the other.

"They're on their way," she said, not even bothering to take off her coat. I didn't ask who *they* were.

I trusted her enough to know that some names don't need breath.

She paced my living room like she was remembering old tactics. She's wearing holes in the hoping they'll give her something useful if she steps in the right place.

"You with me tonight? You ready?" She asks opening the front door.

"Yeah. Let's go." I grab my purse and keys, taking her invitation to escape a quiet that was starting to feel haunted.

"This ain't just about Vince anymore," she says as we wait

for the elevator, "it's deeper. He's pulled threads that fray more than just your name. And Yari," she pauses to look at me as the elevator doors open, "even with all my scars, I still don't know the shape of him, but I know betrayal when it fogs a room."

I swallow hard as we stepped into the elevator. I just wanted things to be normal again.

I stand behind the bar the next morning, watching the way the light hits the cracks in the brick walls like a dancer rehearsing their steps.

Arias is rearranging centerpieces for The Belle's Ball, talking color palettes and wine pairings like we weren't about to be walking into a war while dolled up in sequin dresses and beaded ballgowns.

I nod along through half the conversation, only catching a few phrases.

"Pressed florals on the name cards."

Nod.

"Jasmine-scented programs."

Nod.

"Open mic near the end of the evening. You sure?"

I nod again. Because even if I wasn't sure, I wanted to be.

It felt like everything around me was waving in and out of service. I couldn't piece together a complete thought.

My head was pounding and the lights were starting to cause a migraine.

"Hello, Boss Lady? Are you ok?" Arias questions with concern.

"Huh? ... Oh! Yeah! Well, no. I have a migraine. Let's take 20. I need to escape these lights," I respond using my hand like a visor.

"How about we table all this for the afternoon. I'll get the girls ready for tonight and we can go over final things in a few hours."

Her suggestion sounded like heaven.

As I rub circles into my temple, I hear a different voice, clear enough to break through the background noise.

"Or," says the voice behind me, soft but steady, "she can grab some lunch with me."

The hairs on the back of my neck stand to attention. I turn slowly.

He's standing just past the archway, hands in his pockets, eyes soft but certain. Jarell.

Dressed in black. Simple. Clean. No cologne I could name, but smelling like home. Cedar, sunshine, and something that made my knees quiver.

"I didn't mean to interrupt," he adds, glancing at Arias, "just thought I'd borrow her for an hour or two."

I blink, still pressing the heel of my hand to my forehead like the migraine might spill of my skull.

Jarell stands waiting, as if he knew there was a storm I'd been holding in my chest since the envelope.

Arias looks between us, sensing something I hadn't said. She gave me the smile women give each other when they know not to ask. I'm sure she felt my heartbeat skip.

"I'll go check on the seating chart," she offers, disappearing before I could nod.

The quiet between us is intentional. He's waiting to see if I'd flinch or fold.

"You good?" he finally asks.

I lower my hand, "I'm managing."

He nods, "I figured a little air and something warm might help."

"You planned something?"

"Sort of," he shrugs. "It's nothing wild. Just... not here."

My instinct was to say no. Too much was spiraling. Too many details begged for my attention. But that's the thing about grief wrapped in chaos. It tricks you into thinking you don't need kindness. I knew I needed this, and so did he. He always knew.

I exhale slowly, "Give me five."

He didn't tell me where we were going.

We drive in silence for most of the ride, music low, filling in for conversation without asking for attention. Every now and then, his fingers drum the steering wheel. Not fast. Just enough to let me know he was still thinking.

The car finally slowed in front of a place I hadn't seen in years. A little bistro tucked between a bookstore and a flower shop. The kind of place where time forgets to keep moving.

"This used to be our spot," I whisper, more to myself than him.

"I know," he says. "Thought maybe we could give it a second life."

He doesn't rush me. Just opened the door and waited for me to decide if I was ready to step into memory without drowning.

I am.

The host leads us to a corner table. The same table from that one afternoon sophomore year when we skipped class and split a lavender crème brûlée. The chairs were new but the energy of the place hadn't changed.

He waited until we finished ordering to speak again. Letting the silence breathe.

Then he leaned forward.

"Yari...," Jarell lifts his water glass, the condensation catching sunlight like it had something to say.

I look up.

"I don't need answers. Not right now. But I need truth. Even if it's quiet. Even if it's unfinished. Tell me."

My stomach twists. In... *relief.* Finally, someone was asking for truth without demanding clarity.

I open my mouth to respond, but my phone buzzes against

the table interrupting.

A text, the number unknown.

> Unknown Number [2:11 PM]: Just
> remember… people show up when they
> want to be seen.
> Ask him who was with Vince.

My hands go cold. I flip the phone over, face-down.

Jarell notices, "Everything okay?"

I force a nod. But something in me has shifted just enough for me to remember, not all healing is linear. And not every truth shows up in your own voice.

I press the screen face down against the table, swallowing the lump that has risen quick and hot in my throat. The message echoing louder than our silence.

Ask him who was with Vince.

I look up at Jarell. He was still watching me. Open. Calm.

I hated that I even had to wonder. Who would even know I was with Jarell right now and why would I have to ask about Vince slimy ass.

"Can I ask you something?" I probe, voice softer than I intended.

"Anything."

"Have you seen Vince?"

He doesn't flinch but his jaw ticks slightly.

"Not lately. Why?"

I study him.

"No reason. Just a name I've been hearing more than I'd like," I offer.

He nods, "He's been a shadow for a long time. That's how people like him move."

I let it hang there, the not-quite-lie. The truth wrapped in something polite.

I nod in agreement, starting to wonder if shadows were just people in disguise. If harm could dress itself as help and hold your hand.

Maybe now wasn't the time to press. But I'd felt the shift.

Even the quietest storms start with a change in air pressure.

We don't rush out, don't say much either. Just finish our meal and pay, stepping into the sun, and let the afternoon wrap around us, a quiet question neither of us was ready to answer.

The walk to the car is slow, measured. Like neither of us wanted to break whatever peace had grown between the tension.

He opens the passenger door for me, but stops me before I climb in.

"Yari…" he said, his voice low, almost unsure, "If I finally read…will you listen?"

I meet his gaze. Not wide-eyed, not searching. Just present.

I nod slowly, "If it's from the truth, I'll hear you."

His exhale was deep and long. He's been carrying the weight that question longer than he realized.

I was back at Cream before my body realized I'd left.

My phone lights up with another message from the same unknown number.

> Unknown Number [3:33 PM]: Hope
> you've reinforced the doors this time.
> Not every ghost knocks.

There was that lump again. Before I could swallow it a text from Dion appeared.

> Dion [3:35 PM]: Entry cams up. Back lot
> secured. No movement since Thursday,
> but we watching.

I exhaled, not in relief but in awareness.

That night, the wind shifted like it was trying to bring something with it.

Standing in the doorway of Cream, I stare out at the streetlights seeing if they held the truth.

Poochi's truck pulls up slowly. She steps out first. Two others, shadows I don't recognize, follow her. Something about their walk felt safe.

"This is Nyra and Roman," Poochi says. "They don't talk much, but they don't miss much either."

Nyra nods at me. Her eyes soft, hands calloused. Roman simply tips his chin.

Silent and loyal bloodhounds. Guarding against the ghosts showing up with keys. They didn't ask to come in, they waited.

Roman stands like a statue made of storm clouds. Nyra offers a gentle smile, the kind that says *I'll fight for you before I even know you.*

Poochi gives them a nod, and they follow her through Cream's front door like they already know the floor plan. Maybe they do. People like that don't forget blueprints. Especially ones built on wounds.

Standing by the threshold for a beat longer. The city hums its warnings and I let hints of hinoki, jasmine, and concrete wrap around me.

Then following them inside, I watch as Roman ran his fingers beneath the hostess podium, stopping to tap a hollow spot.

"Unsecure," he mutters.

Nyra kneels near the bar, eyes scanning the line of the baseboards looking for their tell.

"Someone's been watching the staff entrance," she says, "lint's too fresh. Someone brushed up against it yesterday."

I don't ask how she knew, I just believe her.

Arias looks up from her clipboard, wide-eyed, "Y'all

redecorating or...?"

"No," I answer, "we're reinforcing."

She doesn't press, just nods and pulls her curls into a bun, "Can I be of any assistance?"

"We usually work alone," Nyra spits before looking at me. "You trust her?"

My brows rise in response, "Yes, she's like my other arm."

"Since you seem to only have been born with two arms, we'll vet her first. Then my darling..." she says leaning in to meet Arias eyes, "and only then can you assist." She extends her hand and Arias shakes it before heading to the booth near the back corner.

"Damn," I say into the silence they leave behind.

"Nyra don't play. I'm going to have Dion run me footage of the activities that's been happening near this entrance," Poochi says, passing a black case to Roman.

We all have our roles. Today, mine is to breathe and pretend the air didn't feel different.

The streetlights hum as we pull away from Cream. The city looks soft in the dark, all blurred halos and distant horns, but I knew better. Beauty can hide a lot of danger, and I'm tired of mistaking one for the other.

When we pull up to my building, Poochi squeezes my hand once before I get out. She doesn't say anything, she doesn't have to.

My loft feels colder than usual when I walk in, as if the space felt my absence.

Dropping my bag by the door, I take off my earrings and quickly tie up my hair. The last thing I do before stepping into the shower is call Dion.

"What's up? I got eyes on you. It's looking good!"

"Good, thanks. Do me a favor would you?"

"Ok, give it to me."

"Run the back lot again," I say, "and check those rooftop

locks. I don't trust how the wind's been moving lately."

"Got it. Get some rest, we got you!" Dion reassures me.

I hang up. Trying to put my nerves to rest.

I light my candle without a prayer. Just breathing slowly. Burning it long enough for me to try and remember who I am.

I watch the steam crawl through the bathroom, carrying stories the walls weren't ready to release. Each layer of clothing felt heavier than it should've, like memories had stitched themselves into their seams. I peel them off slow in surrender.

Under the water, I let the silence soften me. No music, no mantras, Just the rhythm of my breath and the heat of knowing I was still here.

Still here, feeling a kind of tired that no amount of sleep could cure. So, I let the droplets rinse off the questions I couldn't ask. Let them trace the parts of me I'd been hiding, even from myself.

By the time I left the steam and slipped into bed, the candle had curled to half its height. The room smelled like Kyara, Oud Vanilla and Egyptian Rose. Love like silk, kissed across my collarbones, and only truth remained, nothing false could stay. Now I knew the difference, between rest and running. Between quiet and warning.

The crack in the wallpaper hadn't widened, but it hadn't healed either. It just sat there in between.

Tonight helped me realize that not everything that's broken needs to be fixed. Some things just need to be acknowledged.

I know that feeling all too well.

Poisonous Poppies

Yari

The morning light climbs through my windows like a gentle caress. Soft, quiet, and full of apologies. The light touches my loft like a lover, lingering on my collarbone, slipping beneath silk, warming every window like it knows this will be the last time.

I move slower than usual, letting each gesture mean something. My robe drags softly across the floor. The kettle whistles. I was making rose tea. I stir honey in with one of those fancy candied spoons.

I sit barefoot at the counter, eating mango slices and a bowl of mixed berries. Saxophones and Trumpets hum from the record player, like they're keeping secrets.

I open my skylight windows. Let the breeze brush past my edges. Let it remind me I am alive. Let it carry away the pieces I'm no longer obligated to hold.

The air smelled like peace and promises: Kyara, lemon balm, and something else, something beautiful. Like my rooftop flower garden had burst with blooms that perfumed the air above the loft.

On the stool beside me sits a tiny card. Scrawled in gold ink: *The Belle's Ball – A Bloom to Remember.*

I read it twice. Then close my eyes. Today was supposed to be beautiful. But beauty doesn't always warn you before it begins to bleed. I let the words stitch themselves into my memory. Neat, sacred, irreversible.

Tonight isn't just an event., it's a celebration. A symphony for the version of me that survived.

As I get dressed, I trace the story written in my skin. Constellations mapped across my body, drawing soft, invisible lines from mole to mole with my eyes. Each one a punctuation mark in a sentence I was still learning how to read.

The mirror catches me in the act. And this time... my reflection doesn't flinch. She looks back steadily. Not perfect, not untouched. But aware and present. Like she finally knows she belongs to herself.

The gown waits on its hanger. Bias-cut silk, the color of cream touched by dusk, the gold and blush beading accenting it effortlessly like wet moonlight.

I pin my curls half up and leave the rest wild, like a garden that refuses to be tamed. But before it touches my skin, I reach for the small amber bottle, *Requiem Bloom.* I hold it like a relic, thumb tracing the edge of the glass as if memory is etched there.

I unscrew the cap slow. Let the weight of the scent rise like a prayer uncapped. I don't rush.

One wrist. Then the other. Rubbing them together gently, like I'm waking something ancient. A drop behind each ear, where secrets gather and lovers lean close. Then the dip of my collarbone. A kiss of scent for the parts of me that hold me upright when nothing else can. I press my fingertips to the bottle's mouth once more, just barely, and anoint the space at my heart. Just above the seam where the dress will meet my skin. Where breath has broken once and bloomed again.

The fragrance curls around me like silk remembering fire, rose and pear, smoke and prayer. A story without need for a single word.

By the time I step into my gown, the scent has settled. Not loud, but certain. A final note in the song of becoming.

Tonight, I don't just wear perfume. I wear the confidence of myself.

Cream shimmers in the low light like it has something to prove. Guests float in, draped in jewel tones and soft silks, laughter brushing the walls like perfume. The quartet plays in the background, the clink of flutes punctuating the night.

I walk the perimeter slowly, absorbing it all. The candles, the polished glass, the ribbon-tied menus resting like promises on each table.

Then I catch my reflection in the hallway mirror, the vintage one we'd reinstalled last fall. A touch of nostalgia, Arias had called it. But it wasn't nostalgia that stopped me. It was the faint crack in the lower right corner. Barely noticeable now, but I knew it by heart.

André hated that mirror. Said it made the room feel broken. He told me to cover it. I had. But tonight... I left it uncovered.

The Belle's Ball wasn't just a soft reopening. It was a reclamation. A whisper to the world that I was still standing. Still curating. Still here.

I named it in honor of Monroe Belle University, the place that taught me how to speak before I ever understood my voice. We sent invitations in thick cream envelopes with gold foil script:

An Evening of Legacy & Light.

Arias had convinced me it needed to be more than a return. It had to feel like a coronation.

"I want the women who built you to see what you've built," Arias had said. "And I want them to smell expensive roses while they do it."

So, we filled Cream with flowers, everywhere.

Magnolias drape like ancestral hands from the stairwell, their creamy petals brushing softly against the bannisters, fragrant with Southern memory.

Blush roses curl into the chandeliers, suspended in glass globes and gold fixtures like blessings mid-bloom. White tulips crown each table in low, glass bowls. Their stems wrapped up in silk ribbon, their petals open wide like they have nothing to hide. Lavender sprigs tucked into each linen napkin left the scent of calm on every lap.

Orange blossoms and freesia fill the entryway, subtle but arresting, clinging to the air like anticipation.

Even the bathrooms are laced with florals. Single-stem peonies floating in cut crystal, eucalyptus hanging in the steam like ritual.

The air didn't just smell like florals, it carried them. You could taste the jasmine on your tongue. Feel the gardenia wrap itself around your wrist like perfume. It was sacred and lush, like someone had taken a whole garden and taught it to whisper.

A pianist played near the front. Nothing too emotional, just enough to cradle the hush between the clinking of champagne flutes and murmured names from Monroe Belle history.

And then, the harpist. Young, radiant, braided crown on her head, fingers moving like breath. Beside her, a violinist, warm mocha skin, eyes closed, bow moving slow and deliberate. All women, all beautiful, all melanated.

It doesn't feel like entertainment. It feels like an offering. Like every note was stitched with legacy. Like the music had been waiting for this moment just as long as we had.

Cream didn't just sparkle. It came to life.

I continue taking it all in, before the laughter could clutter the room. Arias was already pacing the front desk, clipboard in hand.

"Lighting is soft but not sleepy," she says, half to herself. "And the stemware came in crystal, not pressed glass. They're gonna feel this, Yari."

I nod, slowly. "Feels luxurious in here."

She smirks, "Exactly the vibe."

Just then, the pianist took a break. And before the next set could begin, one of my old playlists must have slipped into the queue. A song drifted in, low and familiar. The kind that coils behind your ribs when you're not looking. I hadn't heard it since our second month of dating.

I looked toward Arias. She catches the shift instantly, crossing the room with her phone in hand, and swapping it mid-note. She doesn't say a word. But she looks at me like she knows.

I nod, just enough for her to see it, and keep walking. I round the corner to the back lounge, needing a breath, just one. Somewhere between the candelabras and the curated smiles, I could feel my nerves beginning to whisper again.

Then she gestures to a single table by the window. One reserved for alumni guests who'd flown in. There, folded neatly a top a magnolia blossom napkin, was an old Cream coaster. From our first run. The kind with the original logo. Soft gold embossed on matte ivory. We'd only printed fifty. They were never meant to last.

"Who found this?" I ask, brushing my thumb along the faded edge.

"Isaiah," Arias says. "He was organizing the back bar setup and said it slipped behind one of the old drawers. Must've been there since the first month."

I blink, saying nothing. We both know some things don't

return unless they're ready to be seen.

I run my finger along the curve of the Cream lettering, thinner than our current font, a little uneven. Back then, we didn't have a brand team. Just a prayer and a printer. That coaster was a relic. A timestamp. A quiet reminder of what it looked like before the world started watching.

"Do you want me to move it?" Arias asks.

I shake my head.

"No. Leave it."

Because something about it feels like a whisper. Like the past tapping gently on the shoulder of the present, not to haunt, but to hand off a baton.

And I have a feeling this wouldn't be the last time the past came bearing gifts. This isn't just an event. It's a rebirth, and everything has to sing.

I walk to the bar next. Run my fingers over the polished oak. Watching as the bartender lined bottles with silent reverence.

"We have a new drink list," Arias adds behind me. "The headliner? Strawberry sage spritz. With a salt rim. Thought you'd appreciate the nod."

I do. I smile, but it didn't reach all the way. Not because I'm not proud. I am. But something tugged at the edges of the room, like a draft from a window I hadn't noticed was cracked.

Guests began to arrive in waves. Legacy dripped off their shoulders like perfume. Women in pearls. Men in linen suits. Quiet elegance. Heavy presence. And somewhere near the piano, Jarell appears.

He doesn't walk in like a man trying to be seen. He comes in like a breath. Like a pause between songs. Just enough. He didn't speak to me right away. Just nods. I nod back.

We both know the language. We aren't fixed. We aren't even clear. But we aren't fractured. For now, that's enough.

The Belle's Ball unfolded like a slow pour. Smooth.

Intentional. There was laughter, gentle clapping. A moment when the Dean of Monroe Belle raised a toast in my honor.
I hear my name echo against the walls. It didn't sound broken this time.

The night was beautiful. I could feel the love draped over the building like silk.

Imani and Nevaeh waltzed over, Arias in between them like a proud escort.

"Yari, babes, it's beautiful in here," Nevaeh beam, drawing me in for a hug.

"It is," Imani adds. "You really bounced back, girl. *Cream* is still the shit. Business ain't slowing down anytime soon." She high-fived Arias, who grinned in agreement.

I blink back the tears building behind my lashes. I was so tired of crying, but these are the good kind. The kind that cleansed.

"I wouldn't be able to do any of this without y'all. You've held me down, for real." My voice cracked. "Thank you."
They smiled like they knew. Like they'd been waiting for me to stand up again.

"Excuse me, ladies," I say, gently stepping back. "I need to freshen up. I don't wanna mess up my makeup."

I slip into the bathroom, leaning over the sink, and exhale slowly. The tears come anyway. Quiet, hot, grateful. I dab the corners of my eyes. Take a breath and look at myself.

I wasn't the same woman who stood here weeks ago wondering if I'd survive it all.
Tonight, I wasn't just surviving. I owned my power. *And It Felt… Good!*

Then…his voice.

"Good evening, everyone… I'm Jarell. Is it okay if I read for y'all?"

I froze.
What?

Jarell?

Reading *his* poetry?

He never shared his words, not with anyone. Always said he was too honest for the mic. That his truths weren't for the crowd.

"I was hoping by the time I got up here," he continued, "I'd be able to spot the lady I wrote this for…"

I gripped the edge of the sink. My breath hitched. He was looking for me.

"She did say," he added, voice thick, "if it was truth, she'd hear it. So… truth is all I have tonight."

The pianist shifted melodies, like they'd rehearsed this without knowing it. A blend of harmony that sounded like 90s love songs laced through the room. Slow, aching, familiar. The harp hummed alongside her, and the brass, sax, trumpet, found their places in the song.

I rushed to blot the rest of my tears, my heart galloping. I needed to *hear* him. And what he gave me… was everything.

You ever heard a voice,
So full of home that
You ain't realize you was homeless 'til it left the room?
That's you.
I ain't known quiet,
until your silence.
A room once full of saxophones
Felt like static
When you weren't in it.
Baby Girl
You move like Sunday morning after a Saturday storm.
Like blues before it broke,
Like rhythm that knows its way back.
Like me

Before I forgot how to dance.
I've been walking through my days
On mute.
Tasteless.
Weightless.
Living in grayscale
Since you left the room colored.
I didn't know how much I needed balance
'Til mine walked out with a silk robe on.
Didn't know how bland the world could be
Without your voice seasoning my name.
You ain't a song, Baby Girl.
You a whole genre.
You the ache in Donny's voice.
The forgiveness in Anita's hum.
The heartbeat behind Marvin's questions.
You the balance in the bridge
Where the pain and peace meet.
You steady
And I've been crooked too long.
I need you.
Not as a crutch
But as the compass I was too prideful to follow.
I was drowning in silence
While you were the sound
Of everything I swore I didn't deserve.
While talking soft to the walls of your loft
Like they listened better than me.
You reminded me
That love ain't loud,
It's loyal.
It shows up with strawberries and sugar with a pinch of salt
On a Thursday morning

When the world's falling apart.
I messed up.
Took the sacred
And called it familiar.
Treated the divine like it was disposable
And I'm sorry
For leaving you holding the weight
We were both meant to carry.
So, if grace has another verse left for me
Let me carry my part.
Hell, let me carry yours too
If it gets too heavy again.
Let me be your rhythm.
Your exhale.
Your always.
I know now...
Without you,
My life hums off-key.
The world don't sound right.
The light don't sit right.
My chest don't rise right.
And I'd trade every lyric I've ever known
Just to be the baseline you trust again.
I love you.
Louder this time.
Softer too.
With both hands.
And a back strong enough to hold us
Even when the melody breaks.
You remind me of rhythm.
Of home.
Of the parts of me that still deserve music.
And I'm here.

Louder.
Softer.
Still.

When the last word fell from his lips, there was a hush. The kind of silence that kisses a room after a miracle. Then applause, soft at first, then rising like a tide.

But I couldn't move. I stood just outside the curtain. Shaken. Seen. Surrendered.

Jarell stepped off the stage without another word. Not toward the crowd. Not toward me. But upstairs, back to the private suite where those moments had once damn near broken me.

My feet moved before I could question them. I hadn't been up there since that night.

When I reach the suite, he's standing by the window, hands in his pockets, eyes low.

"Jarell…"

He turns. And I swear, whatever was left between us rushed into that space like a tide.

"I meant every word," he said. "I didn't come here tonight to make noise, Yari. I came to make it right."

"I know," I whisper, voice small. "I heard you."

"I was scared," he admits. "Of failing you. Of needing you too much. Of being needed by someone that pure. But I see now… you weren't asking me to be perfect. Just present."

"I didn't want you to carry everything," I say. "Just something."

He steps closer. "I'm ready now. For all of it. Yours. Mine. Ours." And when his hand find mine, I don't pull away.

We don't say I love you, we didn't need to. He'd already sung it, line by line. And I had heard every syllable.

His eyes meet me at the truth. We had been dancing around

this desire for so long. But I know now. Jarell had seen me, just as I always hoped he would.

His hands wrap around the small of my back, pulling me closer.

"Just be my Yari," he whispers. "I'll handle the rest."

His voice was velvet and smoke, full of weight and want. His eyes… they caressed me. And for the first time, I understood what it meant to be seen by a man.

Before I could respond, he held my face, and kissed me. And it was deeper than oceans. He wasn't a boy trying to win. He was a man… who had finally come home.

He finds his answer in my body language. And for the first time, my melt wasn't out of desperation. It wasn't because I thought I had to give something away to be wanted. It was because I had no choice but to receive it. To receive *him*. Because what was finally for me, was more sacred than words could describe.

It's Jazz and It unraveled me with all its mood swings and honesty and promise and noise. And for a moment, the music, the guests, the past all blurred.

There's only this. Only us.

Eventually, the night calls us back to the present. We return to the lounge hand in hand, fingers laced like a new kind of promise. And when our people see us, they don't clap or cheer, they just *smile.* The kind of smile you give when you know something sacred has just taken root.

Xavier caught sight of us first. He raises his glass and knocks his knuckles against the mic with that familiar, lopsided grin.

"Now I don't wanna make it weird," he says, "but I think we just witnessed a love poem come to life."

The crowd chuckles.

"To Yari and Jarell, may the next chapter be softer than the last. And may we all be lucky enough to find someone who sees our broken parts and stays anyway."

Glasses clink, laughter rings, and even Arias lets out a proud sigh and mutters, "Finally."

It isn't loud or wild, but it's enough. A moment carved in champagne and stillness.

The night begins to dwindle. The music quiets as heels come off and guests trickle toward the doors in clusters of joy. I slip away for just a second, to drop off flowers gifted to me by guests at the front desk, to grab a last-minute thank-you card for the harpist, and to breathe.

That's when I see it. At the front desk, nestled between a thank-you card from the event planner and a tray of comped champagne tokens, is a floral arrangement. Small, minimalist, stark red poppies. No note, no vendor label, no delivery record. Just poppies.

My breath catches. I hadn't seen them in years. Not since Vince handed me one on a random Tuesday. No occasion. No card. Just a smirk and a...

"Because it reminded me of you."

Back then, I thought it was sweet. Thoughtful. Now I know better. It had always been a warning. The kind of bloom that poisons slowly. That looks too bright to be safe. That lingers longer than it should.

A chill sweeps across my shoulder blades.

Arias walks up, mid-sentence about something mundane, seating charts or champagne costs. She pauses when she sees my face, then follows my gaze.

"That yours?" she asks quietly.

"Not in the way you think."

She steps between me and the flowers, her body moving on instinct to shield me.

"Want me to get rid of it?"

I shake my head. "Not yet." Because even poison teaches. And I needed to know what's blooming next.

I slip out onto the private side terrace for air. The one no one ever really uses, except staff on breaks or guests who need a moment to themselves.

The door clicks shut behind me. The breeze lifts the hem of my dress. I let it. Everything in me needs a minute to exhale.

And that's when I see it. Tucked between two bricks of the terrace railing, a folded square of thick paper, cream-colored, just like our RSVP cards from back in the day. The kind I used to handstamp myself, when I still believed the right font could make people feel something.

I unfold it. No name, no signature, just one line, in blocky, familiar handwriting:

You've always been a flower, Yari. But flowers rot too.

My breath catches. The ink looks fresh. The words, specific, intimate, intentional. I stand there too long, clutching paper that suddenly feels like it was pulsing in my hands.

By the time I turn around, the terrace is empty. No footsteps, no breeze, the weight of something resurfacing that should've stayed buried the only thing left.

I reach for my phone with trembling fingers and my thumb hovering above the screen before I even know what I'm about to say.

Text Poochi. Now.

That was the instinct. My spirit didn't have time to debate it.

Yari [11:22 PM]: You up?

Three dots, then nothing, and them a reply.

Poochi [11:23 PM]: Always.

Poochi [11:24 PM]: You good?

I stare down at the message. My heart is pounding out a rhythm I don't recognize. Not quite fear. Not quite rage. But the kind of knowing that lives in the pit of your stomach when God is telling you... look again.

I snap a quick photo of the note, fold it back neatly and slip it into my clutch for evidence.

Yari [11:26 PM]: Not really.

Yari [11:27 PM]: I need you.

Another pause. Then:

Poochi [11:28 PM]: Say less. I'm on my way.

Somewhere behind me, the music inside builds for a final slow jam. The night isn't over, but something has ended. And something else, something ugly, has just begun to bloom.

I stand there, frozen in silk and suspicion, surrounded by beauty but unable to enjoy it. The stars look the same, the city hums like nothing has changed, but I have. And I can feel it in my bones, something is shifting under the surface. Unseen, unspoken, unfinished.

I take one last deep breath and head back inside.
I need to shake hands and smile, even though something in my gut is telling me to run.

"There she is." The house mother of The Beta Bellas reaches out for my hand. "This was beautiful, young lady. I am so very proud of you." She squeezes my palm before kissing my cheek. "You've outdone yourself. I'll be in contact. We've got a few events coming up: interest meetings, a gala. I'll be sure to let the board know you're the woman for the job."

I smile through my inner panic. I need Poochi here, now.

The music had fallen to a soft lull. Empty flutes lining the bar. Half-eaten desserts leaning on lace napkins like they can't finish the night either.

Cream is winding down, like a breath that had finally been released. A few guests lingered, exchanging last laughs and long hugs. The glow is warm, but the air feels thinner somehow.

Poochi arrives not long after my text, wrapped in a trench coat and carrying a heavy silence. Her eyes scan mine and she doesn't need to ask questions. She just stands beside me, unmoving. A quiet anchor in a storm I had yet to name.

Jarell eventually finds me again, gently grabbing my hand. "You ready?" he asks.

Not really, but I nod.

We say our goodbyes slowly. Nevaeh, Cameron, Imani, Xavier, Arias. Everyone peeling off into the night one by one, until Cream is almost empty again. Almost how it began.

Jarell and I step outside, Poochi anchored at my other side. The street's quiet. The the glow of streetlamps feel like safety, and the cool breeze kissed your shoulders like a lover.

"I'm going to pull my car around and take you both to Jarell's," Poochi says, unhooking her arm from mine.

"Thank you," I whisper.

"No worries. I gotchu. I'll be right back." She disappears around the corner.

Jarell leans down and kisses the side of my head. "I'm proud of you, baby girl," he says, lifting my chin before kissing my lips.

"Thank you." I blush. I hadn't ever thought about what I'd call him if we ever became what we are.

"Damn. I forgot something," he says suddenly, patting his pockets. "My notebook. The brown one. It has everything in it."

"I'll wait right here," I smile, "You know I'm not leaving without you."

He kisses my lips again. "You better not. I need you." He grins the kind of grin that makes you believe the mornings are worth sticking around for. Then he jogs back toward the doors.

I turn to face the street, heels clicking softly on the pavement as I wander a few feet forward. I can still hear music inside Cream, playing faintly. Like a memory that's already fading.

Then, **gunshots.**

Pop. Pop-pop.

Fast.

Sharp.

Close.

I spin around. But before I can scream, I hear the click of heels approaching fast. Then an arm, a grip, a voice I don't recognize, and pain, from where my wrist twisted behind me. A sharp cry stole from my throat before I can even say his name.

The world spins. My body crashes into something cold and metallic. **A van,** unmarked, with its doors swung open like a mouth waiting to swallow me whole.

"JARELL!"

It's all I had time to yell before a hand smothers the sound. Before the night swallows me and the van doors slam shut behind me.

Epilogue
Blood In The Garden

Poochi

I don't take long.

I swing the car around like I said I would. Looped the block once, music low, nerves steady.

It's quiet, late-night Roseville quiet. The kind that *usually* means peace.

I park in front of Cream, headlights flashing across the sidewalk, but I don't see them. No Yari. No Jarell.

I turn the music lower but don't cut it off. The engine sits idle.

Check my phone, one message waiting. A photo of the note.

You've always been a flower, Yari. But flowers rot too.

I stare at the screen for too long.

A chill climbs the back of my neck.

I step out the car, scanning the block. Still nothing.

And then, by the curb, half-shadowed under the streetlight, a heel. *Her* heel.

The nude stilettos she swore she'd never wear again but did tonight because "it's a rebirth," she'd said.

I take careful steps toward it, heart thudding louder with each stride.

Next to it, barely there, but real, a too red petal. Pressed into the pavement like it had been crushed beneath panic.

Something wasn't right.

"Yari?"I called out, voice sharp. No answer.

I crouch by the heel, picking it up gently. It's still warm, still hers.

My phone buzzes again. A single text from an unknown number.

Unknown Number [12:52 AM]: 🌺

My fingers tremble.

I looked up at the building, then back at the empty street. The wind's shifted trying to clue me in on the things I don't know.

I am rooted in place, one heel in my hand, a warning in my phone, and the kind of silence that didn't feel accidental.

Something had gone wrong. *Very* wrong.

I wasn't about to let it stay that way.

I toss the heel in the passenger seat and slammed the car door. Not even bothering to lock it.

Cream's front door is cracked open, just wide enough to

make my stomach twist.

I stepped inside slowly, heels clicking like threats against the marble floor. The only sound in a too quiet building. Only the exit signs glowed.

"Jarell?" I call out. No answer.

Then, a low groan. Barely audible.

I move faster, heart pounding in my ears. That's when I see him.

Face down, one arm curled beneath him, the other outstretched like he'd been reaching for something, or someone.

"JARELL!" I cry out, dropping to my knees.

His lip is split. His pulse is faint but present. His breathing rapid.

Theres's blood on his temple, his shirt is soaked through. A notebook clutched in his hand.

I shake him gently, too scared to move him too much. "Jarell, wake up. Jay, come on, wake up."

He groans again, eyes fluttering, mouth parting on a single word,

"Yari," he rasps.

Then nothing, breath, blood, and the sound of my own heart breaking into pieces as I realized that whatever this was, it was never meant to be just a warning.

This was a war.

"Jarell," I whisper, "I need you to hang on."

His eyes flutter open, unfocused. Blood trickles down the side of his face and onto his collar. His breathing shallow, more ragged.

I reach into my coat pocket, pulling out my phone, and hit the contact I'd hoped I would never need.

Two rings, then a low, clipped voice answers, "Yeah?"

Something in me snaps into place at the sound of that voice. The version of me that don't cry, don't beg. The version that *moves.*

"It's me," I reply. "I need a trace, a sweep, and a burner, now. Someone took Yari."

A pause, then, "You sure?"

I look down at Jarell's body. His shirt torn, knuckles scraped, blood still flowing from his wounds. I see the nude heel in my mind, sitting on the floor by the front desk. The petal still pressed in the doorway, a signature.

"I'm sure."

Another pause, longer this time.

"I'll send the address to meet. I'm ten minutes from Cream."

The line goes dead.

I exhale, stand, and wipe my hands on my coat. Jarell stirs, mumbling her name again.

"Don't worry," I say softly, "I got her. I got help coming for you."

His breathing starts to stutter.

"Jarell! Jarell! You have to hold on. I need you to press down, right here," I press my scarf to the gunshot in his side.

I need to get to Yari's.

Then I remembered what she once said, "If you need to, check the drawer under the wine rack."

I look around Cream one last time, all this beauty, all this quiet. None of it felt safe anymore.

Then I turn to the door, grab my clutch, and head back into the night.

Sliding into my car, trying to hold it all in.

Somebody wanted a war?

The recipe for payback's been tested and perfected over the years. It's time to remind them who really iced the CAKE.

A Letter from Yari

To the one holding my story…

Hey.

If you've made it this far, then you know, this wasn't just about love. Not really.

It was about silence. And the weight of it. The kind that buries you slowly while the world calls you strong for surviving it. The kind that teaches you to smile when your spirit is limping. To pour into people while you're running on empty. To perform joy so well, you almost forget you're pretending.

I didn't write this to be understood. I lived it to become real. To remember that I was more than what hurt me. More than what I lost. More than what I gave away just to feel wanted.

There were chapters I didn't want to revisit. Moments I almost edited out because they didn't make me look powerful, but they made me honest. And I owe myself honesty now. Maybe for the first time.

If you saw yourself in any of these pages, in the heartbreak, in the confusion, in the softness I didn't know how to hold. I want you to know I see you too.

I see the version of you that's been overlooked. I see the love you gave that wasn't protected. I see the questions you ask yourself when no one's looking. I see the woman you're becoming, and how hard it is to unlearn needing to be everything for everyone.

Healing is not linear. Desire doesn't make you weak. Wanting to be chosen does not make you desperate. And choosing yourself doesn't mean you failed anyone else. It means you finally decided to stop bleeding for people who never learned how to hold you.

There were nights I laid in bed next to someone and still felt like I was sleeping alone. There were days I stood in a crowded room and felt completely unseen. But I kept showing up. Not because I had it all figured out, but because somewhere deep down, I still believed I deserved more.

And I do. So do you.

I'm still learning what wholeness feels like. Still learning how to take up space without apologizing for how loud my love is or how much it costs to be this soft.

But I made a vow to myself: never again will I abandon my own bloom just to keep someone else's garden alive.

So if you're holding this, know you're not alone.

You are worthy. Even when the mirror's foggy. Even when the people you trusted go quiet. Even when your softness is misunderstood. Especially then.

Take your time. Reclaim your name. Speak your truth, even if your voice shakes. Choose peace that doesn't come with conditions. And remember, your joy doesn't have to be small to make other people comfortable.

Thank you for reading my story. Even the messy parts. Especially the ones I was afraid to say out loud.

Because I'm not just healing. I'm remembering. And that matters.

With love,

Yari

Acknowledgements

First and always **to God**. The One who called me by name before I ever knew my voice. The One who taught me that breaking is not burial, and silence is not death. Thank You for being the breath between the lines, the steady hand guiding every word, every rewrite, every moment I wanted to quit. Thank You for the visions that arrived in dreams, for divine timing that interrupted my plans, and for the strength to carry what felt too heavy. Thank You for peace that wrapped itself around me when doubt tried to choke the page, and for mercy that waited for me on the other side of every surrender. Without You, none of this exists, and with You, everything is possible.

To my **husband**, *MTTM (He knows what that means)*. My safest place, my patience, my home. Thank you for loving me through the chaos of creation, for letting me disappear into notebooks and long nights, for bringing me tea and prayer instead of pressure. Thank you for holding me when I was exhausted, for covering me when I was fragile, and for believing in this story even when my hands were shaking. Your love steadied my pen. Your loyalty strengthened my spine. I could not have carried this dream without you.

To my **family and friends**, thank you for the grace you gave when my world narrowed into chapters and deadlines, for the calls I couldn't answer, the plans I cancelled, the holidays spent writing instead of resting. Thank you for cheering me on even in silence, for understanding that sometimes purpose demands solitude. Your support allowed me the space to fall back in love with writing, not as an escape this time, but as a calling.

To the **ones who came before me**, those whose names live in my bloodline and whose stories were never written; I honor you. Thank you to my ancestors who endured shackles and silence so I could hold language freely. Thank you to the women who stitched strength out of survival, who whispered prayers over generations they would never meet. Thank you to every voice that was muted so mine could rise. You are the ink in my veins. You are the reason I can write without fear. I carry you in every comma, every breath, every page.

To those I have loved and lost; I miss you. Your memory is a compass, your legacy a lamp. I hope I have made you proud.

And to **you**, Beloved reader; thank you. Thank you for opening these pages and trusting me with your heart. May these words find the rooms you thought were locked. May they sit beside you in your quiet places. May they remind you that you are worthy of softness, worthy of love, worthy of becoming.

With reverence and gratitude,

Mahogany Rose

About The Author

Mahogany Rose is a poetic dramatist and literary architect whose work illuminates the delicate intersections of love, legacy, and emotional survival. Rooted in her Gullah Geechee and Creole heritage, she writes with reverence for the women who came before her. Transforming memory into myth, ache into intimacy, and silence into song.

Her signature genre, poetic drama, blends cinematic and emotional storytelling with lyrical language, exploring the truths we inherit, the wounds we carry, and the tenderness required to heal. Through her expansive Mahogany Rose Literary Universe, she builds immersive worlds that honor Black beauty, softness, and sacred resilience.

Beyond the page, Mahogany curates spaces of rest and restoration for women through creative ministry, artistic workshops, and floral sanctuaries. Her devotion to storytelling moves beyond entertainment, it is ceremony, reclamation, and legacy-building.Cream is her debut novel.

To step further into her world, visit www.mahoganytheauthor.com

2 Corinthians 8:10-13

www.ingramcontent.com/pod-product-compliance
Lightning Source LLC
Chambersburg PA
CBHW021410110726
47901CB00008B/2124